PRAISE FOR NEWCOMER

"Due to her excellent writing, Mahasweta Ghosh invites us to travel with her main character, a graduate student, as she experiences the many difficulties encountered by her first journey to the United States. She describes the character's adjustments so well that we are right there with her. Since I have lived in two other countries, I can especially appreciate the path she traveled, and I could identify with many of the situations that faced her. "I recommend *Newcomer* to all who like to read of others' bravery and wisdom."
-Sara Hines Martin, author of More than Petticoats: Remarkable Georgia Women *and* Learning From Wolves: Lessons for Humans from Plant and Animal Life

"Newcomer is the classic American immigrant story. The narrator grapples with feelings of wonder and fear in the New World—giving the American reader a fresh perspective on the ordinary—while looking back at the memories and touchstones of India that give her the comfort of the familiar while entrancing us with exotic charm."
-George Weinstein, author of Hardscrabble Road *and* The Five Destinies of Carlos Moreno

"Today there is such a conflict between cultures, most of that is not understood from a human point of view. These stories in *Newcomer* reflect the human appreciation between social institutions. In this the author provides a passage to India, through a college student who misses a grandmother, to recalling a certain feel of a couch, to a thesis defense that brings cause for joy."
-John Stephens, Author of Return to the Water

"Mahasweta Ghosh is a talented writer whose honest voice and sharp reflections help create, in *Newcomer*, an absorbing and memorable take on what it means to find your place and yourself in a new world."
-Peter Lynch, Digital Solutions Editor, American Academy of Pediatrics

NEWCOMER

NEWCOMER

Mahasweta Ghosh

Deeds Publishing | Atlanta, Georgia

Published by Deeds Publishing | Marietta, GA
www.deedspublishing.com

Library of Congress Cataloging-in-Publications Data is available upon request.

ISBN 978-1-937565-77-0

Books are available in quantity for promotional or premium use. For information, write Deeds Publishing, PO Box 682212, Marietta, GA 30068 or info@deedspublishing.com.

10 9 8 7 6 5 4 3 2 1

For my parents, grandparents, and the entire Ghosh family.

ACKNOWLEDGMENTS

I would like to extend my special thanks to Atlanta Writers Club (AWC) Roswell Critique Group members: Gaby Anderson, Michael Buchanan, Josh Bugosh, Daniel Burke, Emily Carpenter, Ellie Decker, Suzi Ehtesham-Zadeh, Jane Haessler, JD Jordan, Tom Leidy, Chris Negron, Thom Shelton, Marre Stevens, George Weinstein, Fred Whitson, and the others for their endless curiosity—"And then what happened?"—that led the short story *Arrival* to turn into the novel *Newcomer*. I couldn't have done without their continuous support.

My sincere appreciation goes to author Jedwin Smith, my teacher and mentor, for his guidance and support. Taking time from his very busy schedule, he wrote the foreword to the novel.

Thanks to my classmates in Jedwin Smith's class: Carolyn Martin Graham, Sandra Davis, Steve Drage, Shane Etter, Sean Hastings, Susan Jimison, Roy Richardson, Mari Ann Stefanelli and Anne Wainscott-Sargent for encouragement.

I highly appreciate Bob, Jan and Mark Babcock of Deeds Publishing for publishing the book.

Thanks to my readers for their interest.

FOREWORD

I first met Mahasweta Ghosh at a local writer's group. Shy to the point of speaking almost in a whisper, she read six pages of a novel highlighting the difficulties a young lady encounters in the 1980s when uprooted from her home and transplanted to the most foreign of locales—a university in southern Ohio.

My first thought: This is a fairly mundane story.

But then I found out the home from which the protagonist has been uprooted is in Calcutta, India, where the year-round average temperature in that tropical savanna corner of the world is 75 degrees. In winter, the temperature rarely dips below 51 degrees. And now she has stepped off the plane and into the face of not only extreme culture shock, but also a fierce snowstorm.

"Such is her welcome to America," Sweta (pronounced Shā-tah) would tell me later.

Looking back on that first encounter, a number of things about Sweta's story stuck close to home, the most obvious of which is the young Indian lady and everyone else she encounters here in the United States are two vastly different peoples separated by a common language—the Queen's English.

Sweta's communication skills, perhaps considered a bit awkward to most Americans, are precision personified. Slang never intrudes into her conversation. Her word choice is dictionary perfect, courtesy of being raised in a country that once was a British colony. As such, there is little she considers "cool" or even "hip."

What also intrigued me were the innumerable trials and tribulations Sweta's main character endures as a "newcomer" to our fast-paced, me-first society. What we consider the norm proves to be as complex as anything Sweta's protagonist has ever encountered, whether it be asking a fellow student where "the lift" (an elevator) might be located, to the extraordinarily high cost of text books, clothing, cooking utensils, and food.

Having spent a great deal of my life reporting from one war zone or another—equally as mesmerized as baffled by the various religions, languages, ethnicities, morals, and cuisines—I immediately identified with the plight of Sweta's main character. And, more often than not, I admired how quickly she adapted, improvised, and overcame all obstacles. Without attempting to be too maudlin, she was a woman after my own heart.

Granted, while she never had to face hostile gunfire, she most assuredly endured the silence and stares of bewildered classmates. And although she would never have to consume the mystery-meat-of-the-day within an embattled city under months-long siege, her diet was vastly constricted by the absence of the traditional foodstuffs of a lifetime.

The war Sweta's protagonist has to confront is first and foremost that of communal indifference. With her family thousands of miles away and, due to living on the tightest of budgets, the staggering cost of a simple phone call a luxury she dare not exploit, the young Indian lady manages to prosper academically. And only when she discovers she isn't alone as a campus oddity—embracing the African, Asian and a fellow Indian community—does her emotional battles become somewhat easier to endure.

I consider it an honor to introduce Mahasweta Ghosh to you—a lady of grace and style, a "Newcomer" in her own right to a country that has made gigantic strides in the past three decades when it comes to the acceptance of diversity.

I commend Sweta because her words are as lyrical as her heart is pure. And the story she lays forth is the perfect example of what makes some individuals stand head and shoulders above the maddening crowd that is our boisterous and oft-confusing nation.

Jedwin Smith
War correspondent,
two times Pulitzer Prize nominee,
and author of *Our Brother's Keeper*

1. Newcomer, 1980

It is the beginning of December. The decade is about to roll over to the 1980s. In the bone-chilling cold of New York City I step out of JFK airport to catch a shuttle to LaGuardia airport. The final leg of the journey to Cincinnati is yet to be completed.

The beautiful red and black woolen sweater, hand-knit by my favorite aunt, and the embroidered light Kashmiri jacket are not suitable for this bitter cold. The fancy black leather dress shoes from Bata Company are allowing ice-cold air to penetrate my feet. People are staring at my dark-green South-Indian silk sari with the red border. My waist-length hair is pulled back into a thick braid so my ears are totally exposed to the freezing evening breeze, which is slicing into them like a sharp razor.

The flight from Calcutta to JFK was not only my first international flight, but also the very first time I left my parents, siblings, extended family and friends, and my country behind. Most of the food served on the airplane didn't look familiar. Moreover, an overwhelming feeling of homesickness suppressed my hunger and prevented me from eating. My stomach is growling now. I am starving.

The long flight included a few hours of layovers at New Delhi and Amsterdam. During the eighteen hours of actual flying time, I dozed off from time to time, but unfamiliar surroundings and jetlag stopped me from falling sound asleep. I have been in-transit during the past twenty-eight hours. My eyes are burning, I am exhausted.

When am I going home again? The assistantship is valid for two years. It's impossible to think of managing to spend two years without seeing my family. But the outrageous airfare is way beyond my affordability.

It's approaching dusk, but the sky still has some residual daylight. Bright lights have just started to turn on. This is the time to return home at the end of a day. Tired and exhausted both physically and emotionally, I am waiting at the New York City shuttle bus stop.

Nonetheless, my thoughts are of home…

I visualize a usual wait at the Howrah Station bus stand on my way home from the university in Calcutta in a typical winter evening.

Every morning I ride a bus from home and come to the Howrah Station to catch a bus to Calcutta University. The British-constructed famous Howrah Bridge over the sacred river Ganges is the first cantilever suspension bridge of its kind. The bridge, partially built in India and partially in Britain, connects the twin cities of Howrah and Calcutta.

Across the street is the entrance to Howrah Railway Station, the terminus for South-Eastern Indian railways. It is the largest railway station in India, as well as one of the largest in the world. Daily commuters are rushing to catch local trains. Long distance travelers with lots of luggage are negotiating fees with the porters. Other porters are busy carrying luggage piled on their heads.

Visitors from remote villages are almost lost, nervous, confused and panicked dealing with the crowd. Families with elderly and children are having a tough time keeping everybody together.

The highly polluted air is stuffed with coal smoke from the long-distance railroad steam engines and the stench of diesel and gasoline fumes.

I board a Route 63 private bus, and fortunately get to occupy a ladies' seat, one of the seats reserved for women, close to the door. Within the next few minutes the bus is packed and passengers barely have room to stand—the daily rush-hour scenario.

I'm almost home. Just a few stops and I'll be there.

"Ticket please, ticket." In his cracked voice due to excessive use all day long every day, the skinny, middle-aged bus conductor keeps loudly requesting fare.

"Here," I hand him the exact fare, an *adhuli*, a fifty paisa coin. They do appreciate exact fares. He hands me a ticket from the stack in his left hand and proceeds with the fare collection. His purse, full of change, makes a rattling noise.

Riding the bus twice daily, most of the passengers and conductors on this route have become familiar faces to one another. Though I don't know them, somehow there exists a feeling of acquaintance. Unknowingly, a feeling of comfort and friendship has developed among the daily commuters. Soon the crowded bus gets busy with friendly conversations.

The lady next to me, wearing a black and blue printed cotton sari, addresses a younger woman in a two-piece brown *salwar-kameez*, "Nira, you look so tired, are you OK?"

In an exhausted tone, Nira replies, "Not at all, just recovering from flu."

"Why don't you take a few days off and rest?"

Nira explains, "First, my son caught it from the elementary school. I had to stay home to take care of him. Next, it was my husband. I can't afford to take any more sick days right now."

"Try to get some rest, girl."

Nira nods.

A middle-aged woman sitting a few seats away asks the woman standing in front of her, "I didn't see you last week. What happened, Mita?"

With enthusiasm, Mita responds, "We went to Shiliguri to attend my sister's daughter's wedding."

Curious women nearby ask almost simultaneously, "How was the wedding? What about the bridegroom? Tell us about it."

Beaming with pride, Mita answers, "Excellent. He is good-looking, an engineer, holds a good job, has a nice family background."

"That's great. Glad to hear it."

Mita continues, "My sister and brother-in-law have been searching for a good match for their daughter over the past two years. Finally, they selected him. We hope to find someone like him when we arrange the marriage of our only daughter."

As the women discuss all there is to be said about marriage, the men have heated discussions about inflation, politics and sports, especially cricket.

The conductor announces the first stop, "Howrah Court, Hospital, and Post office. Please descend."

Hardly anyone gets off in this business area at the end of the day. Homebound passengers get in though. The conductor shouts "All clear" to the driver.

Across the street is the Rifle Club. Only rich people can afford to enroll their children for rifle training courses.

Colorful banners in the Howrah Maidan, the local playground and park, display the upcoming "Inter High School Athletics Competition," an annual event held each winter. My high school excels in academics, but only once in a while we become fortunate enough to capture any sports award.

Going past Howrah Maidan, I witness a regular scene. The sidewalk snack lovers, mostly school and college girls, are relishing the finger licking tasty *ghugni, alu-cabli* and highly popular *phuchka*. The sellers can barely keep up serving them.

The full session of evening walk is winding down. Teenage boys, at the end of football and cricket practices, and other residents of the neighborhood are heading home.

Calcutta experiences a light winter. Woolen sweaters, shawls of all categories—from hand-woven and embroidered Kashmiri shawls for fancy wears to plain ones for everyday use—are seen in abundance.

In addition to sweaters, some extra-cautious mothers have dressed their children in wool caps and scarves, commonly called mufflers. Most of the sweaters display the knitting skills of the women in the family.

Sidewalk hawkers are selling seasonal fruits: apples and oranges. Cobblers are repairing and polishing shoes. Vendors are displaying cheap pens, plastic wrist-watch bands, and knick-knacks. The sellers' loud announcements to lure buyers, as well as the price bargaining episodes, are integral parts of daily business. It is so crowded it's hard to find room to walk.

Established businesses—clothing stores, pharmacies, groceries, confectioners, the beetle-leaf and cigarette stalls, the tea stalls and cafés—are turning on their bright fluorescent lights to attract customers. The mouth–watering aroma of frying snacks fills the air.

At dusk, the unique rhythmic sound of ringing bells and conch-shells in the temples announce the evening prayers and *Arati*. Many passers-by momentarily close their eyes and bow their heads showing respect to The Almighty.

As soon as the bus takes a left turn, I attempt to proceed toward the door. It's a tough task in a jam-packed bus, especially with my heavy book bag. The standing passengers squeeze to make room for me. A woman standing nearby hurries to take my seat.

The two-story red-brick building across the street is our home. On the second floor balcony, with its blooming bright orange-yellow marigolds and red chrysanthemums, Mom is waiting for me. She smiles and waves.

Rexene, our beloved Dalmatian, is waiting at the entrance. She jumps on me, her tail wagging in joy. This is the welcome-home greeting Rexene extends to every member of the family. She licks me, circles me, and enjoys being patted before she settles down.

My brother, a high-school student, is busy with his studies. He is skinny, quiet, and wears high-powered eyeglasses; a brilliant student, a pride in our family of high achievers.

Dadu, our paternal grandfather, a retired attorney, is back from his evening walk. He gets ready for the evening news. *Dida*, our paternal grandmother, is in the middle of her evening prayer session. The fragrance of sandalwood from burning incense sticks floats out of the prayer room and fills the air.

Dad will come home from work soon.

I rinse my hands and face and change to comfortable home clothes and sandals. How relaxing! I'm hungry; moreover, thirsty for tea. Mom serves mouth-watering warm *singaras*, fresh fried hot pockets stuffed with spicy cauliflower and potato curry, my favorite. I relish each and every bite. Delicious! Hot tea with cream and sugar follows. My daylong fatigue seems to vanish.

There is quite a bit of homework tonight. Hopefully, I will be able to finish it and get a chance to read a novel. It's due back in the library at the end of the week...

Suddenly, my thoughts of home are interrupted as I am startled by the sudden rush among the passengers to load their possession in the luggage compartment startles me. My New York City shuttle has arrived.

Running tears obstruct my vision. Howrah, Calcutta, my home, family and friends—each and everybody is there—except me. Why did I come to the other end of the world for higher studies?

Always a mommy's girl, I want to go home to Mommy now. I can't wait to go back to the two-story brick home, where I grew up and lived the entire twenty-one years of my life. Home, sweet home.

A pale-yellow half-moon becomes visible in the light gray dusk sky. Is this the same moon that shines on our courtyard and terrace at home?

With trembling hands and a tearful hazy vision, I board the shuttle.

Joining the Wells State University, a major university in Southern Ohio, as a graduate student in January 1980, I reside in a small one-bedroom apartment in a nearby housing complex occupied mostly by students. A twenty-minute walk up a steep hill gets me to the University.

The First Time Shopping

On my very first day at the university, professor Hewett introduces me to a white American student.

"This is Ken. He is a Ph.D. student soon to graduate. He will take you shopping for the essentials this afternoon."

I nod.

Ken drops me off in front of a kitchen supply store at a small shopping center within a half-a-mile from the university.

"I will be back in an hour," he says and leaves.

I feel totally helpless at the store. I wish someone could help me.

The dinnerware section contains: plates, bowls, cups and saucers—everything shiny white. What's the material? Are these safe? I have never seen anything like this before. I pick up a plate and inspect it. It's really lightweight. The label states: Corning ware.

These cannot be white stone. My grandmother has a white marble dinnerware set reserved for special occasions. They are very heavy and non-glossy.

I am too shy to ask anyone. Since other shoppers are buying, I go for it. It's a big help to find every item with a price tag, unlike India. Costs in dollars are getting multiplied by fifteen and being converted to rupees in my head. Though I am hesitant to spend so much money, I better shop today when I have a ride.

A few dinnerware, cutleries and aluminum utensils—all in the cheapest categories—are what I choose. As I am paying the cashier, Ken returns. He loads the shopping bags into his car.

He asks me, "Done shopping? Let's do the groceries then."

With some hesitation, I mumble, "Um, the departmental secretary asked for my telephone number. I need to buy a telephone." I wait, prepared to hear that he doesn't have time.

He stares at me for a moment which seems like eternity, and then says, "Let's get it."

Ten minutes later, we walk into a department store. This time he accompanies me. As it is I am feeling guilty about taking too long. Walking past a few sections, he leads me to the telephones. Back home I was used to black telephones only. A maroon rotary telephone draws my attention and I buy it.

Ken says, "Please call the telephone company from the department. It takes a few days to get it working."

Our next stop is at the grocery store. He pulls a cart and starts doing his own grocery shopping, asking me to do mine. Everything looks very neat and clean and organized. Hurry up! Hurry up! Hurry up! Keep ringing in my head. Though I would like to see what's available, instead I follow him blindly and pick up: eggs, milk, butter, chicken, bananas, apples, bread, cookies, carrots, onions and potatoes. There are other items he takes but I don't, since I am unsure of what they are.

I have to buy rice. Having no other option, I ask him, "Where is the rice?"

He leads me to a shelf with small bags of white rice. A five pound bag is the largest! We grew up rice eaters. Big jute bags containing 40 pounds or more of rice purchased for family consumption—was quite normal.

Though hesitant, I inquire, "Is there a bigger bag available?"

"Bigger than this?" He looks at me in disbelief. "Let me check." He walks to a store employee in uniform to find out. Coming back, Ken explains, "Since this branch is closest to the University, they sell 20 pound bags of rice for the international families. He went to the storage to get you one."

It must be highly unusual. Looking at the rice bag in my cart, an elderly gentleman standing next to me at the cashier comments, "This will last you for years."

Though it seems rude, I remain silent due to shyness and because "always be respectful to your elders" is engraved in me.

Not only does Ken drop me off at my place, he also unloads the bags to the doorstep. I am very grateful to him. There is so much I want to say to express my gratitude, but I am not sure whether it will be appropriate. "Thank you very much," is all I say.

"You're welcome." He starts his car and drives away.

The First Time Registration

The registration clerk inputs my name and information and gives me a computer receipt. It shows a balance due—$1,100 dollars tuition for a quarter! I don't have that kind of money.

All I know is that the UGS, University Graduate Scholarship, is going to cover my tuition. There is no one I can ask for help. How can I pay this? My head starts spinning. This has to be addressed immediately.

Usually, I have never been too shy to talk, but it started since I got here. The number one reason is my Indian accent. I know I write and speak English well.

Why am I so hard to understand? Why do people keep asking me the same question? I keep repeating my responses until they finally understand me. Out of frustration, every chance I get, I write to ask or respond to a question.

I show the computer printout to the registration clerk, pointing at the balance due amount. There is a long line behind me. I had waited an hour-and-a-half to get to her. Hundreds of students are waiting in the queue, but only four clerks?

She glances at it while chewing gum. Without showing any concern she asks, "Is this your first quarter?"

"Yes." I nod.

"The UGS didn't get processed. Take it to your department. They will fix it."

Her manner of speaking is so casual, as if this happens all the time.

I am confused. Is she right or is she trying to get rid of me just to continue her work? Is she sure our department will be able to fix it? Classes start in two days. What if this does not get fixed? What am I going to do? Who am I to turn to?

I stand still, uncertain about my next action until I hear her say, "Next please." As the next student approaches her, I leave.

In order to arrive early at registration I skipped breakfast this morning. It's lunch time now and I am very hungry. But I cannot waste time to eat lunch. The Engineering building is a ten-minute walk from here. Exasperated, I reach the departmental secretary and show her the form.

Surprised, she asks, "Did you come running all the way here just for this?"

I nod.

She checks a few things, writes something, signs it and returns it to me. "Take it back to them. It will be fine."

The line at registration is even longer this time. Starting over at the end of the line, it takes two more hours to complete my registration.

Finally, my first quarter class schedule is in my hands. Though very hungry and thirsty, I feel relieved as I step out of the building.

The First Class

The schedule shows my first class room is on the 9th floor of the Engineering building. My classes start at nine in the morning. Students are busy rushing to their different classes. After hesitating for a while I ask someone, "Which way is the lift?" Watching his totally confused expression, I repeat the question.

In a hurry, he responds while walking away, "We don't have them."

No lift! Am I to take the stairs all the way to the 9th floor? In Calcutta University we took the lift even to the 3rd floor classes.

A sign in the corridor displays an arrow to the stairs. Disappointed, I follow the sign, only to find out, not one, but two lifts right across from the staircase! Joining the other students, I ride the crowded lift.

In a few days I come to realize the term for lift is elevator.

Initial Impressions about Apartment and Department

Our house back home, a two-story brick building, has fifteen-foot-high ceilings at each level. With a large south-facing verandah, inside balconies and many windows and doors, it's designed to provide natural air flow and excellent ventilation.

My one-bedroom apartment in the apartment complex has low ceilings, an entrance door, a window next to it and another one back in the bedroom. It's not designed for natural ventilation. No window curtains? Horizontal shutters can be tilted to let some light in. Just for privacy, I will keep the front window shut always with the shutters pulled down. Does this provide enough security?

I miss the huge wood-frame windows with wood shutters and vertical iron rods back home. They let so much light and fresh air in, but can be shut to keep the rain out and dead-bolted for maximum security. My bedroom had three large windows, two of them facing each other.

Back home, a kitchen is very private. It's always located well inside the house, accessible only to the family members. Visitors are never allowed in the kitchen. A maid washes the dishes in the courtyard close to the kitchen and brings them back.

On the contrary, kitchen is the first place anyone would see here. Within a few feet from the entrance, it provides no privacy at all. Adjacent to the stove is a small counter and a sink. On the wall are some storage cabinets. Dishes will be done right here? That's all to the kitchen? Just a few square feet, no moving room at all? The kitchen, the small dining space and a sofa set, are crowded next to one another.

The strangest thing is the level of the bedroom. It's partially underground! If I extend my hand out the window horizontally, it will touch the ground! The bed, placed close to the window, gets chilling cold drafts. At night I hang my Rajasthani bedcover on the window frame. It doesn't stop the draft, but reduces it. I bought the bedcover from Rajasthan Emporium in Calcutta. It's all-cotton, thick and very pretty. Yellow, orange and red designs with peacocks and flowers, rows of elephants and camels, are printed on a dark green background. These patterns are common in artwork from the state of Rajasthan, India. The bedcover brings a comfortable Indian setting to the room.

Coming from the plains, I am used to houses built on flat ground. A building always has the same number of floors in the front and the back. The front entrance is always at the same level as the back door. Additionally, a building must start with the ground floor, then go first, second, third floor, etc.

In the Engineering building the front entrance is on the sixth floor, the back one is on the fifth. Built in the 1800s, the front side is the original building. It spans from the sixth to eighth floor. The architecture is elegant; tall columns, wide halls, spacious classrooms, and a broad staircase. Many students run up and down the stairs, but it doesn't look crowded. The elevator is not used that often. The structure reminds me very much of the original buildings at Calcutta University.

The back side is a more recently constructed addition that goes from the fifth to ninth floor. The style reflects space consciousness, with classrooms and modern labs. It is equipped with multiple elevators. The narrow staircase is hardly ever used.

After overcoming an initial confusion, I come to realize that the ninth floor, where most of my classes are, exists only in the back of the building. This is the area for graduate studies in Electrical Engineering.

University Bookstore

I was no stranger to the bookstore zone in College Street, Calcutta. The entire area has numerous book stores, one after another. It's next to the famous Presidency College, Calcutta University and the Calcutta Medical College and Hospital.

The bookstores carried various text books for all levels from elementary school to the doctoral levels. They also carried nontext books published in all branches of science, literature and other disciplines.

As an avid reader of literature, I visited them frequently for newly published works: sometimes a novel, sometimes a collection of short stories—making sure to buy a copy before it went out of stock. Each bookstore had shelves stacked with books. The storage location was usually in the loft area. Often a salesman in the front counter would read aloud the list of books requested by a customer. Another salesman in the loft would send the books to the counter. Just like the libraries, the Calcutta bookstores focused on books only—absolutely nothing else.

I follow the campus map to the sign "University Book Store." The first time I step inside I am stunned. It's a shocking, eye-opening experience!

Shelf after shelf is stacked with writing paper, note books, various pens and pencils, erasers, color pencils, even paperclips and calendars, calculators and batteries, as well as a few items I do not recognize.

One section is reserved for groceries. A refrigerator is full of milk-cartons, ice-creams and items I do not recognize.

Another shelf is full of toiletries such as bar soap, tooth-paste, tooth-brushes, shampoo, and laundry detergents. Most of these items are in smaller packages compared to the grocery stores.

An area for clothes? T-shirts and sweat shirts, light jackets, water-proof hooded jackets and caps, most of them with university logos. So, the university has its own brand of clothes! Is that possible?

A shelf next to the cashier is loaded with lozenges and biscuits, chocolates, mints and chewing gum. Also, a few copies of the daily newspaper and some magazines.

I need a wall-calendar for day-to-day use at my apartment. Any calendar that has nice pictures is outrageously expensive.

My dad used to get dozens of diaries and calendars as New-Year's gifts at work. We always kept a few of the best ones and gave away the rest. Each month displayed some exquisite artwork on expensive, silky paper. It was worth hanging them on the walls just from the decorative point of view. Additionally, every year my uncle living in Switzerland sent us a calendar with Swiss landmarks and scenic beauties.

It's hard for me to settle for a black-and-white calendar without any picture. But that's what I choose for a dollar. It may be an eyesore, but it will do.

Where are the books? This is a bookstore, isn't it?

Looking around I see everything except the books. A sign on top of a staircase draws my attention. It indicates books are in the basement. Finally, I locate the books!

This is more like a combination of a variety store, a clothing store, and a book store!

I am stunned to find how costly textbooks are! Dollars get converted to rupees instantaneously in my head, showing large amounts. That's expensive!

I have some of these books in Calcutta, where they only cost a fraction of this price. Cheap Asian editions, though. Neither the quality of paper, nor the print is as good. So what? Good enough for a student. Had I known this, I would have packed them with me.

The rental office in the apartment complex has charged me a month's rent as the security deposit. On top of that is the price of books! How am I going to afford it? Let me think overnight. I'll be back tomorrow.

As I proceed to leave, I notice the very last copy of a text. What if it gets sold? There is a homework assignment already. I have to buy it now.

Cadbury milk-chocolates have been my all-time favorite. So many varieties of chocolates are displayed in a shelf right next to the cashier. Looking away, I resist the mouth-watering temptation; just can't afford it.

Most reluctantly, I pull out five twenty-dollar bills from my purse. A hundred dollars just for three books!

Departmental Staff and demographics

Pretty soon I realize that the secretaries are a good source of valuable information. Year after year dealing with foreign students' issues, they can resolve most of the problems. If not, they can direct me to someone useful. Since I am hesitant to ask other students for information, the secretaries are a valuable resource.

Bonnie is elderly. She looks like she is in her late fifties. Though she usually has a slight smile in her face, it doesn't take her long to become very serious. She is the most senior among the three secretaries followed by Phyllis, who is in her mid-forties and does accounts related work. Vicky, the youngest one may be in her early-twenties. In a way, she works for Bonnie. All the time Bonnie orders Vicky, "Post this notice on the eighth and ninth floor bulletin boards." "Take these papers to Dr. Biggs' office upstairs."

While I am talking to Bonnie, at the sound of the Xerox copier running in the adjacent room she looks to check who is using it. Professors are authorized to make unlimited copies. The graduate students who are Teaching Assistants (TAs), and Research Assistants (RAs), have permission to make work-related copies. All others must use the coin copier in the Engineering Library that charges five cents a page. Librarians give change for a dollar, if needed. All copies are black and white.

All of the three secretaries are well-dressed and wear a lot of make-up. In Calcutta it's common to complement someone fair-skinned by saying, "She is almost as white as a Westerner. Her lips are pink. She is beautiful."

These secretaries are white and have pink lips. Why do they use so much lipstick and make-up?

The four faculty members—Dr. Hewett, Dr. Biggs, Dr. Rogers and Dr. Norton—are white American males. They have study areas for their own graduate students adjacent to their offices on the ninth floor.

Each graduate student has a spacious desk, a chair and a tall steel cabinet with drawers and a lock and key. Additionally, each student is given keys to the labs, and the graduate students' office. Each key is carved with the writing, "Property of U. Do not duplicate."

Keys are officially issued by Bonnie and signed out by the students. The five-dollar key deposit will be refunded when a student returns all keys before leaving the university.

Three-fourths of the forty graduate students in the Electrical Engineering department are Asian, the rest are American. Most of the foreign students are from India and Taiwan, and a few are from Thailand. Due to the lack of a common language between the North and South Indian students, English serves as the common language. Sometimes Hindi is used. Either way is fine with me.

When it comes to females, there is a Taiwanese woman besides me. She sticks to her husband all the time. Both of them are about to graduate.

There are no black American students, faculty or staff.

Library

The Engineering Library is located on the eighth floor of the Engineering building. Shelf after shelf stacked with texts and journals in all disciplines of engineering, labeled and arranged in order. Three black-and-white pay copiers located close to the circulation desk are available for students' use.

Among the three librarians in the engineering library, Dr. Deborah Bush is the youngest, only about thirty. She holds a doctorate in library science and is the main librarian.

Graduate students are advised to contact her if they need help locating research topics journals, references and cross-references. We hear, starting next year she will offer a one-credit graduate course to help students with how to track research material.

The window-side desks are my favorite. A look outside reveals the infinite sky and makes me feel better.

Snow

Born and brought up in warm weather in Calcutta, the concept of snow is an illusion to me. Never saw it, never watched it snow—naturally, it's a dreamland. All the places that get snow must be paradise. Movie scenes from Shimla, Kashmir and Darjeeling in the Himalayas, and pictures in children's storybooks told me what snow was like. Especially the pictures in the books translated into Bengali from Russian—a very popular kind in my childhood—took my hands and gave me a dream-tour to the snow lands.

Just can't wait to see snow. What does it look like in reality? How does it feel to watch snow falling? How does it feel to touch snow? Must be highly exciting! In the movies it looks like white cotton balls coming down from the sky.

My friends and classmates who visited places with snow make me jealous. Their descriptions magnify many folds in my imagination and create a special place in my heart.

It's getting colder day by day. It may snow any day!

One afternoon, fluffy cotton balls begin falling from the sky and kissing the ground. Most of them melt away, disappointing me. It is just as beautiful and attractive as I had always imagined. I watch intensively. At times it surpasses my expectations. Snowflakes on grass, snowflakes on the branches of evergreen trees. This is what's called snow-white! So soft, so pure, so fulfilling.

The park I walk by gets covered with snow. Kids wearing heavy jackets and hats run happily, enjoying freshly created track marks with joy and pride. Some kids, grinning from ear-to-ear, are busy with snowball fights.

As days go by it becomes bitterly cold. Kids aren't coming to play in the park any longer. People aren't taking walks. The snow stays unperturbed.

I am forced to wear a heavy overcoat with a hood, and heavy shoes. Always I have been a slim girl. The additional weight makes a significant difference to me. Feels like heavy luggage at every step. The walk to the university becomes laborious and time-consuming. It takes twice the time, about forty minutes, to make it.

Not only that the round-trip walk leaves me over-exhausted. The sidewalks, though cleaned periodically and sprinkled with salt to prevent ice formation, often become icy and dangerous. It's not uncommon for walkers to fall and break bones.

I must walk slowly and carefully, watching my stability and securing my balance while carrying a heavy book bag. I have slipped and fallen a few times, but fortunately none was bad enough to draw medical attention.

There are days I go home exhausted and I cry my heart out. This is in addition to the emotional stress of missing my family and friends I left behind in Calcutta.

Snowplows clean the busy streets. Continuous traffic also melts the snow, leaving tire tracks and melted ice-cold muddy water. I walk by a huge six-story apartment house. It's located within a large premise with a garden and is fenced in by a tall brick wall. An iron gate that usually stays closed allows cars to get in and out.

Well-lit rooms in the building reflect ongoing life, but I haven't seen anyone yet. It surprises me. Probably they stay indoors due to the severely cold weather.

It takes me a while to figure out it's a home for elderly people. They live away from their children, grand-children, family and loved ones. The only help they get is from hired people.

In our culture grandparents live with the family. My grandparents have always lived with us. Special diets are provided for them on a daily basis. When they are sick the family physician takes care of them.

When I was twelve, my grandfather underwent an eye surgery. The following few weeks when his activities were restricted, all of us cared for him. I was glad to do my part by reading the daily newspaper to him.

How lonely, isolated and helpless the residents of this old people's home must feel. It saddens me whenever I walk past the building.

Once on campus and inside the building, I breathe heavily while waiting for the elevator, and fearing that I'll be late for class. The average American male students are so tall. If I don't get a seat up front they block my view. From the back I can hardly see the whiteboard. The professors speak with hard-to-understand American accents. Most of them have poor handwriting.

All of these, when combined with my obstructed vision, leave me in a very tight spot. Every morning I struggle hard to get to class early enough to secure a front row seat.

Who knew snow could be so inconvenient and troublesome? Who ever thought snow also has a dangerous side?

Even inside gloves my fingers feel freezing. Sometimes there is hardly any sensation left in them. They become numb. When I return to the apartment I soak my hands in hot water. Hot running water is available all the time. What a luxury!

I need to buy a radio just to stay in touch with the outside world. Besides that, if ever classes are cancelled due to inclement weather or a snow emergency, it's broadcasted on the radio. I wouldn't have to walk to the university to figure it out. A radio can be purchased in the bookstore for less than fifteen dollars. But considering my financial circumstances, that's a luxury. It shouldn't be too long before the winter is gone. I hear spring arrives by late April, just a few more months away. Not that long.

Just the thought of spring and summer cheers me up. I won't have to struggle with snow every day.

The Campus in Winter

Cold weather and a snow-filled campus. The connecting walkways are flooded with ice-cold muddy water generated by thousands of people walking on the snow. The sooner I can enter a building, the sooner I get sheltered from the bitter cold. Every time, before I step out of a building, I have to button up my full-length heavy overcoat, fasten the belt, tie the hood, and put on my gloves.

Once in a while the Calcutta newspaper published pictures of a mountaineering team ready to climb the Himalayas. Looking in a mirror, I think, I look like them. As soon as I step into a building all of the above must to be taken off. This alone takes some of the ten-minute time interval between classes.

Fortunately, the campus post office is located on the first floor of the Student Center building. So is the bank ATM. When I first opened my bank account I had to walk to the bank outside the campus and show my passport and student ID card as proof of my legal status.

Cold and Fever

I am feverish, getting chills, and my throat hurts. Along with a pounding headache, my whole body aches. I am running a fever; but how high? I don't have a thermometer. What is the procedure to see a doctor in this country? How much does it cost? How much do medicines cost? Are they expensive? I am too shy and hesitant to ask my classmates. After all, it's just a cold—nothing serious. Why bother them?

I'm shivering in the cold and feverish. My book bag feels like it weighs a ton. The walk back to the apartment seems endless. I drag myself through the snow. Unlocking the door, I throw the book bag on a chair. I haven't had lunch, I am starving.

Back home in Calcutta, whenever we get sick we become a center of attention of the entire family. Mom gets busy taking temperatures, serving warm milk or hot tea with light, nutritious snacks. She decides on whether to place a house call for our family physician, Dr. Ghosh. He is tall, well-built, bespectacled, and balding with scattered grey hair. Beginning with my grandfather he has, at one time or another, treated three generations of our family.

Dr. Ghosh arrives in his chauffeur-driven black Austin. It has a Red Cross symbol on the windshield. His prescriptions work like miracles. Only once in a while he has to open his medical briefcase to extract a syringe and medicine, and administer a shot—an action I have always dreaded.

He is also a family friend. At each visit he sits down and chats, while enjoying hot tea and snacks. In case of a prolonged sickness, he stops by every day at the end of his morning rounds at the Howrah General Hospital.

But alas! I'm not in Calcutta any longer. There is not a single soul to ask me how I am doing. With trembling hands, watery-eyes and aching body, I somehow manage to make a cup of hot tea. From Calcutta I have brought some non-prescription medicines such as Strepsils sore-throat lozenges and Anacin painkiller tablets. Tea, crackers and medicine. Finally, I crawl into bed and fall asleep instantly.

Rest, medicine, hot tea and salt-water gargle, follow periodically. I'm not hungry, just tired. I sleep without keeping track of time.

Luckily, I start feeling better in two days. I'm very weak, though. But it could have been a whole lot worse. Not a word to my parents. Otherwise, they would be very worried. Missing two days of school has resulted in a heavy accumulation of homework.

Stupid me! I come to know that the university Student Health Center is only a block from our Engineering building. Over-the-counter medicines are available in the campus bookstore. I promise myself never to act this stupid again.

Apartment Life

The three-story apartment house where I live has twenty one-bedroom apartments to a floor. No elevator. The staircase is located close to the center of the building.

The building has oil heating and the temperature is regulated by management. Most of the time it's hot; some nights it's so hot that I can't sleep. Still, it's fortunate we don't shiver in the cold like residents in some other apartment complexes.

I grew up in a two-story family home with abundant sunshine and natural air. I dearly miss my second-floor bedroom, where at dawn the day was welcomed by fresh cool air and chirping birds.

People waking up, the morning shift factory workers leaving for work, the cring-cring bell of the newspaper deliveryman's cycle, the milk-supply van unloading cartons of glass bottles at the milk booth, morning walkers chatting, some religious people heading for a morning dip in the sacred river Ganges—everything around me announced a new day.

Here I wake up to the noise of footsteps on the squeaking wooden floors and staircase, showers running in the apartments next to me, car engines starting, apartment doors slamming shut.

Opening the carton of tea surprises me. It's not loose tea leaves! Small individual packets; each one makes a cup of tea. How to vary the amount of tea leaves? Some people like it dark, some like it light. Why use a fixed amount?

No wonder I couldn't find a tea-strainer in the utensil rack in the shop.

In the morning I am to fix a cup of tea for myself. What a pity! My habit is getting bed-tea served to me with cream and sugar and two thin-arrowroot biscuits every morning. Sipping steaming hot tea, my eyes barely open while sitting in my bed in a half-awake state. Seems like a princely luxury now! Gone are those joyous days.

I sigh long and hard as soon as I wake up in the morning then doze off on the sofa while waiting for the water to boil for tea. I don't even have time to enjoy the tea. It's consumed hurriedly while rushing through morning chores. As it is, the tea has neither the flavor, nor the taste. It doesn't even compare to the Darjeeling tea that I am used to. Far from rejuvenating.

Two dinner plates, two sets of cups and saucers, a few spoons, knives, spatulas, and two aluminum saucepans complete the inventory in my kitchen. That's all I can afford. I end up doing the dishes every day and hating it. I feel like a maid.

It's a good thing that the apartment is furnished, though unfurnished ones rent twenty dollars cheaper monthly. I miss the leisurely comforts of the mahogany Victorian sofa set in the family room and the Burma teak bedroom sets at my parents' home. I took them for granted. Now, I realize fine quality all-wood furniture is a luxury.

Some of the furniture in this apartment almost feels as if it were made of cardboard. The synthetic sofa cushions are scratchy. No matter how poor the quality of the furniture is, at least something is there. Otherwise, I would be sleeping on the floor.

Mrs. Elizabeth Hewett, the wife of my advisor Dr. Timothy Hewett, has provided me with a boxful of household items. Her hand-written note stated these were spares from her guest room, to be returned as soon as I could buy my own. Consequently, I have nice towels, pillows with covers, and a very warm blanket. This means a lot to me. I am so grateful to her. I hope to be able to return them within three months.

She has also packed me some toiletries, including Tide detergent and Camay body bars. These must be the good brands, so I will buy these. Otherwise, I wouldn't know what to buy. Back home, I have always used Bengal Chemical's Glycerin soap in winter. Mysore Sandal soap was my favorite for the rest of the year.

The most compliments I have ever received are for my hair. My gorgeously thick, waist-long wavy hair draws attention easily. Women have asked me over and over again about my hair-care products. The honest answer is heredity. Everyone in our family has gorgeous hair, so there's nothing special about me. We have never taken any special care of our hair. Coconut oil, which is most common in Indian tradition, is all that we ever use. Not even any special shampoo.

I find some coconut oil product in the groceries. Though not the same Shalimar brand we use back home, I am delighted to find it at all. But alas! The problem appears from a totally different corner. Even though I cover my head with a scarf and tie the overcoat hood on top of that, as I walk outside, the coconut oil product freezes on my hair, especially on my scalp. It shows off like a line of sticky-white rice-starch on my parting.

The more important problem is how fast I am losing hair. The change of place and climate I am going through may be the major contributor. Every time I sweep the apartment, bundles of tangled hair show up. It's worst in the bathroom, where I comb my hair standing in front of the only mirror above the sink.

The door and the windows are closed tight due to the bone-chilling cold. The shutters are drawn all the time. Additionally, heat runs continuously. The air feels stuffy. Once in a while I crack the windows a little just to breathe some fresh air. But the shivering cold forces me to close them right away. The exhaust fan in the bathroom helps air circulation, but still, it's not fresh air.

My skin cracks and itches due to the cold and dryness. Calcutta's humid weather has always kept my skin soft and protected. It never needed any moisturizer.

I feel lonely when I am home alone, especially in the evenings and weekends. Though buried under homework and assignments, sometimes I cry my heart out thinking about my family and friends. I miss them so much. I realize how well I am bonded with them, how deeply I am rooted in my country and culture.

The first couple of nights I was unable to sleep due to jetlag. Additionally, I was very frightened, never having lived alone. Often I heard the squeaking noise of tenants walking on the wooden floors upstairs. Every time I heard a squeaking noise I was scared. Basically, I stayed half-awake all night. Gradually, I am getting used to it.

A large parking lot is located behind the apartment building. The parking lot alone could accommodate another apartment house like this. Row after row of cars are parked. Who are the owners? Do all of them belong to the residents? All these cars for just sixty apartments! In Calcutta, there are hundreds of multi-story apartment houses. But only a handful of the residents own cars. People use mass transportation—rickshaws, trams, buses, mini-buses, taxis and trains.

In Calcutta, it's beyond imagination to waste such a vast place just for parking! Many of the high-rise buildings have the basement level reserved for parking only. People who live in individual houses usually park on the streets or in close-by alleys. Some use over-night parking in the neighborhood gas stations, locally known as petrol pumps, in exchange for a monthly fee.

Usually a family with a car hires a chauffeur who drops the kids off at school and the adults at work in the mornings. Later in the day it's the housewife's turn to be chauffeured for shopping or visiting friends and family. The same car picks up everyone after school and after work and takes care of the family's travelling needs in the evenings. Most of the car owners never learn to drive.

On the other side of the parking lot is a swimming pool in a fenced area. A "Do not enter" sign on the gate prohibits admission.

Washing Machine

A look at my laundered clothes right out of the washer has left me perplexed. Everything is light orange. How did this happen? My white clothes are looking really weird.

The apartment complex has a coin laundry. In order to save time and money I put all my dirty clothes in a single wash. My favorite orange cotton sari bled and colored the entire load.

Oh no! How am I going to handle this?

I try to console myself. The undergarments should be fine. No one else is going to see them. Maybe the color from the tinted clothes will fade away with the next few washes. From now on I will sort out the colors carefully.

I remember every morning Mom sorted clothes by color and soaked them in detergent in separate buckets. Whites were soaked in hot water, colors in cold. Our maid used to hand-wash and hang them on the clothesline on the terrace to dry. Now I think that was such a luxury.

Intruder?

One night, a loud metallic noise inside the apartment wakes me up. It must be the neighborhood stray cats knocking down some utensils in the kitchen. The very next moment I remember I am not in Calcutta any longer. The apartment is locked, airtight. There is no room for a stray cat to get in.

Is it a human intruder? This frightens me extremely. My throat goes dry and I can't move. What to do? Should I get up or should I just lay quiet? No footstep, no noise over the next few minutes, which seems like eternity.

Gradually, I muster the courage to get up. Though very scared, I turn on the lights and wait. No noise, nothing yet. Finally, I take baby steps to the living and kitchen area. The cover of the wall-mounted air conditioner unit is lying on the floor.

Why did it fall? Wasn't it attached tightly?

Breathing heavily, I peek through the window. Nothing is unusual. I drink a tall glass of water. Though my heart is still pounding, what a relief!

Rental Office

A much bigger apartment building next to ours is also owned by the same Italian man. The rental office for the complex is located on the first floor of that building. According to the rental agreement, the tenants are to pay by the 6th of each month. I withdraw cash from the bank ATM at the university and pay Julie, the manager of the complex. She is a white woman about thirty-five, tall and strong. There is a lack of softness on her face though, it's rough.

When I give her the rent, she makes an entry in a ledger and gives me a receipt. Then she says, "There is no need for you to come during the office hours and pay in person. You may leave a check in the drop-box in front of the office any time. Most of the tenants do that."

Carefully, I glance at the receipt and keep it in my wallet. I am getting used to writing checks. For the monthly telephone and electric bills, which are much smaller amounts, I mail check payments. The $130 dollars rent, almost a third of my $400 dollar monthly assistantship, is such a large amount that paying it in person and getting a receipt right away, is the only acceptable way for me.

A partially bald, short, white man in his fifties walks in. He is wearing stain spotted blue jeans. He looks at me and says, "Good morning." Before giving me a chance to speak, he tells Julie in an irritated tone, "I'm going to apartment 618 to help the plumber. It's a big job," and then he leaves.

"That's Leo Azoni, the owner of the complex," Julie says.

I am stunned and speechless! As the owner of this complex, he must be very rich. Is he helping the plumber?

Julie notices my confused looks and explains, "He is quite a handyman; fixes many things."

"You mean he does the repairs?"

"Sure," Julie looks surprised. "In your three-story one-bedroom building, there are 20 apartments to a floor. In this six-story building, 18 to a floor. This building is much bigger, nicer and more expensive. It has one and two bedroom apartments and elevators. With this many rental units there are things to fix all the time."

"Yes," I nod. "But I have seen maintenance people around here."

She explains, "We do have maintenance workers, but Mr. Azoni helps a lot too; cuts down the cost."

I am still not convinced. In Calcutta, repair work is done by repairmen only. Fixing things would be considered beneath dignity and status of gentlemen.

Letters from home

Although I live on the first floor, I rush to the stairwell every evening. That's where the mailboxes are located. I receive mail only once in a while, mostly utility bills. But I can't wait to unlock the mailbox and check daily with high hopes of receiving a letter from my friends and family back home.

My parents write to me every week. Even if I got their letter only yesterday, I must make sure there isn't one waiting today just in case. On the days I receive a blue aerogramme from India I am ecstatic. I read it over and over again, almost to the point where it's memorized. I am reminded how loved and cared for I am and how much I am missed.

The letter speaks to me in real-life voices. I forget I haven't spoken Bengali, my mother language, in a long time. Letters make my life worthwhile.

For the time being I don't feel as isolated and lonely anymore. I become quite capable of handling the hardships and the physical and emotional challenges of being a newcomer, a new student, trying for success in a new-world; surrounded by a new culture, studying a new subject: Electrical Engineering.

I write two letters to my parents weekly, on Sundays and Wednesdays. Sunday's letter usually describes everything going on with me and around me. Wednesday's letter is merely a brief acknowledgement that I am well.

Evenings are the loneliest, especially on weekends. That's when I miss home the most. Staring out the window at dusk, while watching the flow of cars on the Interstate, my mind travels to my home at the other end of the world. When will I get to go home? How much longer? My only nephew, my sister's son, will no longer be a baby. At eighteen months, when I last saw him, his vocabulary was so sweet and attractive. Rexene, our loyal Dalmatian with her white coat and black spots, was standing beside me when I left. She sensed something wasn't right.

Mom's letter from last week indicated *Dadu* was having health problems. This week's update stated he was doing much better; but he must follow the doctor's instructions. Usually, *Dadu* is very good at this. Like an obedient little boy, he follows the doctor's orders without any complaint or irritation.

Dida, *Dadu's* wife of sixty-plus years, regularly keeps an eye on his diet and medicine. She pays attention to the entire family, including the maids. It's hard to find someone so beautiful and soft-spoken with such a strong personality. Hardly anyone ever disobeys her.

Her language is so polished, yet her manner of speech is firm. She always wears red-bordered white saris in an old-fashioned style, and a dot of vermilion on her forehead and some on the middle-parting of her grey-and-white thinning hair. Even at seventy-five she is beautiful and pleasant. She must have looked very beautiful as a child bride wearing her traditional red *Benarasi* bridal-costume.

Every day at dawn and dusk she sings religious Sanskrit chants in a sweet voice. I miss that, never realizing it was such an integral part of my day.

We, the grandchildren, have always approached her with our small talk and problems, skipping our parents. Mom and Dad worked full-time and carried all household responsibilities. They couldn't spend very much time with us. We always had great confidence on *Dida*'s advice and resolution skills.

I can't even think of *Dadu* passing away. Customarily, as a widow, *Dida* will be restricted to vegetarian food and white clothes only. Fish, the main course of her life-long daily menu, will be excluded from her diet forever. The wedding signs of vermilion will no longer be on her forehead and parting. I can't visualize her like that. It will be such a stern reality, well beyond my imagination.

We have always known *Dadu* and *Dida* as an undivided entity.

Introduction to Anand

After the third week in the Semiconductor Devices class, a tan, skinny student steps forward to talk to me. With a distinct foreign accent he introduces himself "I am Anand. I just arrived here as a graduate student from Thailand. This is my first quarter."

Just like me, someone else is also a newcomer from the Far East! I am so delighted that it feels as if he is from my neighborhood.

Anand says, "I did my undergraduate in electrical engineering in Bangkok. Some of my professors were Indian. At first sight I recognized you as an Indian."

I comment, "Ananda means happiness in my mother language, Bengali, which originated from Sanskrit."

He sounds glad. "Anand is short for Ananda. Our Thai language has many words from Sanskrit. There will be many common words between us."

"Your last name starts with the word Hema. It means gold."

He is happy to explain, "My ancestors were goldsmiths. My last name reflects their profession."

"Lord Buddha had a great disciple named Ananda," I mention.

Anand confirms this. "That's who I am named after. We are Buddhists."

I comment, "Lord Buddha was an Indian. I have visited a Buddhist temple in Calcutta. Buddha Gaya, where Lord Buddha attained Enlightenment, and Sarnath are famous places for the Buddhists."

He nods. "People from Thailand go to India on pilgrimages."

A tape recorder kept next to his seat makes me curious. "Why do you bring it to class?"

"I don't follow the American accent well. Replaying the lectures helps me study."

I admit, "I have problems with accents, too. But, I rely on the textbooks."

As soon as the professor enters the class, we hurry back to our seats.

Handling Money

Just like in India, where one hundred paisas make a rupee, here one hundred cents make a dollar. Yet, the unfamiliar coins cause me inconvenience and confusion. The ten cent dime is smaller than a five cent nickel. The dime is close in shape and size to the siki, a twenty five paisa coin. A quarter resembles an *adhuli*, a fifty paisa coin. I must pay attention to the coins.

A one rupee bill is blue, two rupee is red, and five rupee is green. Accordingly, a ten rupee and one hundred-rupee bills are blue; whereas, a twenty rupee bill is red. That's how the multiples go. A one rupee bill is the smallest; a ten rupee bill is bigger than that. A one hundred rupee bill is bigger than ten rupee. Illiterate people identify bills by color and size.

Contrary to that, all bills are green and the same size here. One must be able to read the number on the bill in order to use it.

I have never handled a checking account before. It's is a new concept to me. I have to have a checking account in order to pay utility bills by checks and mail them. Back home bills are paid in cash in person.

Measurement Systems

I grew up with the MKS system. Converting from the MKS (meter, kilogram, second) to the FPS (foot, pound, second) system is another hassle.

An American classmate asks me, "My parents travelled to New Delhi, the capital of India. How far is your home from there?"

"Calcutta to New Delhi is about fourteen hundred kilometers," I reply confidently.

He looks confused. "How many miles?"

Thanks to our education system for fast capability in mental math, I calculate in my head and reply, "About nine hundred miles."

Weights are a little bit easier. Approximately half-a-kilogram makes a pound. In the grocery store I use this continuously.

It's good that no conversion is needed for time; a second stays the same in both units.

I also have to deal with measuring and calculating problems in many tests and homework assignments. One of my tests came back with the comment from the professor, "Please use the American system." He also deducted five points. In a hurry to finish a problem, I forgot about the conversion.

In the post office, while the clerk uses the cash register to calculate the amount due, I put down three dollars and eighty-four cents, the exact change, on the counter. He looks at me in disbelief and comments, "We don't work that way."

Does he think of me as a psychic?

My Vocabulary

The accent of the very word "schedule" leads me to change my mind. We have always uttered it with a silent "c." Whenever I mention "class schedule," "exam schedule," "bookstore schedule," "library schedule" or "lab schedule" no one follows me. After the first few attempts I spell it out only to hear a relieved voice, "Oh, you mean schedule." Americans sound it with full emphasis on the "c".

Time after time I go through the same tug of war. What a hassle! Finally, sick and tired of it, I decide to change my accent. It's their country and their university. I have had enough. I need to be understood without so much of a struggle. I compromise and start to sound out the "c" in "schedule."

Clearly, this is just the beginning.

Supermarket

What a grand collection of bread is in the bakery section of the supermarket. Breads can be prepared in such a wide variety? I am pleasantly surprised to find breads containing raisins, nuts and even fruits. Cakes contain these ingredients, but I never knew breads could, too.

We are rice eaters. Our occasional menu includes home-made Indian style *chapati, paratha* or *luchi*, whether dry or puffed in oil. Sometimes regular flour loaves are bought from the bakery.

So many kinds of cakes and pastries are available all the time? Delicious and tempting! Only a few look familiar; the rest of them belong to the unknown category. We relished the wide variety of Indian desserts at home, but eating a cake rarely happened.

In the supermarket's fresh fruits and vegetable sections, are winter vegetables of cauliflower, cabbage, tomatoes, green beans, green peas, beets, carrots and ladies fingers, known as okra, are plentiful. So are the winter fruits like apples, oranges and grapes. Apples and grapes are quite expensive back home, often beyond the reach of the common people; but not here. The year-round supplies of bananas, potatoes and *brinjals*, known as eggplants, are also abundant.

But there are produces that I grew up with that I haven't located yet. On the other hand, there is a big collection that's unfamiliar.

The supermarket concept for groceries is new to me also. Growing up in Calcutta, I have seen individuals selling produce in a common grocery market. Many of them sell just an item or two. The fruits and vegetables vary from season to season. They are sold and consumed immediately after they are harvested.

We are used to waiting for winter to eat winter fruits and vegetables. Similarly, we wait for summer in order to obtain a wide variety of mangoes, black-berries, cucumbers, lichis, melons, pineapples, guavas and ripe jackfruits. The fragrance of ripe fruits fills the air, even at a distance from the fruit market. Similarly, the fresh-fish-market smell may be detected while passing by the neighborhood.

A wide variety of juices are also sold in supermarkets here. Apple juice, orange juice, grape juice and mixed juices. I never knew such a variety of fruit drinks were available. For us, it's a common practice to eat fresh fruits instead of making juices.

We do use fruits to make various chutneys. In summer, mango roll-ups, known as *aamsatta*, are prepared. So are many mouth-watering pickles, called *aachar*, made with mangoes, guavas, limes or berries. All of these are home-made, using family-recipes containing savory spices. Then they are sun-dried in glass jars in courtyards or terraces. These are consumed year-round as snacks or with meals.

I use corn oil for regular cooking. The label shows a picture of an ear of corn. Once in a while we ate corn as a snack. It can be used to produce cooking oil, too? Mustard oil, with its stringent quality to clear sinus and mucous membranes, is the most common cooking oil in Bengal. South Indian cooking uses coconut oil.

Supermarkets load the groceries in big brown paper bags. Shoppers carry new bags home every time they shop!

In Calcutta, every household has sturdy grocery bags made of cotton, jute, or nylon. Separate ones are used for fruits and veggies, fish and meat, and rice, etc. The bags are washed and re-used for a long time.

Mass Consumption

A blouse-button gets loose in the washer. I will sew it back, but I don't know where to find a needle. Eventually, I come to know that the supermarket sells needles and thread.

What is this? A circular box containing a whole bunch of needles of different sizes! One, two, three, four—all together, twenty-four needles: from the small ones for fancy clothes all the way to the large ones that can be used with knitting wool.

Just a small needle for mending is all I need. Having no other choice, I buy the needle-collection most reluctantly. I doubt whether I would use all of them in my lifetime. More and more I realize things are packed to be sold as a unit, not as an individual item.

In Calcutta, the neighborhood stores, locally known as 'stationery stores', sell needles individually. Almost whatever they sell—candies, cookies, toiletries, pens and pencils—can be bought as a single count. In the university bookstore, lead pencils are sold in a twelve-pack, ball point pens in a ten-pack, candies and cookies are in packages.

It looks like "No individual sale" is the way of doing business here.

The same philosophy applies to groceries. Six-packs or twelve-packs of dessert when all I want to eat is just one or maybe two pieces. If I buy a pack, I end up eating all of it. At one point, they don't taste as good any longer. I end up consuming the entire content just to spare myself the guilt of wasting food.

Packs of candies, packs of cookies—feels like I'm being persuaded to consume more and more—a lot more than necessary.

Why are so many outdoor lights kept turned on at night? Not only the parking lot stays well lit, so does the pool area. Parking spots and walkways circling the apartment house stay lit, too. I have also noticed at the university that too many lights stay lit unnecessarily. What a massive waste of electricity!

Paper towels and paper napkins to wipe hands, tissue papers to sneeze. It's stunning to watch how frequently paper products are used at each and every step on a daily basis. What a thoughtless consumption and waste of paper! Why don't Americans use cloth towels and cloth napkins? Why don't they carry cloth handkerchiefs like us?

Student Habits

It seems striking to me that students write only on one side of a page. They never flip the page to use the other side. What a waste of paper!

We have always used red-and-blue pencils for marking the books. Multi-color markers are used in abundance here.

Students consume snacks, juices and soft drinks while class is going on. I am not used to this at all. We were never allowed to do anything like this in Calcutta.

Students here drink just a few sips of water at a time. We drink a lot of water, not just a few sips. Water fountains are located on each floor of the Engineering building. But the drinking water is way too cold for me. We are used to drinking water at room temperature whether at home or at school. I keep trying different water fountains. Finally, I find one at the corner of a ninth floor hallway across from the elevator. Water is not cold. May be that's why other students do not care to use it. I am happy to have found drinking water. What a relief!

Food Issues

I never learned to cook. I can barely fix a cup of tea or fry an egg. Can't afford to buy a toaster yet. There is a long list of higher priority items. In the morning I warm up bread slices in a cheap aluminum saucepan. They frequently get burned and taste bad.

My breakfast every morning is two slices of bread with butter and grape jelly, followed by a tall glass of warm milk. The milk tastes great here. Breakfast keeps me going for hours.

I have learned the hard way to be careful when warming milk. The day it foamed and spilled over, the mess was too big to clean. Even after cleaning, the odor of burned milk lasted for days.

Most days I survive on steamed rice with boiled potatoes and eggs. I use butter generously and sprinkle some black pepper instead of jalapenos, since they are unavailable. Far from being monotonous, it tastes great and satisfies my appetite. I grew up a rice eater. The rice at dinner is so fulfilling.

To begin with, the rice never turned out right. If I added less water, it didn't get boiled enough to be consumed. If I added too much water, it ended up being mashed rice instead of nice, fluffy rice grains. After daily trial and error, it's getting better.

The parboiled rice we are used to consuming in Calcutta is not available. "Long grain white rice" sold in groceries is my only choice. This is not the delicious fragrant "Basmati rice" from the fields of Punjab. It's barely white rice devoid of any fragrance and taste.

I never had any interest in cooking. Always, I have intentionally avoided the kitchen. Now-a-days I really regret not learning to cook. Who knew cooking would turn out to be so hard and complicated? Who knew it was going to be such a required skill?

So many items are available in the groceries, but I struggle with meals every day. At my earnest request my mother, an excellent cook, sent me some recipes in her letters. Traditionally, Indian recipes mention a dash of this and a pinch of that. No particular measure is used. No mention of time and temperature, either.

It's extremely hard for a novice like me to experiment with them. Moreover, statements like "when almost fried," or "when almost boiled," make no sense to me. I have no idea about the phases.

Over the weekend, sometimes I attempt to follow my mom's recipes to fix a cauliflower and potato curry or an egg curry. Each attempt turns out to be a total failure. Some days the vegetables don't get boiled enough. Other days they become over-boiled and mashed.

Some days it goes even further. Not only the vegetables get burned, along with it the aluminum pan gets burned, too. This puts me through the challenge and struggle of cleaning the pan. I bought just a few utensils. All of them are needed all the time.

Totally disappointed with myself, I eat rice with the burned vegetable choosing the least burned pieces due to lack of any other item.

Foods cooked in corn oil instead of mustard oil, don't taste as good.

The food court is located within the Student Center building. That's where I have lunch. The fast food place, McDonald's, is conveniently located at the entry level of the Student Center. At lunch time students wait in long queues. It helps to eat either before or after the regular lunch hours.

I don't eat beef. Never have. The place stinks. The only item available for me is a fish-fillet sandwich. That stinks, too. I don't know whether it is the kind of fish used or the preparation itself. I load up the sandwich with ketchup, hold my breath and take a bite, just for the sake of eating a lunch. The food has to hold me till dinner after I get home.

The university dining room is decorated well with individual tables for four, nice chandeliers and a warm, inviting atmosphere. They serve a variety of food. Their menu changes often. It caters to the deans, senior faculties, guests and visitors. They can afford to pay for steak dinners and expensive desserts. Once in a while a junior professor or secretary eats there mostly to celebrate a special occasion. Students cannot afford to use the dining room on a daily basis.

The ice cream shop in the food court is frequented by the students; especially the female students. It stays crowded most of the time. I visit it only once a while, though I really enjoy ice cream. There are so many delicious varieties and flavors available; most of them I have never known before.

Foreign students must count every penny. Local students get to go home and eat well on holidays and weekends.

Grocery Shopping

Sometimes students from the university ride together to the grocery store. I barely know them and don't feel comfortable joining them. Basically, I don't like to accept a favor.

About 3:00 PM every Friday at the end of my classes, I walk to the local supermarket. Coming back to the apartment with loaded brown paper grocery bags is not easy. First, I catch a bus. Then it's a tough twenty minutes walk down the hill from the bus stop. I keep it limited to a single bag.

There is a one-room neighborhood grocery store on the first floor of a house on my way to the university. It's about five minutes walk from our apartment house. It's owned by an elderly, white-bearded gentleman from Italy. His English is hard to follow. On my way home I stop by there to buy eggs or half-a-gallon of milk or bread. He charges much more than the regular grocery stores. But it's the convenience that works in favor of me. The other attraction is that he sells smaller packages, like half-a-dozen eggs, half-a-pound of butter, etc. I don't have to buy a whole lot.

On my Birthday

As a child I had big birthday celebrations with extended family and many friends. Since high school it gradually became a family affair including only a few close friends. The celebration was simple, not extravagant, yet meaningful. It was something worth looking forward to.

Dad had superb taste. Every year for my birthday he bought me a sari, most of the times silk, his favorite material. I was highly complemented wherever I wore it. Other relatives gave me money. My brother and sister usually bought me books, good examples of, "It's the thought that counts."

My birthday is coming up within the next few days. I have looked at the calendar then looked the other way. It's like, so what? No one knows here, neither do they care. I come home to receive a blue aerogramme. The address is in Dad's handwriting. A letter from my parents! This is unexpected. I received their weekly letter just two days ago. Impatiently, standing right there in the common passage in front of the row of mailboxes at the bottom of the staircase, I open it.

It's a special blessing letter for my birthday. Dad wrote a few lines. Just like his reserved yet caring personality, his letters are short but deep and meaningful. Suddenly I realize words are becoming hazy due to my tears. "This year I don't need to place an order for *gulab jamuns*." Just a single line conveyed how much he missed me. It touched me so deeply, I couldn't resist crying. Because they were my favorite dessert he always made sure we had plenty of them available on my birthday. One year *gulab jamun* was unavailable in and around Calcutta because of an official ban on milk desserts due to the scarcity of milk. Dad ordered a generous quantity from a confectioner outside the banned area and sent someone over to get them. I was so surprised and excited!

Mom's letter is more emotional and elaborate. "You love sweets, so make sure to eat a cake on your birthday. Just like other years, I will hold a special prayer for you with homemade rice pudding offerings, the traditional way of praying for a long and prosperous life..."

On my birthday, I sit down at the library between classes and focus on reading the letter, at least for the thirtieth time. Each and every line along with punctuations has been memorized by this time. It means so much to me. Holding back my tears, I write down a reply expressing my love and respect for them. Not a word gets written about any hardship. It would be so hard on them. I make it a point to mention that I had some strawberry ice-cream, my favorite, at lunch.

After mailing the letter at the campus post-office, I stand outside in the open. The sky above me reassures my connection to my motherland, my roots. It is the same sky that extends over my parents' home too, though far across the world. It must be the middle of the night there now. Maybe the sky is star-studded maybe not. Is it a full moon, or a new moon, or somewhere in between? I have lost track of the lunar calendar.

Though thousands of miles separate us, the bonding is as strong as ever. There is no gap in that. I owe it to myself to return to my roots. In these lonely moments I become more and more determined to finish my studies and return home. To spend my entire life here, away from my loved ones, would be so empty and meaningless.

As it is, I feel uprooted. Both of my names, the formal one and my nickname, are lost. I miss my names badly. My official first name is too long and hard for Americans. My nickname, the one that is integrated in me—the name I hold nearest and dearest to my heart and soul—has always been restricted to my family and close friends. I never even mention it here. Its only existence occurs in letters from home. My parents still address me with my nickname in their letters. The official address carries my full name.

Being a daughter to my parents, a member of our family, I never realized what an integral part of me it has been, until I got here. People have no idea about who I am, what my family background is. The fact that I come from a well-reputed, highly educated family doesn't mean anything here. We grew up with, "Remember the family's reputation and behave accordingly." We always kept up to it. This has been instilled in me in such a way that even in the other end of the world, I live up to it. My self-esteem is high. My lifestyle is reserved. But there is a certain kind of emptiness I sense. I feel like I am nobody here. I could have come from any family, been anyone's daughter, any status, any value, and it wouldn't have mattered.

Spending an isolated and uprooted life here is like living in exile. Spending a few years for education is all that I foresee.

Saraswati Puja

Saraswati is the goddess of education in Hindu religion. The auspicious celebration of worshipping the goddess means a lot to students. The local Hindu Bengali community has arranged for the celebration to take place at the lounge of an on-campus dormitory on a Saturday in February. I am delighted to know this since I am too shy to ask anyone for a ride. The student contribution is five-dollars per head.

After the religious performance the lunch follows. The traditional lunch menu on the day of Saraswati Puja is pretty much standard. *Khichuri* is cooked with fried *Moong dal* and *Basmati* rice, with plenty of clarified butter, better known as *ghee* in Indian cooking. Deep fried eggplant, cauliflower and potato curry with green peas, and chutney made with berries or tomato and raisins. The fragrant vegetarian lunch usually ends with milk desserts like *rosogolla, sandesh* and pink sweet-yogurt. It is a lunch worth waiting for.

Everyone present is speaking in Bengali. A portable cassette player is playing Bengali folk songs and Tagore songs. What a comfortable and festive environment! For a split second it creates the illusion I'm in Calcutta.

Since university students and faculty members are involved, use of the lounge is free of charge. The projector, a property of the university, is also free.

The after lunch special is the Bengali movie "*Atith*i," based on a story by Tagore and directed by the famous director Tapan Sinha. The big tape rotates and the projector shows the movie on a white wall. It takes us back to countryside Bengal and we are mesmerized.

Fifteen-year-old villager Tarapada, the main character, is totally indifferent to the materialistic world. Heavenly innocence beaming on his face, his mesmerizing flute recitals, and his gypsy mind-set capture the audience. His quiet departure at the end of the movie, leaves us sad.

Overwhelming feelings follow me home and stay with me for the rest of the weekend. Staying lost in the world of nostalgia, I escape from my world of stern reality.

The Engineering Library

Located on the eighth floor of the Engineering building, this library is usually pretty crowded with undergraduate and graduate students. Shelf after shelf stacked with texts and journals in all disciplines of engineering are labeled and arranged in order. Three black-and-white pay copiers located close to the circulation desk are available for students' use.

Among the three librarians Dr. Deborah Bush is the youngest, only about thirty. She holds a doctorate in library science and is the main librarian.

Graduate students are advised to contact her if they need help locating research topics journals, references and cross-references. We hear, starting next year she will offer a one-credit graduate course to help students with how to track research material.

The window-side desks, away from the entrance and the circulation desk, are my favorite. A look outside reveals the infinite sky and makes me feel better.

I also enjoy a mental escape while watching a section of the campus. There are more classes in the mornings and longer duration labs in the afternoons. Consequently, more activities can be watched in the mornings. Busy students carrying heavy book bags are rushing from one class to another. The ten minute break between classes is not long enough, especially if the classes are in different buildings and stairs or elevators are involved. The huge clock on top of the clock-tower rings loudly at each hour, marking the beginning of a class period.

In the afternoons it's common to watch students leaving the food court in the Student Center after lunch, still sipping soft-drinks. Then there are students leaving the university bookstore with bags full of merchandise. These thick plastic bags carry the university name and logo. They are quite fashionable and sturdy.

Telephone Bill

I need to ask Dad for some paperwork. Getting it answered by letter would take three weeks minimum. A telegram would cost a lot too. There is enough time, but I am so lonely and I miss my parents so much that I want to talk to them. I want to hear their voices. The urge is irresistible. Finally, I indulge myself, though I am determined to keep the conversation very short.

The telephone company informs me it will have to be an operator-assisted call; hence, expensive. The operator gets Dad on the line. At first, Dad is anxious about what has happened to me. After assuring him I am fine, we talk. Mom and Dad's voices make me feel as if they are standing next to me. So soothing! So comforting! So supportive! It becomes increasingly harder to hang up the phone. I get carried away.

They keep reminding me, "It's costing you too much. Hang up."

While Mom keeps talking, I overhear Dad telling her, "Don't talk too long. She has to pay the bill. Hurry up."

Though I meant to end the conversation in five minutes, it stretches to eighteen minutes.

I am so happy and enthusiastic after talking that I cry. The fact that—I am not alone, I am very much loved and cared for and missed—has been re-established. I have strong roots that are well-anchored.

It's needless to mention cutting corners will not be enough. I will also have to give up a few necessary things to pay the ninety-dollar bill. Still, right now, it feels like it's worth every cent of it.

Mr. Kapur's Indian Grocery Shop

Mr. Kapur's Indian Grocery shop is located within fifteen minutes walk from the university. They bought a two-story residence on the main street and use the front room of the main floor as the store. The store is at the road level. They live upstairs. They have a three-year-old daughter, who follows her mother around the store. Mrs. Kapur does catering on the side. Her husband teaches college part-time.

One side of the store contains a shelf with cooking appliances, utensils and pots and pans. A stainless steel pressure cooker looking almost like the one my mother has, displays a fifty dollar price tag. That's expensive! What difference does it make to me? I don't know how to cook. There is an appliance called the Rice Cooker. A rice cooker? I grew up a rice eater, but never heard of such a thing. There are common stainless steel utensils and dinnerware imported from India and priced accordingly.

They have just started selling synthetic Saris imported from Japan, each selling for about twenty dollars.

They sell big bags of Basmati rice, the famous fragrant rice from India. Only people with cars can carry them home. But two-to-five pound bags of various lentils, fresh vegetables, oils, ghee, spices, and fresh homemade desserts and snacks are also available. Enough ingredients are available to fix a good meal. If only I could cook!

My eyes couldn't help but notice my favorite dessert, the fluffy gulab-jamuns floating in sweet syrup. Irresistible! My mouth waters. Haven't had them since I got here. I will buy a dozen and savor them over the next few days.

Mrs. Kapur reads my mind and encourages me, "Fresh and homemade. I made them last night. Really good."

I can't wait to go home and start eating. "How much are they?"

She answers casually, "Two for a dollar."

That's outrageous! I don't believe it. Just can't afford it. I try to conceal my feelings. With a deep sigh I pay for five pounds of *musur dal*, the red lentils, and a half-a-pound of turmeric powder, and exit the store disappointed. Steamed rice and lentils will be my meal.

American Vocabulary

American vocabulary is so monotonous! In Bengali we say the same thing in so many different ways. We ask the same question using different words. Whereas Americans use the very same words over and over. Sounds like all of them are reciting standard scripts. Likewise, their responses are also standardized. Are they aware of this?

Something I hear throughout the day:

"Hi, how are you?"

"Good; how about you?"

"Doing great."

"That's good to hear."

Beginning from early childhood we learn English based on grammar and spelling. I still remember my schooldays having to memorize appropriate prepositions, phrases and idioms, studying for the English examinations. Maybe most Americans learn the language colloquially. The striking difference between their English and ours is easily distinguishable.

Our education system makes us write a lot. Also, the schools put an emphasis on handwriting. Consequently, most of us have good handwriting. The majority of the American students, even many of the professors, do not have good handwriting. Some write illegibly.

I am having difficulty getting accustomed to daily American vocabulary. All the time, I hear "I love it!" "I hate it!" "I think so." "I don't think so." "I don't care." There is so much emphasis on "I." Don't others matter?

How does a family feel if everyone is so strongly opinionated and so self-centered? Where is the emphasis on family values? How do they interact with extended families?

According to our upbringing, "I hate you!" would be considered an extreme statement. Not to like someone is acceptable. But there is a wide range of feelings between dislike and hatred.

A poem framed at the departmental secretary's desk in the main office ends with: "The least important word is "I." These students really need to comprehend this.

The frequent use of the superlative degree is very annoying. "The best movie ever," "The worst class offered," "The greatest campus in the world," "The best professor in the world," "The fastest car in the world."

English grammar is structured with "good, better, best." A comparative degree does exist. The superlative is not the only choice.

Moreover, the United States is one of the countries in the world. "Best in the USA" is far from being the best in the world.

What an arrogant way of talking! The arrogance hurts my ears and my feelings. Just "Please" and "Thank you" do not express all the politeness required. Much more is needed.

In our language we hardly ever say "Please" or "Thank you." These are expressed more in the tone and the manner of speaking, inflexion in voice as well as the choice of words. Bengali is well-known as one of the sweetest languages of the world.

Whether in English or in Bengali, I never use curse words. My upbringing excluded these. A vocabulary is a direct reflection on the culture of the family. Use of bad words is below etiquette and courtesy. No matter how upset we are, we can express that in formal words.

I hear students talking among themselves freely using profanity, as if it's just a manner of speech. Though I recognize very few bad words in English, I get irritated. How do they utter these? What a shame! Doesn't anyone mind?

The profane words burn holes in my ears. I look away and pretend not to hear. Going through school, college and the university back home, I never did hear such profanity used in an educational institution.

Epidemic

An epidemic of mumps and measles breaks out. In order to keep it under control and prevent it from spreading any further the state health department sends representatives to perform mass inoculations at the university. Thirty-nine thousand students plus the staff in two days. Students who had mumps and measles, or who have been inoculated in the past, are exempted. But everyone else, including those who are not sure, must be inoculated. This is the category I belong to.

I have always dreaded a syringe. Waiting in the long queue I feel even more nervous. As I enter the Student Center lounge, the location for the activity, I ask an outgoing student, "Was it bad? Did it hurt?"

He nods and leaves. I keep hearing the six-feet-tall athletic American guys around me asking the same question. What? They are nervous too! That's humorous. I am not so frightened any longer. As my turn comes I step forward trying to locate a syringe, but can't find any. Standing next to a tall cylinder I feel a sharp pressure in my upper arm.

The nurse assures me, "It's over. You did just fine."

For mass inoculations they are using high pressure air instead of needles.

Disability

Why are there so many left-handed students? Back home I hardly ever saw anyone writing with their left hand.

Actually most of the people in India think of being left handed as somewhat abnormal and shameful. Children are forced to use their right hand. One of my girlfriends back home, though truly left-handed, writes with her right hand. She does everything else with her left hand.

Making room for handicapped people among normal people is an aspect of this society that has highly impressed me. There are so many disabled students and staff in the university. They move in wheelchairs and perform their daily chores. People do not look down upon them or pity them. They are treated just like everyone else. Wheelchair accessible paths make it possible for them to navigate from building to building, to food courts, to the Student Center, the bookstore and the libraries.

There is a doctoral student in our Computer Engineering Department. He is white, skinny and short, and wears high-powered thick glasses. The lower part of his face looks abnormal.

It distorts when he speaks. He walks normally, and goes up and down the stairs without difficulty. Only once in a while, if I run into him, we exchange a formal "Hello."

My classmate Ben explains to me, "He was born that way. It's a disorder."

Though embarrassed, I admit, "I have heard him talk a lot to others. But I don't understand what he says."

"To begin with, it's hard to follow him. People get used to it after a while."

I have really noticed that no one treats him pitifully. He is treated like everyone else. Neither his friends and family nor the rest of the society have forced him to believe he was born with a cursed life and would live as a cripple for the rest of his life. I am highly impressed.

In India, even a little abnormality or handicap is often treated like a disgrace to the family. The handicapped person is subjected to a shameful life, hidden away from the public eyes. The person wishes for death every day while waiting for it. How inhuman!

There are families in India who have a different outlook, but they are rare. Even the number of schools for the blind and disabled is low compared to the need.

A school for the "deaf and dumb" is located next to the Science College in Calcutta. Many of those students used to ride the same bus with me. The teenage girls in uniform were always happy and communicated among themselves in sign language, and laughed frequently. I never saw any of them sad or worried. I used to wonder if being sad and complaining a lot about everything was a trait only for normal people? Those who have so much complain about the little they lack.

A student, a boy about ten, was always accompanied by his adult sister. She used to drop him off at the school every day. One day at Howrah Station, while I was waiting for the bus, she approached me. "I need a favor, please. I have to go to work early today. When you get off the bus could you please make sure that my little brother gets off with you?"

"But his school is across the street. It's a major street with lots of traffic," I replied.

"Don't worry about that. He knows how to cross the street."

Even after her reassurance I continued to hesitate. But noticing the polite appeal in her desperate face, I agreed.

She explained this to her brother, and had him stand next to me before she left.

The entire way, about forty minutes, I remained doubtful and anxious. What if he didn't want to get off with me? I didn't know his language. How was I going to convince him? I could not leave him alone on the bus. If it took too long I would miss my class. Since I lacked the ability to communicate with him, I really shouldn't have agreed.

My heart started beating faster as the stop approached. To my surprise, he got up with his book bag and approached the door toward the conductor. As soon as the bus stopped, he left without even paying attention to me. Carefully checking the traffic on both sides, he crossed the street and walked to his school. I felt so stupid! He was much more intelligent and independent than I thought.

A few months later, I ran into his sister. She said, "My brother asked why he didn't see you in the bus any longer. I explained to him that you had graduated."

Missing friends

I miss my friends back home.

Just after completing the Master of Science degree in Science College, Calcutta, one of my classmates got a good job; out-of-state, though. He sent us some money to celebrate his position. About twenty of us gathered at a confectioner's shop, locally known as *"Mistir Dokan,"* and had tea and snacks. Because of the very plain rank of the store, the money spent per head was nominal. But that didn't matter. The enthusiasm, the joy of celebrating a classmate's job, was so exciting! Everyone in the shop heard about it.

Science College had a cafeteria with plain wooden tables and chairs. Food was cooked in the adjacent kitchen. The steam, the smell, the heat, the hissing sound of boiling water for tea coming from an extra-large aluminum kettle, loud orders being placed, loud conversation among the students and cafeteria crowd—was the regular scenario.

There was also a big table with benches outdoors where many preferred to eat. Classmates and friends carried on loud conversations about professors, classes, tests and exams, politics, inflation, and events in Calcutta. To spice up life, to make it more realistic, some chattering and gossip was also a part of it. Young students, so full of life, energy, and enthusiasm! Passive participation was fine, too. Some liked just sipping a cup of tea while listening to the ongoing discussions, or just watching the flow of life.

I miss all of this. Suddenly my life has become so isolated that some days I long to hear just a few words in Bengali, my mother language.

Student Life Here

Here, in the university, I hear the students talking, especially on Fridays, "Let's go out and party tonight."

I am not interested. Going out drinking and partying has never been a part of my life. I would much rather stay home and read literature.

University classes proceed with lightning speed. No breathing time between tests. In Calcutta University the final exams are taken once a year, or once in two years. Just keeping up with the classes year-round and studying hard over the three months' examination preparation period right before the finals was enough to score really well.

Whereas over here, the university is based on the quarter system: winter, spring, summer and fall. Each quarter lasts about three months. As soon as classes begin, homework and projects are assigned. After a month or so midterm exams are held; and after ten weeks, finals. Most of the time, in addition to the final exam, a percentage of homework, projects and midterms contribute to the final grade. This makes each of them important. There is no room for procrastination. Winter quarter finals are scheduled to take place in the beginning of March.

The university assistantship that covers my tuition and pay is based on a good performance. If I don't perform up to the mark, it will be discontinued. This leaves me no choice. I am solely dependent on the assistantship. I don't know a single soul in this country who could lend me a helping hand. That thought is carved in my brain, and I work accordingly.

I'm surprised to see how comfortable the students are with calculators. Pressing the keys with their left hand, they write down numbers with their right. I've never used a calculator before. In my early education we memorized tables. Further down the road we used log tables. It takes me a while to find the digits and proper keys on a calculator. This is a major inconvenience, especially in tests. Consequently, I lag behind the class.

My Mom

Broken-hearted and worried due to poor grades at the end of the first quarter, I am ready to give up. Everything—the loneliness, the homesickness and culture shock, the unaccustomed winter, food problems and financial hardship—has taken a severe toll on me. My grades this quarter are barely passing, way below my expectation. How did I get these grades? I expected better. I have worked very hard. If this isn't good enough, I am never going to make it. I am on the verge of collapse.

Exhaustion, disappointment and frustration overwhelm me. I don't feel like eating. I go to bed without dinner. It feels as if I am in a deep hole, surrounded by never-ending darkness. I try to fall asleep, but keep tossing and turning in bed.

I am restless. Hopeless. There is no one to turn to. No one I can talk to help ease the load. Tears keep flowing in my lonely, dark room.

After a while I go to the window and look outside. A few cars are running on the interstate, even this late at night. The headlights appear small and dim from a distance. Although dark and cold, it's a clear night with bright shining stars. If I quit and return home now, how am I going to look my mom in the eyes?

My mom's student life flashes before me. Her elder sister was married at age twelve and she started bearing children at fourteen. Mom's sister's marriage, the overwhelming dowry, the impact of that on the family's finances and the hardship the younger siblings had to undergo that had turned Mom against getting married early. Though this was normal in that time and place, she rebelled. She vowed to be independent.

Having to convince her parents not to negotiate marriage proposals until she finished high school was bad enough. After finishing high school at fifteen, Mom was determined to go to college. Neither her village in East Bengal nor any place nearby had a college.

There was a college in the city, where her paternal aunt lived. Grandfather requested his sister to allow Mom to live with them and attend college.

The fast and direct response was, "Your teenage daughter is very beautiful. She is also old enough to get married. Letting her live with us and go to college will be a huge responsibility. We will not accept that. But, in the future, if one of your sons wants to do it, we will accommodate him."

This was the end of that approach. But Mom was persistent. "I want to go to college. I don't want to get married now."

"No way," replied her father. "You are my daughter. It's my responsibility to get you married. I will arrange for that. I cannot afford to put you through college, pay your hostel expenses, and pay for your wedding. College is out of the question."

Mom, the second daughter among three girls and four boys, was well aware of the financial situation. Being stubborn and determined however, she appeared in an All-India competitive examination and secured a women's scholarship. She broke the traditional chain. Her journey began.

Mom came to Calcutta in the mid-1940s, stayed in a women's hostel and attended a women's college. During her overnight train journeys between her hometown and Calcutta, she, the teenager, travelled alone. India was ruled by the British then. Women in those days wouldn't think of doing it.

Mom's scholarship barely covered her minimum expenses, but she prevailed. The hostel didn't allow light in any room past ten o' clock at night, so she studied in the bathroom using a lantern. In two years she got the I.A. (Intermediate of Arts) degree. Two more years were required to get the B.A. and graduate.

But due to the intense political situation Mom's dreams were shattered. The "Independence Movement of India" was in full swing against the ruling British. Hindus and Muslims had turned against one another causing communal riots and killings. Circumstances were getting worse and worse day by day.

Finally, the British left India, but only after slicing it into India with a Hindu majority and Pakistan with a Muslim majority.

On August 15, 1947 India became independent. The State of Bengal was split into East Bengal and West Bengal. East Bengal went to Pakistan. West Bengal stayed as a part of India. Most of the Hindus from East Bengal fled the country and migrated to India.

For the Hindus in East Bengal, land owned by generation after generation of forefathers—the land of birthright, the home and the hometown they had known as their very own—disappeared overnight. There was no safety, no security, no promise of life the next day. Landlords and affluent people, who owned hundreds of acres—wealthy due to their land-oriented income—became landless instantly. Men were killed. Women were raped and murdered. Thousands died like bugs.

Under these circumstances Mom secured a job in a suburb of Calcutta. She brought over three of her younger siblings, two brothers and a sister from East Bengal. They lived with her and attended middle school and high school. Mom, the daughter who fought so hard with the family to get an education, suddenly became a powerful provider.

It took years before the turmoil settled down somewhat. Her parents and her other brothers eventually were situated near Calcutta.

Mom got married—with no dowry, of course. Even after having three children, two girls and a boy, Mom's desire to graduate from college stayed dormant, but never died.

Friends and relatives dropped by at our home all the time. Some came just to visit, some out of necessity. My paternal grandmother, the eldest of six girls and two boys, had a large extended family on her side. My paternal grandfather's elders had already passed away. Since he was the senior-most on his side, relatives came to get his approval on family issues and to seek favors. Some came to get his permission to use his name in invitation letters for weddings, etc. It was customary to use the name of the eldest man alive on the father's side, even if he was a first or a second cousin.

Friends and relatives in close proximity usually visited for a few hours. They were always offered snacks and tea. Anyone present at lunch or dinner time always had a meal with us.

Out-of-town relatives often arrived without prior notice. They were extended hospitality and requested to stay with us. No money or help was ever expected or accepted from them.

Some came to shop for weddings. Shopping in Calcutta offered a better choice at a much more reasonable price. They stayed a few days and returned with suitcases full of various saris, a bridal costume, a bride-groom's costume, and gold jewelry.

Some made the trip just to negotiate marriages for their family members.

People who came for doctors' or specialists' appointments often stayed two to three weeks to complete a re-check before returning home.

My father had two cousins who lived in Europe. Because their hometowns were at remote places, they always spent a few days with us on their way to and from the Dumdum International Airport in Calcutta. We enjoyed their visits, especially because the topics of discussion were so different. What they did when it snowed; they no longer ate rice and fish on a daily basis; their surroundings were way too different from ours. We absorbed these discussions like story-telling, our eyes popping out in amazement.

Our grandmother was the lady of the house. She was more in the managerial role, whereas Mom had to make sure everything was done properly. If a few guests suddenly dropped by half-an-hour before lunch, she made sure another pot of rice was cooked to accommodate them. Mom also cooked special items for special occasions. Serving food is a part of our culture, and she frequently did that.

Though we had a live-in cook, and a maid who came twice a day to clean the house and do laundry and the dishes, Mom was always busy. Every time people visited and stayed, it added more to her responsibilities.

In the midst of these activities Grandfather, a retired attorney, made sure the students in the household were studying seriously. An extra-large room on the first floor was used as the study. This room was isolated from the rest of the house, connected through only one door. My aunt had graduated from college and was continuing her studies at the university. One uncle was in engineering, another in medical school. The students shut the door and concentrated on their studies.

The engineer and the doctor graduated and went abroad for higher studies. After my youngest aunt finished her masters and got married off, Mom started thinking seriously about going back to college. She always carried in her heart a burden of inferiority for not being a graduate in a highly educated family. She knew my grandfather, the head of the household, would have to grant her permission for further study.

One morning after breakfast, while Grandfather was reading the daily newspaper in his room, Mom approached him very nervously. As customary, she had her head covered with the end of her sari and stood at a distance. Grandfather was surprised to see her. He glanced at her and gestured with an interrogative look.

With a trembling low voice Mom said, "I want to study for a B.A."

Grandfather stared at her intensively for a few minutes. She stood helpless, almost shaking, and ready to collapse.

"Want to go to college?" He asked in his usual serious tone. He paused. "Get me the Byakaran Koumudi and Julius Caesar."

Both of these books were required as foundations for a B.A. Byakaran Koumudi, authored by Pandit Vidyasagar, was the basis of Sanskrit grammar. Though clueless, Mom retrieved the books from the study and brought them back to him.

Grandfather glanced through pages and asked her a few questions.

Years had passed since Mom had been a student. She answered nervously and unsurely.

"Hum." Grandfather thought for a while. It seemed like an eternity to Mom. "You will make it. Go ahead."

Overwhelmed with joy, Mom bent down and touched his feet to show her gratitude and get his blessings. She was too emotional to speak.

Mom registered in a local college for the morning session. Her college hours were 6:30 to 10:30 AM. Her days revolved around all sorts of responsibilities: college in the morning, work during the day, household chores and responsibilities in the evening and at night. All three of us children were in elementary school at that time. In the evenings when we saw her for the first time, our complaining and whining poured out. Whatever else happened in the household took higher priority over her studies.

Though she never got a chance to focus on her studies, she was desperate to get her degree. She knew this was her one and only golden opportunity and she couldn't let it pass. Every morning she woke up at 3:30 AM and tiptoed down the stairs to the study hall. No alarm clock, no footstep, no noise that could disturb others fast asleep. Without any exception, she studied two hours before daybreak.

Her motivation and dedication were rewarded when she passed the B.A. exam. Her lifelong dream of graduating from college finally came true.

We, the three siblings, were ecstatic. We jumped and yelled in joy. We made sure to announce it to all who visited us. It was customary in our family to write letters to keep in touch with the friends and relatives who lived at distances. In each and every letter we made sure to convey the great news in capital letters.

My paternal grandfather was excited to say, "There is no age limit for education!"

I am sure my dad was happy too, but he was the quiet and reserved type. Moreover, it wasn't appropriate to celebrate a wife's success. Without his help and compassion Mom would have never made it.

Previously, some of our jealous relatives had made sarcastic comments, "Look at her, a mother of three, gets up in the morning and goes to college. Never heard of such a thing. How absurd! How funny! Ha! Ha!" They were over-confident that Mom was not going to succeed. We never responded to them. I am sure Mom's graduation was the best possible response, a slap on their face...

I had lost track of time. It must have been hours. The dark sky is gradually getting lighter. Stars are disappearing. The eastern sky is preparing for the sunrise. The interstate near the apartment complex is coming back to life with rushing cars.

To this day, I haven't been able to fathom the kind of iron will, motivation, determination, and strength of mind that would allow a teenage girl from a remote village to break the traditional chain and become victorious.

I cannot quit studies and go home a loser. To suit this system, I have to try even harder with a better strategic approach. I have heard the first quarter is the toughest for foreign students. This was my first quarter.

If I quit now and go home, how could I look Mom in the eye? My efforts have been no match for her struggle, not yet. I could never do this to her.

Considering the extent of sacrifices my parents made to assure our higher studies, quitting is impossible. Their determination and sacrifice to be sure that their children get a great education cannot go unrewarded.

Dad's elder brother lived and worked out-of-state. Dad, the eldest son living in the household, had too many family responsibilities. In addition to his highly responsible full-time job, he was the pillar of support in our joint family. The same applied to our extended families, uncles and aunts, first and distant cousins. It was his sense of responsibility and his willingness to help that put him in that position. As a result of Partition—the separation of India and Pakistan—many of our relatives were still struggling. Their unemployment and instability led to numerous problems. One relative could not come up with the registration fees for his final examination in college, another one really needed a job just for his family's survival, yet another suffered from physical ailments. Everyone knew approaching Dad would resolve the problem. Dad always stood shoulder-to-shoulder with them and helped them.

In our family, he carried not only the financial but also all other responsibilities for everyone: siblings and parents. He negotiated marriages for his sisters and helped his brothers go abroad. He was there for everybody. Consequently, Dad had very little involvement with us, his children. Though he lived with us, he was kind of a distant person. We hardly ever approached him for anything.

My grandmother's magnetic attraction was her magnificent ability to read storybooks aloud and tell stories. Her facial expressions, inflexions in her voice, and the pauses—all were remarkable. We could see everything happening right in front of us. She read to us after lunch every day. We could hardly wait for that. Probably this was what made all of her children and grandchildren passionate about reading and helped them excel in education.

Spring

The spring quarter begins in the middle of March, 1980. The weather is pleasantly shifting away from severe winter. It feels as if spring is not very far away. Between regular cold days some days are nice and warmer. A few nice and sunny days at a stretch and the bone-chilling cold is gone. Snow begins melting away little by little. My eager and impatient wait for spring usually ends in a big disappointment, as it gets colder again. It's like revolving in a circle.

Finally spring arrives. It stops snowing, and ice and snow stay melted. The sidewalks are no longer slippery. I can walk without watching every step and being scared of sliding down. I get rid of the heavy overcoat and get used to a lighter jacket again. No scarf, no gloves, no hat. Without the excessive weight it's such a light and relaxed feeling. What a relief!

I get to see other residents not buried under overcoats, scarves and hats. I start to recognize them by face. On my way to and from the university I see other people walking, too. Many students enjoy a walk in this pleasant weather.

Tulip stems peek out shyly. Chirping birds are heard at the crack of the dawn. On my way to the university a garden belonging to a single-story family dwelling looks flooded with red, yellow and orange tulips. What an attractive, colorful combination as soon as the winter waved goodbye! I pause to enjoy the flowers. There is a few square foot patch of land next to the entrance to my apartment. Colorful tulips will look nice there. After some hesitation I address the elderly gentleman, probably the owner of the family dwelling, busy working in the yard.

"Beautiful flowers. Where can I get the seeds, Sir?"

His prompt reply, "You can buy the bulbs from me right now."

It's beyond my comprehension. A shocking eye-opener! An established gentleman is asking a student for money just for some seeds! What kind of country is this? Is it a part of their culture? Back home it's a pride to share seeds and plants with others. Offering money would be considered offensive.

While standing confused I hear his words, "But you may not want to buy now. Fall is the time to plant tulips."

Campus in Spring

In the beginning of spring, a crew of uniformed employees from a landscape company work diligently to prune the bushes and clean up the yards. They throw away the piles of yard debris. After lawn mowing and removing dead grass, they fertilize the yards. Automated sprinkler systems water the huge lawns a few times a week.

Watering the grass! This is new to me. Calcutta is warm and humid, and especially in the monsoon season it rains excessively. Grass stays green as it is.

Within the next few weeks light-green new grass peeks out. Gradually the lawns look green, healthy and full of life. Some signs are put up asking people not to step in the grass. But that does not stop some students, especially when they are in a hurry switching classes.

Big trees are also clipped, and dead branches are removed. Fresh new leaves peek out. These are not the mango, berry, grapefruit, *neem* and *banion* trees that I am used to seeing. These are all unknown to me; so are the bushes.

The campus looks beautiful in spring. Most beautiful are the beds of colorful seasonal flowers. White, purple, red, violet, blue, yellow, and orange decorate the ground. They are unknown to me, too. Some of them have just a few petals, some have a lot. Some are very small, some are medium sized. As I walk past the flowers, however, I hardly ever smell any fragrance. All these flowers but no fragrance?

People are busy cleaning and maintaining their yards. A few residents of the old people's home start coming out of the building and walk within their premises. Some lean on walking sticks; others are accompanied by attendants in uniform. Poor elderly people living away from their families and surrounded by strangers! I cannot bear to look at them any longer. It's beyond my imagination to think of my grandparents not living in our family. I feel lumps in my throat. Heart breaking!

Spring in Calcutta

In Calcutta's mild winter, some leaves turn yellowish before shedding, others stay green year-round. At the arrival of spring, the big, tall *Krishnachura* tree in our neighborhood gets flooded with newly-bloomed bright red flowers. The tree looks spectacular as if it has been painted in glowing red. Fresh new leaves in many trees and the cooing cuckoos announce the arrival of spring.

Programmable Calculator

In the winter quarter the undergraduate Microelectronics I class got me used to using a calculator. I purchased an ordinary scientific and engineering calculator for frequent use like most of the students in that class.

During my second quarter, the spring quarter, I go a step further. A giant step! I take a high graduate level semiconductor device engineering course. The professor recommends the use of TI-59 programmable calculator. When it comes to long and complicated expressions, it will be indispensable for homework assignments and tests.

A programmable calculator! It has been three months only since I got acquainted to a basic calculator. The programmable calculator is a brand new concept for most of the students in our class. That makes me feel really good. I will learn how to use it along with every one else. The TI-59 will also be used in upcoming courses. It is well worth the money.

Just like the other students I end up buying one. It costs about two hundred and fifty dollars. I am not in a condition to spend that, but "Necessity knows no law."

Thin magnetic strips are used to input complex equations and expressions. Many standard parameter values can be stored in memory. Initially, it takes me time to input the long and complex expressions on the magnetic strips. After a few trial and errors I learn to program the magnetic strips and process them.

As a few buttons are pressed sequentially, long expressions are evaluated superfast. That's really convenient! Once that is done, the calculations process quickly, and outputs are shown. What used to be step-by-step time-consuming calculations, using an ordinary calculator—turns out to be fast and efficient now! The first few times I watch admiringly as it functions. How easy and convenient!

Though this is an advanced course, coming from a physics and math background, it is not hard for me. I hope to score very well.

Women's Image

Anand tells me, "It surprises me that so much emphasis is put on women's independence here. Why do they make such a big issue about women going to college, having a career? My mom has been a high school teacher in Thailand all her life. We never thought of her as being exceptional and liberated. It's quite normal."

I agree. "It surprises me, too. While waiting for the elevator in the Engineering building people ask me, 'What brings you here? Are you visiting someone?' One man even says, 'You must be lost. Let me help you find someone.'

In a matter of fact way I always reply, "I am a graduate student here.

'Really!' The disbelief, the shock, the not-yet-convinced expression in their faces, offends me. Women engineers are not uncommon in Calcutta."

Lady doctors, the common term for women physicians, are very common in India. Especially the OB/GYN field is dominated by them due to patients' preferences.

Bishop Woods

Right across the street from the university is a ninety-acre park named Bishop Woods. All winter long it was covered by snow. With the arrival of spring the snow has melted away revealing bushes, a kids' playground, jogging trails and walkways. Bright green new leaves, spring flowers, joggers and children frequent the park adding liveliness to the area. Mothers don't stay behind, either. They walk, too, pushing baby strollers.

The fresh look of colorful spring flowers, though I don't know what they are, attracts me. Sounds of giggling children absorbed in playing draw my attention. I wish I could spend more time in the park.

A sign at the park's entrance lists the plays and variety programs to be performed this season, including Shakespeare's plays. I am eager to attend these, but the high pressure of graduate studies makes this impossible. I'm always running against time. There is always something that must be done that very day. When am I going to be able to finish the work? An additional inconvenience for is me getting used to the grading system. The final letter grades are based on class average performance. Basically, it's the statistical Gaussian distribution. Locally the students call it the "bell curve." The level where most of the students perform becomes a B. I have to outperform most of the students in the class to score an A. In graduate level a B is merely passing a course.

At times I have done very well in midterms and finals, and expected an A. But my final grade was a B. This is so frustrating!

At other times I get caught by surprise ending up with an A. I must have outperformed the class.

A major lab assignment is due this Monday. I end up spending the entire weekend in the lab working on it. It's a relief to submit it on time. But there is no time to sit down and relax. I have two tests on Wednesday. Though I am exhausted, I must continue to study.

Over the weekend I couldn't find time to buy groceries or to cook. Consequently, I am surviving on steamed rice with boiled potatoes and eggs. Besides that, it has been bread, butter and grape jelly, cookies, apples and bananas, milk and tea. At the university my lunch is always a fish fillet from the fast food store. Once in a while a side order of french-fries. At times I'm nauseated at the sight of fish fillet, the same item day after day. I load it up with ketchup, cover my nose and swallow it somehow. Still, I can't figure out an acceptable alternate menu.

The other day I overheard a classmate, a six-foot-tall all American man, venting out to another student, "No time for myself, no social life. Study, study and study some more. No break in the weekends. What kind of life is this? Is this a life at all?"

Someone who is born and brought up here, a product of this social and educational system, feels the overwhelming pressure, too? This must be quite normal. I'm not the only one! His statement brings so much comfort to me, boosting my confidence and reassuring my endeavor.

Our apartment house has a big outdoor swimming pool in the back, next to the parking lot. People are preparing to re-open the pool. First it's thoroughly cleaned, then painted in blue. The surrounding area also gets some maintenance. The lounge chairs are scrubbed and painted. So is the fence around the area. Everything looks nice and fresh. The pool will open to the tenants sometime in May.

Joggers frequent the street. Mothers with babies in strollers, relieved to get out of captivity indoors, are a common sight.

Finally, some laughter, some movement can be seen outside. This makes me feel like I still dwell in a world surrounded by people. Coming from a crowded metropolitan city, I often felt isolated during the winter. I couldn't help but wonder, "Where did the people go?" That left-alone feeling is subsiding gradually. Now I am convinced people truly lived here, just not visible outside.

Next week is the mid-term week; three exams and a project due. Friday evening as I enter the apartment after buying groceries I feel like crying. I have a mountain load of studies to be done, but the apartment really needs to be cleaned. The bathroom and the kitchen space are dirty. Fortunately, I live on the first floor with a concrete floor, just like back home. I use a broom and a mop, the old fashioned way. The second and third floors of this house have wood floors. But cleaning is impossible this weekend. I will have to ignore it. On top of everything, I have a killer headache.

There is no time for cooking even, let alone cleaning. As usual, I will survive on steamed rice with boiled potatoes and eggs, toast with butter and grape jelly, apples and bananas, and tall glasses of milk. Tea, crackers and a pound cake will serve as snacks. I have to cope with the fast speed of the educational system.

In Calcutta when exams approached, there was special treatment at home. The family revolved around the exam schedule. As it was, there was hardly any chore assigned to the students in the family. Then during the exam period it was extra special. Mom checked on me and served nutritious snacks frequently at my study table. Sometimes milk and cookies, sometimes ready-to-eat sliced fruits. If I ever fell asleep she made sure I was comfortable.

In the morning as soon as I woke up and went to the study table, Mom brought fresh hot tea with milk and sugar and a few cookies. Breakfast was served later. Lunch and dinner were the only times I shared meals with everybody at the dining table.

And now? If I starve no one cares. What a drastic change of situation!

I crave rice and fish with gravy; the very basic dish I grew up having at every lunch and dinner. The frozen fish I purchase from the grocery smells so bad, I end up throwing it away. Breaded fish doesn't work, either. Chicken drumsticks turn out to be a somewhat better choice.

Mom sends me easy-to-cook recipes, one after another. The blue air-mail letter from India is left open on the counter top as I follow her step by step instructions. Nothing works. Sometimes she sends recipes for fresh fish dishes. How would she know what I get here? Additionally, trial and error in the kitchen is expensive as well as time and labor consuming, a hard-to-afford combination.

India Students Association Movie Day

The first Saturday of every month at 1:00 PM, the ISA (India Students Association) shows a Hindi movie at the Student Center auditorium. They rent the big reel movie from an out-of-state dealer. The rent along with shipping and handling costs about sixty dollars. Using a projector from the university it's shown in the auditorium. A student ticket costs a dollar, non-students three. ISA recovers the cost, and the surplus goes to their fund.

While watching a Hindi movie, once the characters and scenes from India become lively on the screen, I get so absorbed that I stay mesmerized and spend a few hours in India...

Family scenes: members of a family interacting; siblings picking on each other; women in saris; family dinners with ongoing discussions. Joint family, better known as an extended family here, consisting of grandparents, uncles, aunts and cousins; people attending social occasions with family and friends.

Indian cities during rush-hour traffic: bus stops crowded with office workers and students boarding regular buses, red double-deckers and trams; students in uniform; girls wearing double-braided hair styles walking to neighborhood schools. Fancy school buses with students from well-to-do families; people riding rickshaws, bicycles or walking. In major intersections, police officers using hand-signals to direct traffic and help people go across the streets.

Neighborhood stores: grocery markets, pharmacies, dessert shops, roadside tea shops, small corner shops selling beetle leaves and cigarettes.

Indian village scenes: rice and wheat fields; mustard fields full of bright yellow flowers; farmers dwelling in mud huts with hay roofs. Some of them are preparing the soil and planting, some are reaping crops.

Everything looks so important to me.

...At the end of the movie I encounter a rude awakening and get back to reality. Such a painful reminder of how much I miss home!

A Hindi movie is such an attraction that many families drive an hour or two to attend. After the movie most of them visit Mr. Kapur's store to buy their monthly groceries. It's a big business day for the Indian grocery.

The Indian families bring their children with them including infants. As the adults are absorbed in watching the movie, the children get restless and start running around outside the auditorium. The place is safe, the parents are not worried. Sometimes the noise reaches a peak disturbing everybody, but the parents remain oblivious. The kids get out of control and break the glass of the fire-alarm window. The movie stops due to the loud alarm. Everyone abides by mandatory evacuation of the building and wait outside on the lawn. The Fire Department shows up with fire engines and figure out the children are at fault. This isn't the first time this has happened. ISA is strictly ordered to stop it.

At the end of the movie ISA volunteers clean up the auditorium. There are crumbs, empty packets of snacks, and empty pop cans all over; once in a while dirty diapers, too.

A student volunteer picks up an empty packet of potato chips and comments in an irritated voice, "What do they think of us? Servants, huh?"

The ISA president, a doctoral student in Mechanical Engineering, responds in a lighter voice, "Exactly so. While watching Indian movies they seem to forget they are not in India any longer. They leave a mess behind expecting servants to clean it up."

The volunteer asks, "This is disgusting, time after time. Isn't there any way to stop it?"

The ISA president shakes his head in disapproval. "What to do? I try. I mention it every time before the movie. Nothing changes."

This is the only time I am able to watch a movie. I can't afford to buy a TV, not even a black-and-white one.

Meeting the Rajan Family

During the intermission at an Indian movie I meet Deepthi, a South Indian woman about my age. Just like me, she is a newcomer. She is married to a Dr. Rajan, who works in the university hospital. We instantly relate to each other how much we miss family and friends. Both of us are going through extreme culture shock.

Next day Deepthi calls me with a lunch invitation for the following weekend.

I am so excited to visit the first Indian family in USA!

I step into their apartment which is right next to the University Hospital. A nice bouquet of red roses in a vase in the living room draws my attention immediately.

"Beautiful roses! I haven't seen roses in a while." I keep looking appreciatively.

"Don't talk about roses. They are expensive. The bouquet costs eighteen dollars."

I look away. Yes, it is a lot of money to me. But, isn't it below courtesy to mention the price? Is she trying to brag?

The saga continues. Deepthi is wearing gold bracelets and bangles, earrings and a necklace, while bragging about how well her parents covered her with gold jewelry at her marriage.

I wear gold earrings and a bracelet, always. Also, I have some gold jewelry. Unlike me, Deepthi brought everything over. I came here as a graduate student, whereas she came to spend her life. There is a big difference between our purposes.

Another Indian gentleman, a friend and colleague of her husband, joins us. The lunch is so plain: rice, lentils, green-beans and yogurt. They are vegetarians. An invited guest could be served just this? They seem comfortable, however.

As Bengalis, we are famous for being gourmets. Our menu contains many vegetarian and non-vegetarian items. We are also well known for milk desserts.

The two men keep discussing sports and politics by themselves.

The entire time Deepthi shows off her status. I know she is a physician's wife.

She mentions, "As soon as the weather gets better, I will start taking driving lessons." She pauses and smiles like a winner. "My husband wants to buy me a new BMW."

I am clueless about the price of a new BMW. It must be expensive. Usually students drive old, sometimes even damaged cars. I swallow and say, "That's good."

Deepthi proudly announces, "I am already a member of the local ladies club. We meet for a potluck lunch once a month. The appetizer I fixed last month was so well appreciated."

Though this doesn't matter a bit to me, I try to sound excited— yet fail. "How nice."

"I am planning on the item for next month."

"OK."

Right before leaving, I am truly offended by her husband's comment: "Being a doctor, I don't know how you survived walking to the university in this winter."

Obviously, I am not the only one. Other students did, too. Wasn't he a student once? Didn't he struggle at all? The comment pierces my skin and strikes my heart like a sharp arrow.

What happened to Indian hospitality? Being polite and making a guest feel welcome and comfortable are mandatory.

They drop me off later in the afternoon. Though very insulted, I get out of the car and say good-bye to them politely.

This family dwells in a world so far removed from mine. I may be a struggling graduate student, but I will not allow myself to be humiliated like that again. I will maintain my distance from them.

I am much more educated, and much more sophisticated than Deepthi. My goal in life after getting my Ph.D is to become a professor or a research-scholar. As I wipe away my tears of insult, I keep reminding myself that just being someone's wife is not good enough for me.

Alexander Petrov

In Microelectronics II class senior professor Dr. Petrov speaks English with a heavy Russian accent. Paying undivided attention is a must to keep up with the topic. He used to teach Engineering in Russia, and has been doing the same here over the past twenty years.

He has a serious, very reserved disposition. It's to the extent that students think twice before asking a question. No light comment or light atmosphere is allowed in his class. It's striking to find such energy and dedication he applies to teaching.

Short and robust in appearance, Dr. Petrov has an almost square face and salt-and-pepper gray hair balding on the temples. He is scheduled to retire next year.

There are different versions of stories that circulate about him. He deserted his family in Russia and moved here; he has family here, but no one likes him; no one keeps in touch with him, so he keeps to himself. This lonely professor's life revolves around the university.

I have never paid too much attention to gossip. How much do the students know? Just because Dr. Petrov is a dedicated professor, he doesn't have a personal life?

He owns a small single-story home across from the university. Some businesses have offered him an outrageous amount of money to purchase the house. Without a second thought he sticks to his opinion: "Only five minutes walk from the department. It's worth a million dollars to me."

I overhear a conversation between two students. One says, "Though Dr. Petrov is retiring, nothing is going to change in reality."

"What do you mean?"

"He will continue to teach here, even after retirement."

The other student asks, "Is that possible? For how long?"

"As long as he can keep teaching. In a nutshell, he will donate his time to the university."

"Really! Are you serious?"

"Not only that. His will authorizes the university as the sole inheritor of all of his possessions."

I am simultaneously confused and surprised. I have never heard of anything like this before. Usually relatives inherit. Really rich people donate to hospitals or religious or charitable organizations. But leaving it to the university? Strange!

Parking

Within a block from the university, while waiting for the traffic light to change one morning, I notice something.

A student with oriental features steps out of his rusted and dented car carrying a heavy book bag. Right away an elderly woman comes out of the house in front and blocks his way.

In an irritated voice, she points to a short yellow metallic cylinder and claims, "It's illegal to park in front of a fire hydrant. You can't park here."

So, the yellow cylinder is called a fire hydrant? I don't have a clue about what that is. But I have noticed no one parks next to it, not even on a crowded day.

The student, while glancing at his wristwatch frequently, tries to say something in a hard-to-comprehend accent. Sounds as if he is running late for class.

The woman raises her voice and screams, "If there is a fire close by, the fire engine depends on the fire hydrant for water. Do you understand how dangerous it is to the neighborhood to park here?" She pauses. Then she threatens him with the ultimatum, "If you don't listen to me, I will call the police right now."

This works like a charm. Instantaneously, he drives away with a long face.

Poor fellow! He will miss class today.

Students who pay monthly parking get to use the students' parking lot on campus. University faculty and staff have reserved parking lots. They breeze through parking their cars. But the students who park free in the adjacent neighborhood face a hard time, especially in the mornings. Often they end up parking at a distance, walking a good bit and consequently either getting in late or missing the class.

Back home the fire engine is called the fire brigade. Most frequently, neighborhood people run to the spot as soon as they hear the scream: "Fire! Fire!" They fetch buckets of water from household reservoirs, roadside tube-wells, and try to put out the fire. Sometimes, without a second thought, they jump in the fire to rescue people. Small, even medium fires are often extinguished before the fire brigade arrives.

Host Family Program for International Students

A lady named Susan Wallace contacts me through the university's International Students' Office, offering to be my host family. This is a new experience to me. She will keep in touch with me, take me out, and invite me to her house. This is supposed to help me get familiarized to this culture and feel as if someone is there for me.

She extends an invitation, "Would you like to join us for dinner this coming Saturday? I will give you a ride."

I hesitate somewhat. Deep down I am delighted to get a chance to go somewhere other than the university.

"Yes, please."

Mrs. Wallace says, "That's great! I will pick you up at 6:00 PM. I look forward to meeting you."

Getting a chance to become acquainted with an American family— participating in a family dinner, listening to a dinner conversation— is a great opportunity. How exciting! The excitement washes off my nervous and awkward feelings.

What should I wear? It has to be a sari, to show my Indian heritage. I will choose a nice silk sari. I have to make sure the Wallace family approves of me. I can't show up empty handed to an invitation. That's below courtesy. What do I take as a gift? From India I brought a couple of fancy sandalwood letter openers carved with exquisite hand-crafted designs. The fragrance of sandalwood fills the air as soon as the knife container is opened. One of them will make a nice gift.

Mrs. Wallace comes to pick me up as scheduled. She is a tall and slender white lady of about fifty. I am nervous and excited simultaneously.

She parks the car in her driveway and unlocks the house to let me in. I don't see anyone around. No introduction to anybody?

The living room is downstairs, across from the kitchen and dining area. A very well decorated home. Also, there is a yard in the front. It must be an expensive house!

She is so happy to get my gift. She places the knife on her study table to let the air fill with the sandalwood fragrance.

It turns out she is a divorcee. Her son is in college on the West Coast. Katie, her twelve-year-old daughter, is upstairs in her room.

This is unbelievable! I have seen many widows and a few spinsters back home. But a divorcee living with her children, running her own household? Is that even possible? It's a brand new concept.

To my dismay, it's not a family dinner at all. Katie says hello to me, puts some food on a plate and takes it back to her room. She wants to eat dinner while watching her favorite TV program.

Can someone eat dinner in the bedroom? Moreover, does someone have a choice not to dine with others in the family?

Ms. Wallace and I dine together. She keeps talking about her graduate student life, and her classmates from India. During her one semester study in London she met many Indian families. Just like us, she is drinking hot tea with cream and sugar, a habit she picked up in London.

Currently she is taking some Yoga classes, and truly enjoying them.

I eat some salad and two dinner-rolls with butter. She offers me some fried chicken. But a distinct smell—maybe from the oil or the grease—keeps me away. A piece of cake with walnuts is what I truly cherish. Delicious!

In our culture, repeatedly insisting a guest to eat more is an essential part of hospitality. Unlike us, she doesn't do that.

On a mention about her ex-husband she comments bitterly, "He wasn't the kind of person to get involved with foreign students."

Mrs. Wallace stays in touch with me with a once-in-a-while telephone call. A few months down the road, I invite her to a South-Indian classical dance performance at the university, organized by the India Student Association. The tickets are expensive, but I get a student's discount.

She arrives with her boyfriend. She had mentioned him before, but this is the first time I meet him. A white gentleman in his early-fifties, he is bespectacled and balding, and doesn't talk much. Apparently, they enjoy the program, and thank me for the invitation. I am happy to be able to reciprocate somehow.

What happens next is not clear to me. Her phone calls taper off gradually.

I keep hoping and waiting for her. Is she very busy with her life and her boyfriend? Sometimes I wonder whether she married and got busy with her new life.

Rape

RAPE! How horrible! Unbelievable! Oh my God! Why did I come to such a dangerous town? In Calcutta women are revered so highly. Being raped is unthinkable! If a woman raises her voice in the street and accuses a man of misbehaving, the public gather and beat him up right away. Bad guys don't dare attempting such an act. Calcutta is far more congested, crowded, and polluted. Pick-pocketing and thefts take place all the time, but not rape. Respect and safety do exist for women.

It was reported in last night's local news on TV. A twenty-year-old female student left the university library at 9:00 PM. As she was walking back to her apartment in the cold and dark, she was attacked and raped within a mile of the campus. She was hospitalized in a critical condition. The attacker remains at large.

I don't have a TV. Neither do I have a newspaper subscription where it made headlines today. Therefore, I have not heard of the incident until I went to class this morning. It has become the talk of the day. The atmosphere at university is very different today. Campus police are alert and in-sight.

The news is giving me chills. I walk to my apartment every day. This could have happened to anyone. But I do make sure to get back to my apartment in daylight. In the evenings and nights I study at home without any exception. When I walk to the university for my first class at 8:00 AM, often it's not clear daylight. But the streets are not empty, and many cars go past me.

I am on the verge of collapse. I need to run away from this place. I feel like taking the next flight home. Let me pack up and leave. Under the circumstances it doesn't even cross my mind that I couldn't afford to buy a plane ticket. I am confident that in an emergency situation my parents would definitely send me the money.

I can't sleep; lay half-awake at night. Even a little sound frightens me. Is someone trying to break in? Didn't it sound like a push? Is anyone trying to slide the front glass window open? A wood stick is placed inside to block the window from sliding. It's not supposed to slide. Time after time I walk to the front-door eyehole and check. Often I peek through the shutter just to make sure no one is around. I am even frightened to take a shower. The running water will mask the noise of someone trying to break in.

An apartment building this big is noisy all the time. Starting about five in the morning tenants are getting ready for work, cars are starting and driving past my room. People are returning home at all hours, parking cars and shutting car doors. Telephones are ringing and televisions are playing in other apartments.

The squeaking noises of wood floors, the footsteps of residents walking upstairs have given me company all this time, kind of helping me deal with loneliness. But now, even the slightest noise or movement alerts me. In Calcutta, buildings have all-brick construction and concrete floors. Sound doesn't travel as easily through the walls or floors. Most of it travels through open doors and windows.

The laundry room is only about thirty yards away. Rows of washers and dryers are used at all hours. Though I make sure to do my laundry on Saturday afternoons during daylight, sometimes I have to wait until a washer or dryer is available. Some choose to do it at odd hours to avoid the rush. Tenants carry their laundry in the laundry baskets and walk past my apartment all the time. Now I am suspicious about them, too. Who knows what their real intention is?

How can I live like this? It's good my parents don't know. I must be careful never to mention it to anyone in India.

On campus, dormitory buildings for students are relatively secure. Twelve-story buildings, three in a row, stand across the huge university parking lot. Each floor has sixteen apartments. Most of these are studio apartments, shared by two students or a couple. One-bedroom apartments can be rented by three students or a couple with a child. Two-bedroom apartments are mostly occupied by families with kids. Four students share them rarely.

One of the buildings is reserved for undergraduate students only. The other two allow graduate students, faculty and staff. Because of their crowded nature and lack of privacy, crowded lobbies and elevators, plus the high rent—regular American graduate students, faculty and staff hardly ever live in the dormitories. They prefer to live off-campus, enjoy a private life and drive to the university. The foreign faculty with short-time appointments and the foreign students usually do not have cars. They reside in the university housings.

The dorms are expensive, but the proximity to classes, banks, groceries and the campus health center makes them very convenient. The students come home for each meal. Also, it's on the bus line if they ever decide to take a trip downtown. Because of the large concentration of kids, the school buses stop there, too.

The lobby, the laundry room, and the kids' playground are full of foreign nationals. Indian and Bangladeshi women wearing sari or *salwar-kameez*, middle-eastern women with their heads covered and unique dresses, and African women in colorful clothes are seen all the time. Most of them spend a lot of time socializing in the lounges while their kids play in the playground. These women are mostly students' wives, with abundant time to kill. Most families do not own cars. In the very few that do, women don't drive. All these factors keep them confined. Loud conversations in a variety of languages are heard. Chatting and spreading gossip is an integrated part of the lifestyle.

Legally, they are not allowed to earn any money. But some of them babysit behind the scene. Students let them babysit their kids while they attend classes, and pay them an hourly rate.

When someone takes the elevator inside the dormitory, as soon as its door opens at a specific floor, the confined hallway air carries the flavor of cooking spices and gravies that announce the country of origin of some of the landing's residents.

The campus police patrol frequently, especially after dark. During final examination preparation weeks the Central Library stays open until midnight. Campus police cars are seen even late at night and in the wee hours of the morning.

All this time I wanted to stay away from that congested lifestyle. But the rape case shakes me so bad. I am going to apply for housing in the graduate dorm. If I could move there today, I would. But their rental starts in September at the beginning of the academic year. I'll have to share an apartment and face the consequences. At least I will be safe there. It's a matter of priority. I will trade peace and quiet for security.

A white American woman, about twenty-five, lives by herself in the apartment next to me. When I started living here she introduced herself while walking her dog. "Hi, I am Lisa, your next-door neighbor. This is my dog, Brandy." She looked compassionately at the big brown golden retriever standing next to her. "I have seen you walking with your book bag. Are you a student?"

"Yes," I nodded.

"I am a receptionist at a doctor's office about five miles from here."

I have seen Brandy on a leash, tied outside Lisa's door. Brandy is very affectionate, well-behaved, a loving and caring family dog. As I come and go she sniffs me, wags her tail and expresses that she likes me. I like Brandy. I pat her sometimes. The other day I was eating toast while standing in front my window. Brandy kept watching and licking her mouth in a greedy manner. She was almost begging for it. I couldn't help but giving her half of it. She enjoyed it thoroughly and licked her mouth clean. Lisa doesn't know this. I wasn't aware it was improper to feed a pet without the owner's permission.

Running into Lisa in the laundry room, I mention the rape case and ask, "Aren't you frightened?"

Surprising me she responds, "Not really. It happens all the time. I'm careful."

"Aren't you afraid to live alone?" I ask in a hurry.

"Brandy will take care of me."

"Certainly," I nod in agreement.

I've made a fool out of myself. Why didn't I think of this? I am so embarrassed. Brandy will definitely protect her owner.

I feel some relief. If someone tries to break into my apartment at odd hours wouldn't Brandy bark? I think, she will. Dogs have a very sharp instinct. "Just be careful. Last summer there was a rape case right here," alerts Lisa.

My eyes are popping out, my heart is beating fast. "You mean, in this building?"

Most casually, she answers, "Yeah. A young woman, a tenant on the second-floor, was doing her laundry alone at midnight. She got raped in this laundry room."

"Oh my God! It happened here, too?" I almost start shaking. "Why was she doing laundry that late?"

"I don't know," she shrugs.

I mumble, "What happened to her?"

"She survived. But no one was arrested."

I always lock my apartment door as well as the dead bolt. Before going to bed at night now-a-days, I put a chair next to the door and pile up aluminum utensils. If someone pushes the door, the pots and pans will make a noise loud enough to wake me up. Hopefully, Brandy will bark.

I feel somewhat relieved. Maybe I will sleep better tonight. I really need to sleep well. Anxiety and tension have taken a toll on me.

From that day onwards, when I am home, the chair stays blocking the front door.

Lisa's choice

This morning as I step out to go to the university, Lisa is about to enter her blue car. I am surprised to notice she is expecting. I have seen some people visiting her now and then, but I am not sure about which one is her husband. Maybe he comes and goes because he has to live elsewhere for his job.

The mailman has delivered some of Lisa's mail in my mailbox by mistake. I knock on her door to give them to her.

"Come in," she says. While arranging a few roses in a vase she comments, "I am sure you have no idea about these flowers."

"What do you mean? These are red roses. Pink and red roses bloom on my parents' balcony. The fragrance fills the air!"

She asks in a suspicious tone, "Do roses bloom in India?"

"Yes, of course."

Most reluctantly, she comments, "On television I have watched so many times about the drought in India. I thought India was too dry to grow anything. While I was in high school once we donated our pocket money to the relief fund."

I realize she is not convinced about roses in India.

A few days later, one evening, I am surprised to watch a middle-aged woman leading Brandy to her car.

She walks to me. "Hi, I am Ann, Lisa's mom. She is in the hospital. She delivered a daughter this afternoon. I came to take the dog home."

A daughter! I am so excited. "Congratulations, congratulations. That's great!"

Ann gives me a stern stare. No excitement. Not even a smile. She walks to the car with her head down. Most seriously she starts the car and leaves in a hurry.

What's this? Just doesn't make any sense. I stand confused.

Two weeks later I see Lisa walking Brandy.

With an ear-to-ear smile I ask excitedly, "How is your baby girl?"

She stares at me blankly. She almost recites, "I work full–time. Additionally, I have Brandy to take care of. I couldn't bring my baby home." At the end her voice cracks. She enters her apartment and shuts the door.

I had bought a small toy for the baby. I don't even get a chance to give it to her. The situation leaves me perplexed.

After much thought, I come to a conclusion. Who is going to take care of the baby here? Lisa must be keeping the baby at her parents. They will take great care of her. I am sure Lisa goes to see her every day. Under the circumstances, it's a good arrangement.

Virginia, a resident of the second floor, sells cosmetics door-to-door in this apartment building. Showing me catalogs she has insisted that I purchase items, but without any result. She always stays up to date with all the happenings around here. On my way back from the university, I see her at the school bus stand waiting for her son.

Virginia steps forward and asks, "So, have you heard about your neighbor, Lisa?"

Excited I respond, "Sure! She has a baby girl, about three weeks old! I haven't seen the baby, though."

She looks at me astonished, and continues in a slow but serious voice, "No one has seen the baby. Not even Lisa."

"How is that possible?" My ignorance gets established really well.

Virginia hesitates for a while. "Lisa is not married. She has put up the baby for adoption. The adoption agency gave her a picture of the baby. Lisa showed it to me." She sighs, "Such a pretty baby girl, big blue eyes."

ADOPTION! I couldn't have been more shocked had it been a bolt from the blue. ADOPTION! In the streets of Calcutta I have seen the wretched poor street-dwellers without any means to feed or raise a baby. Even they do not put up a baby for adoption.

Waving her cosmetic catalog like a hand-fan, Virginia makes a comment that sounds like a monologue, "Lisa wants what's best for her baby. She will grow up in abundance with nurturing and caring parents—that's all Lisa wants. She is an ideal mother."

Spring Quarter Ends

In June, at the end of the spring quarter, we get a two-week break. Nature has displayed it all over that summer has arrived. It gets really hot during the day. Running an air conditioner keeps it cooler. The kids are enjoying a three-month summer vacation from school. Three months! This is something I've never heard before. September to May is the school year. They get to enjoy three months vacation before they start the next grade. No homework, no anxiety of exams, total freedom. They are delighted with the long vacation time. It shows on their faces, conversations and activities. Playful children are giggling and talking in the parks, riding the seesaw, going up-and-down the slides. Some of them are wearing swimming trunks and enjoying swimming pools, seeking refuge in water from the summer heat. In most of the cases parents or life-guards keep an eye on them.

I am so jealous. Our school system in Calcutta followed the calendar year. New grades began in January. A month-long summer vacation started in the middle of May. Consequently, the half-yearly exams took place right after the vacation. We had a month of religious holidays in autumn, around October. The beginning of December was the time for annual exams. Needless to point out, both of our vacations were loaded with homework assignments and exam preparatory studies. Enjoying a three-month long vacation with no strings attached to study? Beyond my imagination!

Adults do not lag behind having fun in summer, either. The tennis courts and swimming pools are busy. The swimming pool in our apartment complex is hardly ever unoccupied. To begin with, I am not comfortable with their swimming costumes, because so much is exposed. Especially on weekends, the residents crowd the pool. They try to achieve a little bit of tan on their otherwise white skin.

Music

After much hesitation and justification of the expenditure, I purchase a radio. Tuning the channels I discover a gold mine! Every Saturday evening from 6:30 to 7:00 PM a German music program is broadcast. I don't have a clue about the language, but the rich music touches my heart. The rhythms and beats, the flow of songs—everything together, I sense a deep-rooted familiarity.

Maybe my longtime practice of Indian classical music has created the bridge. No matter how busy I am, I always make time to listen to this program. It soothes my heart and soul. Never knew that music was so powerful that it could overcome a language barrier.

The country music channel also turns out to be my favorite. John Denver's song "Take me home, country roads," makes me tearful—as if, my homesickness feelings were expressed. Do others go through this, too? Somehow, it offers me consolation.

Rexene

I miss Rexene, the family dog I left behind, especially whenever I see dogs. She must be wondering a lot about me. Does she realize I will not be back soon? This morning I wake up to realize I have been dreaming about her...

Rexene has just finished her evening walk on the third-floor terrace. She is licking dust off her silky white Dalmatian coat with black spots. This is the season for kite flying. The sky is colorful with kites. As they race against one another, the losing kite falls.

Suddenly a kite lands next to her! Rexene gets ecstatic. She drags it with her teeth across the terrace and performs the victory run. The string, still attached to the kite, follows. She feels like a conqueror.

But this game is always short-lived. Pretty soon the drooled-wet, colorful, thin-paper kite rips apart. Placing her front paws on whatever is left, she sits and breathes heavy while guarding it. Not that anyone is coming to snatch it from her, but she still likes to show off her ownership.

At dusk Rexene comes down to the main floor. A drink of water from her water-bowl in the kitchen balcony helps refresh her.

When Dad drinks tea after returning home from work, Rexene sits next to his single-seat sofa. She gets a biscuit, but not just another tasteless dog-biscuit. It's a regular tea-biscuit—crunchy, sweet, and so tasty. Everything the family eats is tasty, but not her food. Even her regular fish and rice dish is specially cooked without any sugar, salt or oil.

Rexene loves Didi, my elder sister. She is great! Almost every day Didi sneaks out some fish hidden under the rice on her plate. Both the fish and the gravy are delicious! Rexene licks her lips as she enjoys the aftertaste.

My brother and I are not as generous; definitely not Mom. Dad often lets Rexene have some fish or meat, as if he didn't want to eat it himself.

Now-a-days my brother comes home only once in a while. He attends a college out of state. Fortunately, the girls live at home and attend nearby colleges. When they return home at the end of the day, Rexene extends her welcome-home greetings. She runs to the front door, circles them and licks them. She does the same for Dad, too. However, the girls are more her playmates.

Disciplining comes from Mom, yet everybody says Rexene loves her the most. She is often called as Mom's shadow, or her youngest daughter. Yes, she does follow Mom around the house quite a bit.

The most awful person is Moti, the maid. Rexene totally dislikes her. Just last afternoon Moti went to the terrace to get the dry clothes from the clothes-line. What a scene she created! Screaming on the top of her voice she complained, "Ma, look what the dog did!"

"What?"

"She pulled down the bed sheet and laid on it. It is full of dirt and dog hair."

What a terrible accusation! It sounded like the worst possible sin was committed. Rexene pulled down a clean dry bed sheet and rested on it. What's so bad about that?

Doesn't Moti carelessly drop tea-cups or saucers breaking them sometimes? Mom has to remind her to be careful so many times. Isn't that a lot worse? At least, Rexene doesn't break anything.

She hears Mom's serious scolding voice, "Rexene, where are you? Why did you do it? It has to be washed again. Can't you rest in your own bed?"

Rexene is guilty. With her head down and tail tucked between the hind legs, she takes refuge under Mom and Dad's king-sized bed. This is a safe and secure spot that no one else can reach.

Moti makes a big issue out of nothing. She is such an expert at fussing! She complains frantically, "Ma, the dog chewed my sandals. What am I going to wear?"

As if the entire neighborhood needs to know that. What a drama-queen!

Rexene hates being mentioned as "dog." Didi's girlfriend remarked the other day, "You have made a human out of Rexene by pampering her." Rexene totally agrees. She is not just any dog—she is a member of the family. The street-dwelling stray dogs can be mentioned as dogs. Rexene is nothing like them.

The slippers were halfway worn out, anyway. It's not a good day for Rexene. Mom scolds, "Have you ripped a sandal apart again?" A light slap on her back accompanies. "Where is my spanking stick? Let me get it."

Rexene doubts whether it exists. At least, she has never seen it. But the mention of it is certainly unpleasant. She reaches her hiding spot under the bed, fast.

Mom comforts Moti, "Don't worry; I will buy you a new pair."

The very next day Rexene notices her wearing a pair of new sandals. Just because of Rexene, Moti gets a new pair. Shouldn't she be pleased with Rexene?

Not that Rexene likes all the friends and relatives that visit, either. The ones she dislikes, she barks at them only once or twice. After all, they are family guests. She has to be courteous to them.

Rexene can't stand stray dogs. The very mention of the term irritates her. The leftover food from her bowl is often given to them. What nonsense! Whenever she sees them from the second floor balcony wandering in the street or resting, she barks at them and orders them to leave at once.

She has voiced her discontent so many times, still they don't seem to care. This home and the place around it is her territory. How dare they—a bunch of street-dwelling dogs with dirty coats and patches of wounds from street-fights or pebbles thrown at them by naughty boys— trespass on her territory?

Rexene has a clean and shiny white coat. She is bathed regularly with dog soap and towel dried. But she hates to take a bath, and tries her best to get away. That's when she gets jealous of the stray dogs. They don't take baths. How nice!

"Rexene, come here. Here is some fresh bread for you." Rexene tries to pay attention. Did Ma mention whether it is homemade round bread or a store-bought loaf? She loves the loaf and hates the homemade whole wheat puffed bread.

Round bread, again? No way. She walks away, disappointed.

She sits on the third-floor landing and relaxes. A while later she is alerted by my comment, "Rexene has wasted food again. Let me give it to the stray dogs."

What an audacity! Stray dogs again?

She comes running down the stairs, exasperated. Placing her front paws across the bowl, she stands guarding the bread. Her annoying "Woof," means, "It's mine, whether I eat it or not."

I bend over to pick it up. Promptly, Rexene places a paw on the bread and starts eating. I stand up and laugh, "Rexene eats bread smeared with jealousy."

As soon as I step away, Rexene goes back to resting.

GSA Lounge

The ninth floor of the Engineering building totally belongs to graduate studies in electrical engineering. Classrooms, laboratories, professors' offices, graduate students' study areas and the Graduate Students Association lounge are located there.

The lounge is a medium-size room. Actually, it's half of a regular class room. The other half is used as a storage area for equipment.

The lounge has a wooden round table in the center, surrounded by six mismatched chairs. A TV is on a stand in the corner. A three-seat sofa with floral cushions is situated adjacent to the mail-boxes. A shelf, with small cardboard individual mail-boxes for all of the forty graduate students, is the mail delivery area.

On the other side of the room is a sink and a refrigerator and a little counter space with an electrical pot for hot water. Students who pack lunches often use the lounge to eat.

In general, this is the rest and relaxation area for the graduate students. Some like to watch TV during a break, some chat, others relax while drinking tea or coffee.

Usually, I eat lunch either in the food-court or at my desk. I am not yet comfortable eating with the graduate students around me. Except for the departmental notices my personal mail goes to my apartment. Students who share apartments with roommates often like to receive their mail at the departmental mailing address. Then their mail is delivered to individual mail boxes at the lounge.

This morning, around 8:00 I step in the lounge to get a cup of hot water for tea. As soon I open the door and turn on the light, I find a Ph.D. student from India, fast asleep on the sofa. As he is lying on his stomach, his long legs are protruding off the sofa. His eyeglasses are on the table, his shoes on the floor.

Obviously, he worked in the laboratory all night long. Too exhausted to return home, he walked a few steps and slept in the lounge. This is not an uncommon scenario. I have seen other male students sleeping here before. This is an advantage the male students have over me.

With no intention to disturb him, I turn off the light and leave immediately. I am well experienced with the long exhausting hours in the lab.

Though I do not work in the lab overnight, I have worked many long days and early evenings, especially on the weekends, when the lab is not crowded and equipment is more available.

The Central Library, adjacent to the Engineering building, has a relaxed study area for students. Many three-seat sofas, as well as some two-seat and single-seat chairs are available. It's common for students to use this area to study comfortably while stretching their legs. Sometimes, if too exhausted, I go there to study. The dark blue sofa cushions are made of scratchy materials. But that doesn't matter when I'm exhausted.

Sunday Newspaper and Lunch in Calcutta

One afternoon I enter the GSA lounge to check my mailbox. The Sunday newspaper is on the table. It's unbelievably thick!

It reminds me of the Sunday editions of Calcutta's newspapers. My mind travels to a typical Sunday in Calcutta…

The Sunday paper is somewhat thicker than the weekday editions. Several pages, called the literary section, include a children's section with stories, cartoons and puzzles.

Music lessons on Sunday mornings are followed by listening to a weekly radio program for children. Then we, the kids in the family, hurry to read the children's section before the adults find time to look for the literary section.

Though two newspapers are subscribed on Sundays, *Statesman* in English and *Anandabazar* in Bengali, I wait for the literary section of the Bengali newspaper.

Once in a while there is a to-be-continued story; it's so hard to tolerate a week-long wait. Why do they do it to us? It never crosses my mind I will soon be so distracted with studies, music and games that I will forget about it shortly.

Sunday lunch is the most important family meal of the week. On most Sundays our aunts and their in-laws and other family and friends join us. Not that all of them are invited or expected. Some drop by to visit us for one reason or another. The family rule is to cordially request everyone to have lunch with us.

Specialty items such as *hilsa* fish, goat meat, chutney and milk desserts are included. Customarily, meals are served an item at a time by the women of the family.

The first batch having lunch is always our grandfather and the children. The second one is for all other males, and the third one for all the women.

My mom and grandmother are never annoyed by unexpected late arriving guests. For us, the children, a few more cousins and playmates are always fun.

As they arrive, Mom often goes to the kitchen and tells the cook, "Start another pot of rice." "Fry some potatoes." "Fix a battered fry of eggplants." Sometimes she sends someone to buy a big bowl of *Misti doi,* the sweet yogurt, from the local dessert shop...

"How are you?" The question brings me back to the present and I see Anand.

"Good. But you look exhausted," I say.

He yawns and then replies, "Dr. Hewett's assignment is killing me. I had only three hours of sleep last night."

"Yes," I nod. "We all know how that goes."

He serves himself a cup of coffee and leaves.

I open the extra-thick Sunday newspaper on the table. In addition to the news section, it contains several sections such as: Life and Leisure, Travel, Food, Sports, Health and Fitness, etc. But I am stunned by all the advertisements! Page after page of advertisements look endless.

One grocery store after another, item by item: fruits, veggies, meats, cereals, etc.

Department stores: appliances, clothes, shoes, watches, perfumes, gifts, etc.

Pictures are so attractive with reduced prices—they instantly give the feelings that buying today is mandatory; otherwise, it would be such a loss.

Now I realize what contributes to the thickness of the Sunday newspaper. Still, it's hard for me to accept.

Summer

Summer really isn't going to be any different for me. I am glad that I will continue to remain a full time student in summer. The sooner I finish the degree, the sooner I get to return home to Calcutta.

At the end of summer there will be a month-long break. What an indulgence! But I am also a little bit worried about it. What am I going to do? How am I going to stay busy? Some students are going home on the break. I wish I could afford to go home!

Perhaps I will take a Greyhound bus to visit my girlfriend Lata from Calcutta. The round-trip fare should not be outrageous. She has insisted me to come over and over again. She will be very happy to see me. I will get to meet her husband. It will be a long awaited true break for me. I entertain the thought and become happy.

Summer will be my third quarter. The Microelectronics III course will be offered Tuesdays and Thursdays in the evenings from

6:30 to 8:30. I must take the course to complete the sequence of Microelectronics required of me. But attending a class that late, and then walking home alone at night? I am not that brave.

I run into Bindu, an Indian librarian, who works part-time in the Engineering library. Anxiously, I share my thoughts with her.

Surprising me she laughs and comments, "Why are you scared? 8:30 PM will be daylight in summer."

Daylight savings time, forwarding the clock by an hour, was new to me this spring. She must be joking. The clock does not change in India.

I say, "In Calcutta, it's dusk at 5:30 in the winter and 6:30 in the summer. 8:30 is definitely night time regardless of the season."

She smiles and replies, "It's different here. Summer has long evenings. Then it's suddenly deep night."

Daylight after 8:30? It's hard to comprehend and accept. Still, I am relieved to know that I will be able to walk home in daylight.

The summer quarter starts in late June, 1980. As I step into the Microelectronics III class I am surprised. Where are the twenty-five to thirty undergraduate white male students that were with me in Microelectronics I and II? Not a single one of them is present. This class is full of older people. I have never seen them before. Our professor, Dr. Rogers, is about thirty-five. Many of the students are older than him.

They attend the class wearing nice dress clothes with ties. Most of them wear polished shoes and carry nice briefcases. The atmosphere is very different from our usual classes.

Who are these people? Where do they come from? I don't follow their questions, either. But Dr. Rogers seems to be comfortable with them.

Often they sound like they are bragging, "When I worked with these microchips, it was my experience that…"

The professor nods and agrees with them, and offers them further explanations.

Truly, 8:30 is daylight. When I walk home after the class, people are outside walking and talking.

After the first few classes, I become really worried. If these students know everything to begin with, how am I going to get good grades competing with them? I describe the situation to my classmate Ben and ask him, "What happened to the undergraduate students?"

"Undergraduate students are not in school in summer. They will return in fall."

Concerned, I ask, "Who are the people in the class? Why are they here?"

Ben's explanation opens a new area for me. He says, "Usually, these people are employed during the day. They come to the class in the evening, after work."

"Are they engineering students like us?"

"Not really. Some of them take courses to stay up-to-date with technology."

I ask, "They sound like they know it all. Do they?"

Ben assures me, "Not likely. Most of them are not engineers. But they use engineering products at work. The class helps them get a better insight. Many of them just audit the class. They do not care about grades."

I admit, "I don't follow their questions. Most of them are about practical uses."

"They ask specific questions to help them at work. Those are not important for you."

"You mean, if I don't understand, it will be OK?"

"Sure. As long as you follow Dr. Rogers, you will do well. Forget about the people from industry."

I breathe a sigh of relief.

Summer Barbecue

In the beginning of July summer barbecue is at the home of our professor Dr. Hewett. Mostly, students have been invited. Many of them are my seniors. I know them by face. Also, there are people I don't know.

The front yard has a nice green lawn and a charming flower garden. Different colored flowers unknown to me are in full bloom. I recognize the rose bushes, however.

Entering the back yard the first person I see is Dr. Jordon, a friend of our professor. The elderly professor of chemistry is bragging about his newborn first granddaughter.

Dr. Jordan comments, "My son and daughter-in-law got married six months ago. As you know, the second one will always arrive after nine months, but the first one may arrive any time." Some people laugh.

I am so embarrassed that I am about to choke while drinking Coke. I can feel my ears have turned red. It's that embarrassing. This kind of a crude joke coming from a professor! I don't want to be around him. Who knows what he is going to say next? I quickly leave and go elsewhere.

Dr. Hewett is cooking chicken in a strange looking stove. A student tells me it's a barbecue grill. Whatever that is, I don't have a clue. The professor is cooking chicken pieces, turning them around and sprinkling a liquid on them from a bottle. A couple of students are standing next to him offering to help.

Barbecue chicken appears to me as raw or partially cooked meat. Far from eating, I cannot even look at it. First, I stare away. The place smells of barbecue and smoke.

The air is filled with barbecue smell. I step inside the house just to get away.

Abundant natural light and sunshine in the living room impress me. Big glass windows allow plenty of light. I feel so good. Currently, in my life as a first-floor apartment dweller, with the door locked and window shutters drawn all the time, I miss daylight and fresh air.

It's not natural air in this house, though. It's a lot cooler than outside. The air-conditioner must be running.

I grew up in a spacious house with big rooms, abundant sunshine and fresh air. Big doors and windows, and a large south-facing balcony designed for natural ventilation. High ceilings with ceiling fans in every room provided circulation.

It was one of my first impressions in the apartment house. Americans are so tall, why are the rooms so low? Don't they use ceiling fans? I haven't seen one yet.

Dr. and Mrs. Hewett have two daughters. Beth is ten, and Jane is eight.

Wearing eyeglasses, Beth is reading a book in the living room. My first impression about her is that she is a bookworm; kind of calm and quiet and reads a lot.

She looks at me and says, "Hello."

"Hello, Beth. Which school do you attend?"

"I am a fourth grader at the Indian Hills Elementary School."

"What do you want to be when you grow up?"

A shy reply comes with a smile, "A teacher, maybe. I don't know."

"That's great. Your dad is a well known professor. What's your favorite subject?"

"English and history." She smiles, again.

"I also liked history in elementary school."

Beth says, "Also, I like to draw and paint. Mom takes me to a class after school twice a week."

In my family extracurricular activities like dance and music were always encouraged. We took private lessons. But many families around us considered it a waste of money.

"Would you like to show me some of your drawings, Beth?"

She smiles and leaves. In a few minutes she returns with some drawings. Mostly scenes of flowers, gardens, etc.

"They are beautiful."

Beth's face brightens with a smile. "Thanks." In a minute she asks, "Our library is downstairs. Would you like to go there?

"Sure." I accompany her.

The stairs lead to a spacious area that she calls a game room. A couple of students from our department are playing table tennis.

"Jane likes gymnastics." Beth gestures to show the series of award ribbons displayed on the walls. "She won them."

"That many?"

"She is good. She wants to be an athlete."

I am surprised. Are the little girls encouraged to be gymnasts and athletes? Isn't that too risky?

We enter the library. Shelf after shelf is stacked with neatly organized books. At a glance I notice, besides science and engineering, many of them belong to literature and other categories. Complete works of famous authors, a complete volume of an encyclopedia, and some biographies. Someone could forget about the world in this room.

Beth smiles, "I like to spend a lot of time in the library."

In the dining room upstairs I see a glass *almirah*. It's full of fancy dinner sets, cups and saucers. Beautiful red-and-gold floral designs are painted on them. These must be reserved for use in special occasions only.

The professor's wife, Mrs. Hewett, steps in and says, "I inherited this china cabinet and most of the china from my grandmother. Most of them are antiques. They belonged to my great-grandmother."

I smile. "We also have the custom of passing down dinner sets as heirlooms. Inheritance from really wealthy families includes gold and silver dinner sets. Based on a family's financial status, instead of precious metals, dinner sets are made of brass and copper alloys. My grandmother's generation had heavy dinner sets of expensive alloys."

She asks, "What is used now?"

"The trend is gradually moving to lighter weight and more convenient ones. For my generation it has come to be lighter weight and easier to maintain stainless steel.

"At *annaprasan*, the rice ceremony for about a six-month-old baby, rice is fed to the baby for the first time. It is celebrated with family and friends. At *annaprasan*, we were presented with a silver bowl and a silver spoon as a symbol of the tradition. Now-a-days very few families even follow that."

"Is your family doing well in Calcutta? Do you keep in touch?"

"Yes, we communicate regularly by letters," I reply.

"If you need help, please let me know."

"OK."

Mrs. Hewett shares with me, "Beth must have really liked you. She takes her time to open up to someone. On the other hand, Jane is restless and talkative and makes friends easily. She is climbing the monkey bars with her friends right now."

"Children like me; even babies and toddlers. I enjoy spending time with them."

"You have the exceptional ability to get close to the kids."

I smile. I am glad to hear it.

She changes the topic. "By the way, let me give you a few safety tips. Never use a shortcut through a parking lot."

"Why? Regularly I take shortcuts through university parking and grocery store parking areas."

She shakes her head. "Please don't; especially not after dark. Sometimes women are attacked in the parking lots."

The thought never crossed my mind. I stare at her like an idiot.

She continues, "When you walk on the street if a car slows down and asks for directions, leave right away. Do not stop or slow down to respond."

I say, "OK."

"Never enter an unlit apartment. Before you enter, turn on the light and check that nothing looks suspicious."

I nod. As it is, I am not brave and these alerts are really scaring me. But these are useful hints. Although I am glad she is telling me, I am also shocked and surprised. I have never thought of these safety tips before. Without even realizing how dangerous it is, I have been violating basic safety rules. Because these rules are not applicable to Calcutta I never knew.

Dinner

We hear Mrs. Hewett say, "Dinner is ready."

She mentions to me, "I have used canned vegetables for convenience."

Canned vegetables? I have seen them at the grocery store, but I am not sure what they are. Fresh vegetables are what I buy.

She asks me, "Are you a vegetarian? Some Indians are."

"No, I eat fish and chicken," I assure her. I do not mention that I cannot consume chicken barbecue. As the hostess she would be bothered, just like my mother would have been if someone invited to our family home would not eat fish.

A big serving-platter full of barbecue chicken is placed on the dining table.

I help myself to some cooked green beans, potatoes, deviled eggs and rolls, the only items I know that are free of beef, ham and pork. No barbecue chicken for me, not even a little bit.

Barbecue is being consumed as the main course. In fifteen minutes the barbecue platter becomes almost empty. The professor reminds us, "A second batch is being cooked."

To make up for my dinner, I eat generous servings of walnut cake and strawberry ice-cream.

In Calcutta it's customary to take a dessert to a family invitation. My favorite walnut cake is what I have brought to the party. Everyone else brought something, too. Some brought a home cooked item.

Some of the invited ladies ask me, "This cake is delicious. How did you make it?"

"It's store-bought," is my honest reply.

Questions follow: "Where did you get it? What's the brand?"

How would they know about the dessert-lover Bengali in me? I have made a list of my favorite American desserts, and I indulge myself in consuming them. Rich desserts like walnut cake and cheesecake have become my favorites.

Another lady asks about the recipe of a homemade potato dish. She says, "It's so delicious it's worth putting a lot of effort into making it."

I do not comment. To my spicy Indian palate, the potato dish tasted like nothing but steamed potato sprinkled with butter and salt.

During the party I notice that the professor cooked, served drinks, and helped with cleaning. In Calcutta, men do not do these chores usually. The guests also helped, especially with the cleanup. I watched them, but did not feel comfortable enough to do it.

Back home, it's not customary to accept any help from the guests. It would be considered rude and offensive. Guests are always served. They never help serve.

Customs are based on the socioeconomic conditions. I realize they are very different here. In India people have extended family, maids and attendants.

After dinner and dessert the party ends and I get back to my apartment—to my monotonous life.

Summer Lab Course

Integrated Circuit Fabrication Laboratory I and II are mandatory courses in this department.

I am in the Fab Lab I class. Our professor, Dr. Rogers, presents an introduction: "Integrated circuit chips are used everywhere in electronic system design. Every hardware design engineer should know about the fabrication process of chips. Fab Lab I will teach you about that. Basically, it's starting with a bare silicon wafer and building an integrated circuit chip on it. This is a part of integrated circuit engineering. Since it deals with wafer processing, it's also known as process engineering."

To emphasize the necessity of safety, Dr. Rogers shows us a documentary film from OSHA (Occupational Safety and Health Administration).

He takes us on a tour of the lab and emphasizes, "Controlled environment is the key to the success. Even a little bit of contamination may cause circuits to fail, killing weeks of round-the-clock work. Every step must be taken to assure safety and cleanliness."

Entrance to the lab is through the clean room. A "No food or drink" sign is displayed on the door. When we step on the circular shoe cleaning brush, it rotates and cleans the shoes. Then we put on shoe covers.

Not only a full-length lab coat, but also a head cover is mandatory. I put my waist-long thick hair in a tight braid. Then make a bun and secure it by U-shaped metal hair clips that I brought from India. This is the only way I can get the head cover to fit.

Thick plastic goggles serve as eye protection. They cover the eyes, eyebrows and the sides of the eyes, too.

We tour the different labs that are used for processing the chips.

The Dark Room is almost pitch-black. After our eyes get used to the darkness, the photography development equipment becomes visible. I have done physics experiments in similar optics lab before.

The Gold Room earns its name from its very soft, yellowish light. This is the photolithography lab. Photolithography is used during each processing step to produce a desired pattern on the surface of the wafer. This is how pattern generation is achieved. Most of the setups look familiar to me, much like a chemistry lab.

The Furnace Room is lit by bright fluorescent lights, and contains the high temperature electric furnaces for oxidation and diffusion. This is totally new to me.

The Measurement Lab is used for post-fabrication chip testing. It has a traditional look. Microscopes and other standard equipments used for electronic measurements are set up to help test functionality.

Following the tour I whisper to Anand, "This is like a combination of optics lab, chemistry lab and instrumentation lab. It can't be that hard."

He replies seriously, "I have heard it's the other way around."

On the first day, lab coats, shoe covers, head covers and goggles are assigned to us. The coats and covers are disposable, to be discarded after a few uses.

Every student is also assigned two-inch diameter, bottle green silicon wafers, stainless steel tweezers to handle them, a covered wafer tray and long thick plastic gloves that are resistant to chemicals. Many of the chemicals to be handled are extremely harmful.

Rows of lockers are located in the Clean Room. Each student is allocated one.

"Please write your names on lab coats, wafer trays and goggles. Keep your stuff in your locker," Dr. Rogers instructs us.

After the initial photo-mask generation by photo-reduction, we are ready for the Furnace Room. The furnaces are arranged in two rows. The top row furnaces are too high for me, though they are fine for the men of average height.

Ready to load my wafer, I stand confused in front of the high temperature oxidation furnace.

Dr. Rogers steps forward, "Please, let me load it for you."

From the beginning of my student life here I realized that in order to survive as a female student in this all-male department, I have to work independently. I must prove that I can do anything required of them. When it comes to studies, I work very hard to get good grades. I will not let my height get in the way.

With a firm determination, I tell him, "No, thank you."

I pull over a stool and stand on it. Wearing high temperature resistant special gloves, I lean forward to load the wafer rack into the red-hot furnace. The professor stands right next to me nervously. Anxiety is written all over his face. When I succeed, he seems more relieved than me. As the course proceeds, I perform this task routinely.

Utilizing photolithography techniques, the micro-circuit is gradually transferred to the wafer. This step includes using chemicals, down-to-the-second precision etching, etc. The lighting in the Gold Room is maintained not to interfere with the design steps. In spite of the perpetual running exhaust system, a strong odor of chemicals fills the room.

Standing next to Ben I say, "In Calcutta, my high school and college chemistry labs had large windows providing natural air ventilation. That helped dissipate the odors fast."

"It can't be done in a controlled environment lab," is his response.

He asks, "Did you go through twelve years of school and four years of undergraduate college like us?"

I explain, "It's somewhat different for us. I went through eleven years of school, three years of college and two years of post-graduate studies, and obtained a Master's in Physics."

A scene from the distant past flashes in front of my eyes. In my tenth grade class, the very first chemistry lab in a girls' school, most of us had elbow or waist-long hair.

The instructor lit a Bunsen burner and held a single lock of long hair near the flame. The flame almost jumped and burnt the hair in the blink of an eye.

"You have witnessed how easily hair catches fire. Please have your hair tied tightly before you enter the chemistry lab," he warned us.

That scene stayed engraved in my mind. In a chemistry lab I have always had my long hair in a tight braid or a bun.

There are no open flames in the Fab Lab, and my hair is secured under a head-cover. Totally unaware, my hands reach my head to assure that my hair is not going to get in the way when I am around chemicals.

The SOP (Standard Operating Procedure), a step-by-step instruction manual for the lab course, is used daily. The very last instruction for each day is "Leave Clean."

This two-word rule, apparently innocent, simple and easy, turns out to be a heavy duty chore for me. I never realized how demanding it was.

At the end of a day, after long hard work at the lab, hungry and exhausted, all I want to do is go home. But alas! That's not even a remote possibility. At that critical time I am to be patient and clean up. I am expected to clean and organize everything I used so that the lab is ready the next morning. What a punishment!

I have to admit that my fellow American students are not bothered. They clean up and organize habitually. I face the negative impact of growing up being used to help from attendants, whether at home or at school. There I just did the work and left—someone else was responsible for cleaning up.

I learn the hard way that if everybody cleans up, an attendant is not needed.

I can't find my tweezers. The photolithography lab assignment has to be completed this afternoon. The next phase is scheduled to start tomorrow morning. I search my locker and the lab, but I just can't locate it.

James, standing next to me in the Gold Room, asks, "What's wrong?"

Almost ready to cry, I respond desperately, "I can't find my tweezers. I thought I left it on my wafer tray, but it's not there."

"Go get another one from our lab technician, Mr. G."

I go to his office, but I can't find him. Twice frustrated and anxious, I return to the lab.

James asks, "Got another one?"

"No. I couldn't locate him, either. Who else can I turn to?"

"Not a problem," he answers. He must be joking. How can he? "I will be done in twenty minutes. Use mine after that."

I am highly impressed. He is so friendly and cooperative!

"Thanks, James," I say appreciatively.

I have never even had a conversation with him. Nothing beyond the formal hello, and even that was only if I ran into him face-to-face.

Ready to write my lab report at my desk, I realize I left my lab notebook with the recorded data in the lab. Oh no! As it is I am running out of time. I have to go through the Clean Room just to fetch the notebook.

As I get to the Clean Room I find Gary is about to enter the lab and I tell him my problem.

"I will save you a trip. Let me get it for you. Wait here," Gary offers to help me.

This is saving a trip, indeed. Have shoes brushed, put on shoe cover, lab coat, head cover and plastic goggles. Then undo all on the way out. Just to get a notebook!

"Thanks, Gary," I say as he hands me my lab notebook.

I have learned a lot in this course, both theoretically and hands-on. So far, as a newcomer Indian woman, I have been so reserved and unwilling to carry on a conversation and so determined to maintain my distance from the other students that they have hesitated, too.

But, going through the extra-long-duration fabrication lab week after week throughout the summer quarter accompanied by frustrations and exhaustion just like the other students, I have achieved something special. We have become closer.

While working side-by-side in the lab, I get used to brief conversations such as: "How are you?" "What other courses are you taking this summer?" "What about the coming fall?" "Oh, the Solid State Electronics course? I will take that, too. It's a core course required of all students."

In the process I come to use their names, instead of attaching them to their individual appearances. For example, that tall one is present in most of my classes. Or that skinny one is kind of quiet; hardly talks to anyone.

I don't try to avoid them like before. Finally, I have come to realize they are students just like me. Student life is our common ground. Both sides get comfortable talking to one another—a milestone achievement for me that continues well beyond the lab course.

The tall one present in most of my classes is Tom. He remarks, "You are a lot easier to understand compared to some other Indian students."

I am not sure about what he is saying. So I ask, "What do you mean?"

"Last quarter I took the Digital Design III course. Kris, the TA (Teaching Assistant), is Indian. Do you know who I am talking about?"

"Yes. Radhakrishnan."

"It was impossible to follow him. It was a nightmare. I'm glad that class is over." Tom shakes his head as he breathes a sigh of relief.

How nice! He is complimenting me on my English accent.

It's hard to believe that I have just completed making an Integrated Circuit (IC) chip something I have read so much about. I am holding the two-inch silicon wafer with a design on it. It's unbelievable how a design drawn by computer on red Rubylith film becomes an IC!

Long hours at the lab require down-to-the-second precision timing, excessive cleanliness to avoid any contamination, immense patience, beyond imagination exhaustion, and precise work until finally, the lab work comes to completion. It takes a toll on me.

Testing

At the end of the Processing Lab, it's time for testing in the Measurement Lab. This is where the students find out whether their chips are functional or not. This lab witnesses triumphant and heart-broken students.

I hope my circuits are working. Since the chip design is replicated to make a number of the same chips on a wafer, it's highly likely that at least some of them will work.

Walking past me, Ben comments, "The peripheral ones are usually damaged by tweezers. Avoid them. Good luck."

I complete the electronic measurement setup and concentrate on studying at the wafer under a microscope.

The first few circuits I test turn out to be non-functional. I keep getting more and more frustrated and anxious with each negative outcome. Is this it? Will all my effort and hard work produce nothing?

Finally, I find a couple that respond well, showing beautiful characteristics. I am excited, ready to scream and dance in joy. Instead, I run to Ben's desk with the great news. "Ben, guess what?"

He lifts his eyes from a book and gives me an interrogative stare. "What?"

Ecstatic, I say, "I got a few working chips; three so far."

"Great! Collect some data. It will help you analyze the results and write a report."

Dr. Rogers will grade the lab reports, but that will only contribute to half of the grade. The other half will come from the mid-term and final exams.

Field trip

We go on a day-long field trip accompanied by Dr. Rogers. My very first field trip in America! We visit a commercial fabrication lab owned by a well-known semiconductor corporation, about two hours drive from the university.

A couple of their engineers guide us through their design engineering and process engineering labs.

Because of the commercial environment, they have to secure a high yield to keep the labs profitable. Extremely high standards in cleanliness and controlled environment are maintained. The employees are covered in long aprons, shoe covers, hair covers, masks and gloves.

A better image about the electronics industry develops in my mind.

Conclusion

Dr. Rogers tells the class, "Fabrication Lab II, the next sequence will be offered. It will be an individual project-oriented course, a lot harder than this one. It will require individual circuit design, fabrication, testing, analysis and a written report."

I am glad this lab is over. I don't even want to hear about the next one. I want to get out of this for now. I will handle it when I get there. Not now.

Summer break

The lab course has drained me. The first three days I indulge myself by sleeping a lot. Never realized I could sleep this long. Following that loneliness and boredom take over. How much time can I spend by myself in the tiny apartment? It's common for the students to pass hours and hours absorbed in watching TV. I don't have one. I have watched some TV in the students' lounge once in a while, but most of the programs are not worth watching.

Watching TV for hours? That's impossible! I couldn't do that.

My hobby has always been reading literature. Any kind is fine; but short stories, especially in Bengali, are my ultimate favorite. Starting from the older generation of Tagore, and Sarat Chandra, to the next generation of Bibhuti Bhusan, Banaful, Ashapurna Devi, Mahasweta Devi, Bimal Mitra, Bimal Kar, etal. I have read them all. Courtesy of translations from foreign languages, I have also read Maupassant, Tolstoy and Chekov. While reading a good book I forget the world and lose track of time. Sometimes severe headaches due to hours of non-stop eye strain force me to take a break. But I still dwell in the world of the story. The characters stay alive with me for days.

Throughout my childhood I enjoyed reading *Sandesh*, the Bengali monthly magazine, published by the famous movie director Satyajit Ray's family. U. Ray, his grandfather, started it. My parents grew up with it, too. As children, we used to count the days, watch the mail and wait eagerly for its monthly arrival. As soon as it arrived it was like a hotcake, changing hands starting from the children, to our parents, uncles and aunts, with the afternoons especially reserved for my grandmother. We used to solve the puzzles within the first day or two, and mail the answers right away to assure our names would get published in the following month's magazine. Why were some novels published serially from month to month? We had to wait helplessly. It was so hard. Without being aware of it, I turned into a literature lover in my childhood.

Being an avid reader is a habit I inherited. Novels and books, sometimes purchased, sometimes from the libraries, were always in circulation in our home. As high school students, we were allowed to read *Desh*, the weekly subscribed Bengali magazine. Many famous novels, short stories and contemporary literature were first published there.

A special attraction was every magazine's *"Puja Sankya,"* the special edition published at Durga Puja, the biggest religious celebration in Bengal.

I really miss the Bengali books in my lonely life. That alone could have given me company. I wish I had brought the tiny book *Gitanjali*, a small collection of poems and songs by Tagore.

While growing up, time after time I witnessed how Bengalis, who lived in Europe and the U.S., had pathetically forgotten the mother tongue. What a pity! I used to feel sorry for them.

Bengali is intertwined in my heart and soul. Every drop of my blood has been nurtured by it. Time after time I have been complimented on the cultured version of Bengali that I use. I refuse to give it up. Though my only practice now-a-days is limited to letters to home, I pay attention to my handwriting, grammar and spelling. Fear of losing the language scares me. It would be losing a part of me. Under parental pressure, over a decade of music lessons have earned me the prestigious degree of Sangeet Pravakar. On the local celebration of Saraswati Puja, I earned fame by singing two of Tagore's songs. Though out of touch, I keep singing Bengali songs and keep reciting poems. Sometimes I miss a word or two, but I don't give up. I must stay connected to my soul.

Having no other choice, to get away from the loneliness and boredom, I end up going to the university. The department is almost empty. Just a few foreign students are seen here and there. Only a very few M.S. and Ph.D. students, who are fast approaching completion, keep working hard to take the opportunity of empty labs. The engineering library, the computer center and all other facilities those were so crowded till last week that it was impossible to find a spot, are totally vacant now.

After wandering around awhile, I enter the huge Central Library. I wish I could read some Bengali books. An inquiry at the circulation desk reveals they don't have any.

Startling me, a female-voice greets me in Hindi, *"Namaste. Kya haal hai aap ki?"*

Standing next to me is Bindu Kapur, the Indian librarian, wearing a sari. She used to work part-time at the Engineering library.

I smile back, "I'm fine. How are you?"

"Your finals are over. Relaxing now?"

"Yes. Your sari is beautiful," I complement her.

"Thanks. Why don't you wear saris?"

"Well, I tried in the beginning. Didn't go well at all in engineering. Very inconvenient in labs. Additionally, people kept staring and asking questions all the time. I stopped immediately. It's irritating to wear pants every day, because I have only a few of them. On the contrary, I have dozens of silk saris with matching blouses in my apartment."

Bindu encourages, "You could have worn a sari today. Why don't you wear it to the library or the grocery? It's comfortable to wear and pretty to look at. From now onwards wear saris whenever you get a chance."

She sounds like I owe her an explanation. I hesitate some. "I am not so sure. On a scorching hot Saturday I was walking to the campus wearing a sari to attend a Hindi movie. Just like in India, I had a fashionable lady's umbrella open to block the sun. Everyone on the street kept staring at me as if: "Which planet did she arrive from?"

"It's not customary here to use an umbrella in the sun."

I pour out my grievance. "That wasn't all. Even a police car stopped and kept watching me. What an embarrassment! That was enough."

Bindu bursts out in laughter, I join her soon. She asks, "How far away do you live? Is it a long walk?"

"No, about a mile or so. Do you live in this neighborhood?"

She shakes her head, "Not at all. Anderson Township, about thirty miles away. It's a beautiful neighborhood."

"That far? Is there a bus route?"

Proudly, Bindu elaborates, "No. My elder brother, my sister and I live in the same neighborhood. My brother is a faculty at the University medical center, just two blocks away. My sister is a librarian there. My brother's son and daughter, and my sister's son are undergraduate students at the university. Every morning my brother drives his minivan and drops us off. He picks all of us up at the end of the day."

I become jealous instantly. "Great! You are surrounded by family, even outside India. How fortunate!"

Suddenly a thought crosses my mind. As a benefit of employment, employees' children may attend the undergraduate program here free of charge. Is that why their youngsters go to school here? It's below courtesy to ask such a financial question.

Bindu smiles as she says lightly, "You have gained a lot of weight. Watch it, girl. You arrived nice and skinny. Don't get out of shape at such a young age."

"I sit at my desk, and study and study. Fast food for lunch every day. Steamed rice and veggies topped with butter for dinner. Toast, butter, jelly and cookies along with tall glasses of milk for breakfast and snacks. No wonder I put on weight."

"You are from Calcutta," Bindu says. "When I visited Calcutta, I really enjoyed the Bengali desserts: rosogolla, sandesh, pink yogurt. Delicious!"

"We love milk desserts."

Bindu continues, "The Bengali women are so pretty; just like you. I am jealous."

I am so honored as well as flattered. According to our custom I become shy and say in a low and appreciative tone, "Everyone says so."

She glances at her watch and hurries away, "My break is over. Bye."

The periodicals section keeps a nice collection of well-known worldwide newspapers. Eagerly I pick up a copy of "The Times of India," published from New Delhi.

I recognize the elderly Indian gentleman across the table, also reading *"The Times of India."* He and his wife came over from Calcutta to spend a few months with their son's family. His son drops him off at the library two days a week on his way to work and picks him up after work. This is his only way to spend some time outside home. What a pity!

On the other hand, his wife doesn't mind staying home, cooking and taking care of the grandchildren while the son and daughter-in-law are at work.

The elderly visitors from India cannot drive. They are at the mercy of their children for transportation. In Calcutta they walk to nearby parks. They may ride rickshaws or taxis. They have the freedom to go places. Sometimes a family member or a servant accompanies them to assure safety. Additionally, friends and relatives drop by all the time.

Many of the elderly visitors cannot bear the boredom and the loss of freedom in the confined life. They feel relieved to return to India as soon as possible.

ISA Picnic

The India Students Association has arranged the annual picnic this summer on a Saturday in August. All the students and faculty from India are invited. I am delighted to go to a picnic just to see how it goes in this country. The thought of being around Indians a whole day and being able to communicate to them is tempting.

The venue is Bishop Woods Park right across from the university. It will work out well for me. I will walk to the picnic spot.

I am too shy and too embarrassed to ask for a ride. For the very few social occasions that I am invited to join, if a ride is involved my response is often, "I am too busy. I can't go."

Dr. Mohanti, a post-doctoral fellow in the physics department, went home to Orissa, India this summer and brought back his wife and five-year-old son.

Kalpana, his wife, wearing a sari, is delighted to meet me. She comes from a village in Orissa and speaks Oriya only. She requests that if I speak Bengali very slowly, she will understand it due to the similarity in the languages. This is her first chance to talk to someone since she arrived three weeks ago. She stays glued to me.

Not being used to the situation, she asks me, "How long the picnic is going to be?"

"It's late morning, about eleven o'clock. The agenda shows it will go on till four."

Startled, she almost screams, "What? In this burning heat, am I to stay outdoors all the way till four in the afternoon?"

Sounds as if, she will be happy to leave right away, though her husband and son are having fun throwing a Frisbee.

Prof. Gupta, a professor in the math department in his fifties, arrives with a woman about twenty-five and two pre-school boys. He introduces them to me. "Meet my wife and sons."

Though kind of shocked, I swallow and manage to say politely, "Hello."

After they step away, Uma, a graduate student in the English department, walks to me. "I have heard so much about you. I am from New Delhi."

She starts conversing in Hindi, the national language in India. In a joking voice she asks, "Did you notice the young wife of the old husband? Doesn't he behave like he is dying to please her?"

I say, "I mean, I was kind of surprised at their age difference."

Uma explains, "Of course, this is his second wife. He divorced his first wife. Then he remarried as arranged by his family in India."

"Divorce! That's so sad. What happened?"

"People say it was because they didn't have kids in ten years of marriage."

It saddens me. "Poor first wife! What happened to her? Did she return home to India to her parents?"

Uma replies promptly, "Not at all. She lives right here, in town."

"By herself?"

"Yes. She teaches at a Montessori school and lives by herself."

I comment, "That's usual for Indian women. Whether a widow, or a divorcee, they hardly ever get remarried."

"Not so for Indian men, though. They have no problem jumping into the next marriage and starting a new life. Look at Dr. Gupta, two kids in three-years," says Uma.

As soon as she steps away, Kalpana asks me, "What happened?"

Though she doesn't understand Hindi thoroughly, she has picked up a few words and has become curious. I slowly explain the whole thing to her.

She is in total disbelief. Her eyes are about to pop out. "Absurd! Can a marriage ever break?"

"Yes." I nod.

She shakes her head. "This is a strange world!"

Uma introduces me to Mrs. Datta, the wife of Dr. Datta, a professor in the Physiology department.

She tells Uma, "I am so very jealous of you. Going home to India twice a year! Additionally, your parents and siblings coming over from India to visit you!"

That's a matter of thousands of dollars. In disbelief, I ask, "Is that true, Uma?"

Uma nods. "Yes, it's true. When I first arrived here last fall, my parents and my sister joined me. They stayed three weeks to help me settle down."

"Really?" I am still in doubt. This must be some kind of a joke.

"But that's not all, Uma," Mrs. Datta reminds her, "Then you visited India last Christmas."

"Yes," Uma agrees. "I returned in January at the beginning of the winter quarter."

I am confused. Uma must be from a millionaire family. I wasn't aware.

Mrs. Datta says regretfully, "We get to go home to India only once every three years. My husband and I and our two kids. Four tickets; the airfare is outrageous. I missed my only sister's wedding. My dad was really ill last year, but I couldn't go. He is better now." She sighs, "The long three years of wait! Can you believe it? It seems endless."

"That's right," I agree with her immediately.

Mrs. Datta comments, "Had I realized this before, I would have requested my father to arrange my marriage to an airlines pilot husband, someone like Uma's dad."

So, Uma's family travels free of cost because of her father's job.

In the afternoon Uma and I take a trip to the park's restroom. Oh no! Looks like it hasn't been cleaned in ages. Two trash cans are overflowing with used paper towels. Doors on stalls do not latch. Toilets look like they do not flush properly. The counters and the sinks have stains all over. The mirror is spotted. Even the floor is wet.

How do people use this place? Can a restroom be this dirty in America? I decide to step out.

Uma asks, "Aren't you going to use the toilet?"

"No. It's way too dirty."

She starts laughing. "Well, well, is this your first trip to a public restroom?"

I think about it for a while. "Yes."

"What about the restrooms at the university?"

"They are always sparkling clean."

Uma shakes her head. "Not always."

"Like this? Never," I protest firmly.

"No, not this bad. Janitors at the university clean them daily."

I object, "The ladies room I use in the ninth floor is always sparkling clean. Basically, I am the only one who uses it."

Uma almost falls apart laughing. "Oh, sounds like you are used to the luxury of a personal restroom in your department. In our English department female students and faculty use them. Despite regular cleaning, they get dirty, especially in late afternoons."

I come to realize that being the only female student on the ninth floor of the Engineering building I do have a restroom to myself.

Issues at the Graduate Student's Lounge: Fall 1980

The academic year started a few weeks ago, at the end of September, 1980. New faces appear in the hallways, in the library and everywhere else.

What a shame! What a shame! In our graduate students' lounge food is being consumed without payment. Most likely the newcomer graduate students are the culprits. Most of them are foreign students. They stay at the lounge watching TV and chatting. The refrigerator is within an arms reach. Boiled eggs, bread, peanut butter and jelly are stored there all the time. Just the bare minimum ingredients to fix a PBJ sandwich to hold starving and exhausted students over to the next meal. Often they work long hours in the lab or on projects, and they do not get a chance to go home to eat. Payment for food is based on an honor system. A student is supposed to write down on a sheet posted on the refrigerator what he has consumed, and deposit the price in a locked cash box weekly. Over the past few weeks there has been almost no payment. At the same time the refrigerator is empty without any name in the sign-up sheet.

The Graduate Students Association president, a graduate student himself, has watched this and waited impatiently for two weeks. But nothing has changed.

So, today he posted a handwritten note on the refrigerator: "Due to some students consuming food without payment, the practice of keeping snacks available is being discontinued. We cannot continue to buy groceries without money."

I am so ashamed of the fellow students who are responsible. I am sure everyone is holding the new students responsible for causing an abrupt stop to a convenience that has been maintained over the years.

The Month-Long Season of Religious Celebrations

Durga puja

A letter from my parents mentioned that this year Durga *puja* will be celebrated from Oct. 11th through the 15th. *Puja* means a Hindu act of worship. Durga puja, the most important festival of the Hindu Bengalis, is celebrated all over West Bengal in the autumn. Educational institutions allow a month off to celebrate the festivity period.

Since my childhood, the puja is coming; it's approaching, it's just a month away. Now not even a month, two weeks only, less than ten days, and finally, it's the very next day…What an excitement it is awaiting the arrival, and getting ready for it!

Annual shopping is done to maintain the tradition of wearing new clothes and new shoes. Ads are everywhere. Neon signs, full-page ads in newspapers and periodicals, each try to claim the very best product available.

Our family always purchases the exact same clothes and shoes for my sister and me. We have the same hair-style and the same color socks and ribbons, too. Except for the two years age difference, we could pass as twins. If material is purchased and clothes are custom-made, Mom has to start early. Most of the seamstresses refuse to take orders in the last few weeks prior to festivities. The seamstress comes to our home with her notebook and measuring tape to get our measurements. Mom explains the design she has in mind or shows her a picture.

My brother, being the only son, never has matching clothes with anyone else.

Dad has superb taste in choosing clothes and materials for everyone. He goes shopping all by himself and buys saris for all the women in the family—my grandmother, my mother, all the aunts, including his sisters and sisters-in-law, all the way to our maids. He does the shopping for Dhoti, shirt and pant pieces for all the males, too.

Once my sister and I become of age to wear saris, we will be included in his list.

I do not recall anyone ever expressing negative comments about what he purchases.

Based on the Hindu myth, Durga puja commemorates the victory of Devi Durga over the demon Mahisasura. The festival celebrates the victory of good over evil.

In the past, the puja used to be performed individually by landlords or wealthy families. Now-a-days a local puja is sponsored by residents of the neighborhood.

Dates are decided by the traditional Hindu calendar, which is luni-solar.

Mahalaya, the auspicious new-moon in the month of *Ashwin* (Sept./Oct.), marks the end of *Pitri-Paksha*, the fortnight of the forefathers. People take a morning dip in the sacred river Ganges to perform rituals, and pray for the peace of the souls of their forefathers. Reciting Sanskrit verses from the holy book *Chandi* to praise the Mother Divine is also an integral part of this morning.

Devi-Paksha, the fortnight of the worship of Mother Divine, follows this.

After a long awaited year, in the evening of *Shasthi*, the sixth day after *Mahalaya*, the Mother Divine *Devi* Durga arrives home to her parents. Her daughters Laxmi and Saraswati, and her sons Kartik and Ganesh accompany her. She stands on a lion, the symbol of her majestic strength.

Laxmi, the goddess of wealth, carries an urn full of gold and money. A white owl stands next to her. An owl is nocturnal, a symbolic representation of wealth to be kept hidden.

Saraswati, the lady in white, is the goddess of knowledge. She carries a *bina*, a sitar-like instrument. Books are kept next to her. A white swan is her symbolic representation. Swans are believed to be capable of drinking milk from a mixture of milk and water, leaving the water behind. When it comes to learning, only the good teachings are to be absorbed.

Kartik, the very handsome god of beauty, stands on a peacock.

Ganesh is the god of wisdom. At any Hindu religious performance he is the first one worshipped. A mouse stands next to him as his symbol.

Idols of all of these gods and goddesses, usually life size or bigger, are placed on a large raised wooden platform in a well decorated enclosure, commonly known as a *pandal*.

Kumortuli is the famous area in Calcutta where clay idols are handmade and sold by clay artists. Most often this profession is carried on for generations.

The well-known puja committees contract the famous clay artists far in advance to custom-make their deities.

Line after line of idols are displayed ready to sell. It's generally acknowledged by Indians that Bengali girls are very pretty. Big, dark and beautiful eyes, a head full of black hair, pretty face and a sweet smile are often typical of Bengali women. This general image is reflected in the Kumortuli idols.

In Calcutta if a future bridegroom's parents are too critical about the looks of the daughter-in-law they are looking for, they are jokingly advised, "Since you can't find anyone you like, you better place an order in Kumortuli."

Following Shasthi, four days Saptami, Astami, Nabami and Dashami, are the four days of Durga puja. Many priests are required due to the extensive religious and ritualistic performances involved. Rituals of anjali and arati, integral parts of the worship, are performed daily.

On *Saptami*, the seventh day, the plant *Nabapatrika*, colloquially called *Kala Bau*, is taken to the river Ganges and bathed in the morning. This is an ancient ritual of worshipping nine types of plants.

Anjali, offering flowers to the Almighty, is routinely performed every morning. Lotus is a must. Both pink and white lotuses, marigolds, roses and *shiuli*, the most common autumnal flower, are used. Along with the flowers, *tulsi* and wood apple leaves, sprinkled with sandalwood paste, are offered to the *Devi*.

Extra large dishes of various fruits and desserts are also offered to the divine ones. Fruits such as cucumbers, sugar canes, coconuts, bananas, guavas, apples, oranges and pomegranates are used. Milk desserts like *sandesh, rosogolla*, and sweet-yogurt as well as coconut desserts fill the dishes.

Neighborhood residents, wearing new clothes, gather in the *pandal*. Women appear in new saris and waist-long hair. The married ones wear a dot of vermillion on their forehead and on the parting of their hair.

Repeating Sanskrit mantras after the Brahmin priest, devotees offer *anjali* to the *Devi* and pray for her blessings.

The fragrance of flowers, sandalwood and incense floats in the air.

After the *anjali* the food is distributed among the devotees. Cooked dishes are offered at lunches.

The Mother Divine is presented with new saris every day, along with cosmetics such as hair oil and vermillion.

Aratis are performed in the evenings. Ringing metal bells, Brahmin priests worship the Devi with illuminated open flame oil lamps, camphor lamps and incense sticks.

Ceremonial drumbeats by traditional drummers, the metallic sound from cymbals, and the blowing of conch shells accompany them, while the devotees watch. Some of the devotees dance to the rhythm of the drumbeats.

Smoke from lamps and incense sticks cloud the *pandal*. The combined sound, the fragrance—the entire environment—is unique to Durga puja.

Like their forefathers, many traditional drummers come to Calcutta from remote villages to earn special income.

Ashtami, the eighth day, is the most important—the day Devi Durga killed the demon Mahisasura. People who choose to participate in Anjali only a single day do it on Ashtami. Also, people who have only one set of new clothes wear them on this day.

The special religious performance of *Sandhi*puja marks the auspicious moment that *Ashtami* rolls over to *Nabami*. A spectacular *Arati* is performed during this.

The sadness starts on *Nabami* night. There are famous songs that request *Nabami* night to stand still, preventing the arrival of *Dashami*, the final day of the puja.

Dashami morning reminds everyone that puja is about to end, and it won't return in a year. All the fun, all the enjoyment, is about to be over. Soon it will be time to face reality again.

On *Dashami* special rituals are performed to mark the end of the puja. Married women take part in the ritual of *Devi baran*. They touch the deity's feet and pray for the well-being of everyone in the family for the upcoming year.

A pandal is often decorated with a competitive attitude. Some pandals are designed to look like temples or shrines; others display a specific type of sculpture. Decorating companies compete against one another, trying to achieve the best decorated pandal. The topmost decorators are booked well in advance.

Attractive decoration by electric light displays is another competitive area. Neon signs, blinking lights and multi-colored arrangements are built frequently. After dark, electric patterns display mythical stories.

Local newspapers print photos of the most spectacular displays, and people follow their lead. Famous puja locations draw hundreds of thousands of visitors. Villagers take trains and buses to travel to Calcutta to see them.

Car riders may have general advantages in some respects, but not very much when it comes to *pandal* hopping. Many streets are blocked from traffic to ease the flow of pedestrians. It's not uncommon to separate men and women into two different channels to ease the flow. Security officers patrol to handle the crowd.

It's a pleasure to watch the flow of the enthusiastic and jubilant crowd from the comfort of the second-floor verandah of our home. It reflects popular fashion trends for the year.

Kids are more interested in which lion, the real king of the animal kingdom, looks the strongest and the most unbeatable, and which peacock has feathers that look almost real. Are swans paper-white in real life? The shining decorative weapons in *Devi*'s hands look so real. Are they sharp?

Roadside makeshift snack bars and ice-cream shops do highly profitable business. *Pandal* hopping and eating, eating and *pandal* hopping, the cycle continues into the early hours of the morning till people are too exhausted.

New albums, specially released for the puja, are played loudly and repeatedly. After we enjoy them a while, they become ear-sores.

The noise, the crowd, the restlessness—everything is a part of the celebration.

At the end of the puja, awards are given in different categories such as best idol, best *pandal* decoration, best electric decoration, etc. Winners are announced in the newspapers.

At the end of the day of Dashami the clay deities are immersed in the Ganges.

The immersion procession starts in the evening. Deities are carried in well-decorated open-top trucks to the Ganges. Local marching bands, drummers and neighborhood people perform on the streets as they accompany the deities. A final performance takes place as they arrive at the river. Each deity is carried by a group of people and immersed. Hundreds of deities are immersed that evening. The *ghat*, bank of the river, where immersions are allowed, has police to maintain security.

Accompanied by my dad and uncle we walk to the river in the evening. After we watch quite a few immersions, we sprinkle some Ganges water on our heads, and return home sad. What a depressing thought that Durga puja is over and we must wait an entire year for the next one!

The rituals of *Bijoya Dashami*, the post-puja, starts in the evening. Showing respect to elders by offering *pranams* touching their feet, and best-wishes to siblings and cousins is customary. Afterwards, sweets are distributed by the elders. Every household is loaded with varieties of desserts for the occasion. Just another excuse for sweet-tooth Bengalis to consume desserts.

The milk desserts include *rosogolla, rajbhog, sandesh, chumchum, gulabjamun, monohara,* rice-pudding and sweet-yogurt. Special desserts are homemade with flattened or puffed rice and molasses as well as cocoanut.

This continues over the next few weeks to cover the extended families and friends.

Ours is not a weight-conscious and calorie-counting society. We never hear people pay attention to how much weight they gain during the celebrations from overeating.

It is customary to write letters to relatives living out of town to convey *Bijoya* greetings. Letter writing also continues over the next two weeks. Everyone in my family participates: grandparents, parents, uncles and aunts and children.

Vice-versa, the postman delivers us stacks of letters from our friends and families. Some letters are just formal; many are cordial. Most of them contain at least a few lines about puja celebrations.

After the four days of the puja *Devi* is believed to return to her husband Lord Shiva at Kailash. Based on this, common people relate to Durga puja as a homecoming for their daughters, too.

In real life many daughters and their families come home to their parents during this celebration.

This year puja came and went. I witnessed it only on the calendar. I had marked the dates bright red beforehand. Every day I stared at the calendar sadly, and imagined what was going on in Calcutta.

I visualized the *Anjalis* performed in the mornings; people reciting Sanskrit chants after the Brahmin priest, and offering flowers sprinkled with sandalwood paste. The evening *Aratis* with ceremonial drumbeats, the metallic sound from cymbals, blowing of conch shells, ringing of bells, the whole place covered with fragrance and smoke from the lamps and incense sticks.

One more event to wipe away tears, one more reminder that I am in a foreign country far away from my family. Stern reality!

In the USA, Durga puja is celebrated in some big cities with a large Bengali population. Some cities, due to the large concentration of Hindus living there, have Hindu temples. Nothing like that exists in this city.

In the weekend following Durga puja I spend a lot of time writing auspicious Bijoya-greetings letters to my parents, grandparents and siblings. I try my best to conceal my acute homesickness. Actually, this is just a start. I have a long way to go to cover my extended family and friends. I will do that in the upcoming weekends.

Pretty soon, I start receiving letters with *Bijoya* greetings. It begins with my siblings, parents and grandparents and continues. I am overwhelmed, and wish the letters would never stop coming. So many of my friends and family have written to me; most of them before receiving my letters! I did not even know that some of them had my address. They must have approached my parents.

They offer *Bijoya* greetings, state how they spent Durga puja, and how much they miss me. I feel so important, connected and well-cared for. Though physically I reside at the other end of the world, the hidden thread of affection bonds me to them strongly. I am not alone!

Time after time I read each and every letter. But even that doesn't seem adequate, so I keep them displayed on the table. They will provide me companionship in my lonely life.

Kali puja

On the following new-moon, believed to be the darkest new-moon of the year,

Mother Divine is worshipped in the form of Kali at midnight. Goddess Kali symbolizes *Shakti* or strength. As a destroyer of all evils, she is in a fierce, destructive mood.

*Pandal*s are decorated and the goddess is worshipped, but relatively few compared to the Durga puja.

Bengalis are well-known as dedicated devotees of the Mother Divine. Calcutta has many Kali temples. Some tend to think the very name Calcutta, locally called Kolkata, was derived from Kali.

This is also the night of *Diwali*—derived from the Sanskrit word *Deepawali*—meaning a row of lights. It is the topmost religious festival celebrated in different ways in different states by Hindus all across India.

Every household is decorated with rows of lights at night. Some use candles; some use old-fashioned, open-flame clay oil lamps; and some use electric light bulbs. To exhibit the spirit of the celebration each and every neighborhood reflects the illuminations.

At night various firecrackers and sparklers dominate. Skyrockets go high in the air before exploding. The night sky flashes with colorful patterns. Loud noises and the fumes go on for hours.

In the USA, *India Abroad*, the weekly Indian newspaper published from New York, also reflects the impact of the celebration. Big businesses run ads extending their *Diwali* greetings. Ads for *Diwali* sales—all the way from 22 karat gold and precious stone jewelry imported from India to saris, grocery items such as rice and lentils, spices and especially the mouthwatering Indian desserts—fill page after page.

The local Indian grocery store near the university also stocks up on their supplies of saris and sweets for *Diwali*.

Bhai-phonta

Two days after Kali puja is *Bhai-phonta*, a ritual between a brother and a sister. It expands to cover extended families and distant relatives. A sister puts a sacred dot of sandalwood paste on her brother's forehead and prays for his longevity and well-being; in return she receives gift from the brother. Brothers are served delicious desserts and meals throughout the day by their sisters. This celebration applies to all ages, from infants to the very elderly.

This is the first time in my life that I have missed this very special ceremony. Tears roll down my cheeks as I write an emotional letter to my one and only brother in India.

Welcome from a Friend

About two months after arriving here, past eleven one night, I was busy working on my homework as usual, when the telephone rang. Surprised, I picked up.

An excited female voice greeted me in Bengali. "Lata speaking! How are you? I got your telephone number today in a letter from home. I am so excited; just couldn't wait till the weekend to call you."

I glanced at my assignment. That was due the next day. She couldn't wait till the weekend, so she waited past eleven to get the weekend rate for long-distance calls. There went my homework.

Nonetheless, I was so excited! Lata and I had attended college together. She got married and arrived in the U.S. about a year ago. With great enthusiasm I responded, "I am so happy to hear from you! How are you?"

During our ten-minute conversation Lata said, "Come on, we are friends. Call me every weekend; visit us over the long weekends. What are friends for?" In a warm and welcoming voice she continued, "My husband and I would love to have you over."

Such a cordial invitation! I was convinced that would be a great getaway for me, to speak in my mother language, to share my thoughts with a girlfriend. Now that she had cordially invited me to visit her five hundred miles away, I was thrilled. How lucky!

She kept asking, "When are you coming? When do we get to see you? I can't wait."

"Well," I responded, "I will have a month-long break between summer and fall, before school starts back in September. That will be a good time to visit."

"Sure, sure. Summer is beautiful here. We will take short trips around. I have my own car, no problem. It will be great. Make sure to spend at least a week or two with us. Call me a few weeks ahead and let me know. I will keep calling and stay in touch with you. After all, you live by yourself."

I was beaming with joy, floating in an ocean of excitement! I would take a long-distance bus, as I have heard from students, and visit them. It would be great. A place to go to, someone to visit! What an opportunity to get a break from my monotonous high-pressure life!

I brought a few beautiful new silk saris from India. Two of them with exquisite handcrafted needle-work, were very expensive. One would be a nice gift for her. After all, she was nice enough to invite me to stay at least a week.

We were classmates over a period of three years. But we were never friends, just acquaintances. I never knew she was such a nice person.

Months passed. I waited eagerly for her phone calls. A long-distance phone call was a luxury to me. Tired of waiting indefinitely, I called her.

Her quick response was, "I'm very busy right now. I'll call you later."

She never called. I came to realize she was reluctant to stay in touch. What happened? I questioned myself: What went wrong?

When she was my classmate, her family was struggling with finances due to the sudden untimely demise of her father. An ordinary looking, bespectacled girl wearing cheap printed cotton saris, was how I remembered her. Lata's mother and uncles arranged her marriage to a Bengali professional in Chicago through a newspaper matrimonial advertisement.

Now she has her own house and car, and a good social status through marriage. Maybe she thought about my visit, discussed it with her husband and realized that having a struggling graduate student over was one-sided. No reciprocation could be expected in the near future.

As I have heard from other Indian students, many local Indian families think this way. Students need rides. They cannot afford to reciprocate properly. When they graduate either they return to India or move to the place where they find a job. What's the point in socializing with them?

Why do people suddenly turn so materialistic? That's such a non-Indian attitude.

However, when a student graduates and starts a good job, the scenario changes quickly. Suddenly, the student earns the status of a prospective bride or groom. Indian society suddenly shows immense interest.

In October Lata calls me, "Auspicious Bijoya greetings from us."

Though annoyed, I reply politely, "Auspicious *Bijoya* greetings from me to everyone in your family."

She asks casually, "Didn't you mention visiting us in summer?"

I'm stunned. What's she trying to say? I fail to come up with a response.

Lata tries to sound disappointed. "We were really hoping that you would come."

What a hypocrite! I manage to swallow the insult. "I was very busy."

She says in pity, "I know, students have neither money nor time."

Continued Education

Since the beginning of fall quarter, often I see a tall, bearded white man on our ninth floor. He cannot be a student. He is a lot older than us. Is he a new faculty? I will find out.

Before long, he introduces himself to me. "Hi, I am Jack, a new Ph.D. student here. I completed a M.S. in physics years ago."

"Why don't you go for a Ph.D. in physics?"

He smiles as he replies, "A Ph.D. in electrical engineering will be more marketable, a lot more money."

I can't help saying, "Yes, but…"

"I know. A lot more courses, a lot more work. Also, it will take longer. But I am willing to do that," he says with admirable confidence.

"OK."

Jack sounds regretful. "I wish I did it like you guys, when I was younger. Instead, right after the M.S. I got married and went to work."

"Where did you work?"

"At the telephone company. Now, ten years later, I am divorced. No children, no commitment. I want to do a Ph.D. and go for a teaching career."

"OK."

Though he is older than average students, he is a full-time student and spends his days in the classes and labs just like us.

I am surprised to see someone returning to do his Ph.D. after a ten-year break. I guess, because it is a new concept to me. It must be acceptable in the universities and the society here.

I had no idea that a bigger surprise was waiting for me.

I am surprised to find an elderly woman attending the undergraduate class, Network and Circuit Analysis. She is not only older than the students, but also a lot older than most of the professors. How old is she? Maybe sixty or sixty-five? I don't know. American physical characteristics, especially skin, hair-color, build, etc., are so very different from Indians that I get lost when it comes to estimating age.

Whatever it is, she cannot be a student. Maybe she is a mother or an aunt accompanying a student. What is she doing here? With a book and a notebook in front of her, listening to the professor and taking notes, she acts like a student.

I am not left in the dark much longer. At the end of the class she comes forward and starts talking to me. "I am Sara Burton. You may be surprised to see me here."

Definitely I am surprised as well as shocked, but it's not polite to say that. I admit, "Kind of..."

She elaborates, "I am fifty-six. About thirty years ago I quit college and got married. Two children: a son and a daughter, both grown up. They graduated from college and they work now. I always regretted not finishing college. I felt like I was the only uneducated person in the family.

"In that era," she explains, "It was customary for the wives to stay home and raise a family. That's what I did. It's a different trend now-a-days. Married women go to school. They go to work."

"Yes," I agree.

Enthusiastically, she continues, "My husband retired earlier this year. He encouraged me to go back to college and get my degree."

I ask, "What brings you to engineering?"

Mrs. Burton replies, "I am not sure what to study. I took a few basic classes in engineering math while in college. Not that I liked them, but I followed my boyfriend to class. Electrical Engineering is a big name now. I decided to give it a try. Currently, I am a part-time student, taking just two courses."

I am spellbound. Though decades younger than her, the pressure of studies stresses me out. How can she even dream of this? Is it even a realistic expectation?

In a joking tone she says, "Last week I forgot my homework. My husband came to drop it off. He commented, 'That's your professor? He is just a kid.' Of course he would say that. You all are much younger than our children."

I smile.

"I will talk to you from time to time to update myself about the issues of student life. Please help me, if I need it."

I nod and smile.

"Come to me if you have any question about life. I have a lot more experience than anyone else in the class." Mrs. Burton smiles as she leaves.

In Calcutta the education system is different. Continuity in education is almost mandatory. If someone discontinues school for years, it's not easy to get back as a regular student again. In the fields that require lab, it's hardly ever allowed.

Under the circumstances, I am confused about the education system here. How can she even start back in engineering after thirty years?

Two weeks before the final exams Mrs. Burton approaches me after class. She mentions some medical problems, most of which is beyond my comprehension.

She says, "The surgery is scheduled right after finals. Four-weeks of Christmas break will give me enough time to recuperate. I expect to get well and return in January to attend the winter quarter."

The thought of surgery sends chills down me. I never had one and I am scared to death even at the mention of it.

She keeps talking, "The problem will be scheduling Christmas parties. The entertaining and socializing we do every year will not be possible at all. People will miss my cooking, especially the cakes and cookies. If you need a recipe, please let me know."

I smile back. Desserts are my weakness. But spending time to follow a recipe, buy the ingredients and the baking utensils and make them? Beyond my imagination! I would much rather buy desserts from the grocery store and relish them.

The year rolls over and the winter quarter begins in early January, 1981. It marks the beginning of my second year. I start racing against time, as usual. Surprising me, Mrs. Burton never comes back.

I wonder what happened to her. Did she get really sick and could not return? Did she get discouraged by her grades?

Poor Mrs. Burton! It must have been really hard for her to face the reality.

I try to find consolation. Maybe she is studying another subject and doesn't need to come to this building any more.

2. Newcomer, 1981

Bank statements are delivered by mail every month. I pay attention to each and every transaction. A "waste not, want not" policy has been instilled in me as a result of my upbringing. Self-esteem and pride prohibit me from talking about my financial hardship. Foreign students, in general, are under financial pressure.

Many Indian students brag about how rich their families are in India. Americans are not used to having domestic help. To them, it's a luxury beyond imagination. When Indian students talk about attendants and domestic help, Americans perceive them as descendents from families with princely status. That's far from true. Due to the socio-economic structure, even a middle class family can afford to have a maid.

Vaskar, our classmate, doesn't stop there. At our first introduction he tells me arrogantly, "You know, I am a Brahmin."

I am surprised he brags that he is a Brahmin, the highest caste. Though it doesn't make sense to Americans, they are given the impression his status is above and beyond the reach of common people. He makes the impression that other Indians should be much obliged even to get a chance to talk to him. Moreover, his behavior and gestures portray as if he is in charge of the Indian students and is entitled to pity them.

Obviously, I do not cater to his opinion. Truly, I am disgusted about it. Brahmin, so what? What difference does it make in the university environment? When it comes to academics Vaskar is a poor performer. He always bothers others and seeks help, and copies one after another homework assignment from his classmates. He doesn't do well on tests and ends up getting poor grades. It's hard to put up with such a braggart.

Being a good tennis player is his only positive quality. In general, Americans like sports. He mentions tennis at every opportunity.

Many foreign students without assistantships work on-campus at minimum wage jobs, mostly in the libraries and the bookstore. Foreign students are allowed to work on-campus jobs up to twenty hours per week. But they are restricted from working off-campus. American students work off-campus for better pay. Vaskar doesn't work at all; neither does he get any financial help from the university. He claims his elder brother, an established professional in the U.S., supports him.

Our departmental secretary delivers paychecks the first day of every month. I am so happy on that day. Excited, I walk to the bank off-campus to deposit the check and withdraw cash. On my way back I stop at a special fast-food place and have a fish-fillet lunch with a glass of Coca-Cola. Tastes delicious! While occupying a window seat and staring out at the scenery I enjoy a relaxed lunch. The campus looks so very different from outside. Even the clock-tower that reminds us of time every hour, which sounds dreadful when we are running out of time—looks like a nice architecture from a distance.

There are students who live closer to the university. Not only is the rent higher, but also this area is more congested. Though my apartment is a twenty minute walk from the campus, the surroundings are much nicer. Trees, bushes and flowers decorate the yards. Parents push baby strollers in the walkways. It's relaxing to watch adults and kids throwing Frisbees and playing ball in this family environment. Though I live alone, there is a relaxed feeling.

Whereas, in the university area students are carrying book bags everywhere. They are stressed out, with tired and worried faces and dark rings under their eyes, due to financial and educational pressure. They look exhausted going home with brown grocery bags. They walk to the library, to the computer center and laboratory at all hours. Even weekends and holidays are no exception.

It gets worse during exam weeks. The main library stays open till one in the morning. Many students prefer studying at the library to avoid interruptions caused by their roommate's telephone calls, TV watching or listening to music. Fortunately, I don't have to deal with a roommate. I like to study at my apartment. Usually, I do not go to the university over the weekend unless there is a special assignment at the lab.

Sunset

I walk home from the university facing the west. This side of the town is hilly. Some days I notice the sunset behind the hills. The sun slides down from a circle to a semicircle to smaller arcs, and eventually disappears. The western sky still looks light golden-orange with the residual light. Exhausted from day's work and stressed out by the homework assignments to be done at night, enjoying the sunset is out of the question. Suddenly, I realize that staying in touch with my finer side has become a luxury I cannot afford.

A Cup of Tea

Looking at the ingredient label on the cake that I buy from the grocery, I find it contains so many good items like milk, butter, cream, eggs, etc. But it's way too sweet. I taste nothing but the sugar. What's the point of adding the good stuff? Less than half the sugar would have made it delicious. I guess Americans like too much sugar. It appeals to the common palate.

On the other hand, they drink hot coffee without cream and sugar. They call it black coffee, and relish it cup after cup. Doesn't it taste too bitter?

On the contrary, my cup of hot tea contains three teaspoonfuls of sugar and a quarter cup of milk, just to make it palatable.

I bring supplies to the department and make my own tea. Oh, no! I have run out of tea packets today. I must remember to bring them from home tomorrow. The on-campus fast-food place sells hot tea. It's displayed on their menu board.

As I order, the girl in the other side of the counter hands me a cup of hot water with a tea packet in it. She smiles, "Here you go."

Just a tea packet? Is that all? "I want milk and sugar in my tea, please."

She stares at me as if it's beyond her comprehension. After I repeat my request twice, she asks confused, "You mean cream and sugar?"

Though not sure, I nod. She extends a tiny packet of sugar and another tiny packet that states creamer. How am I going to make tea with so little sugar?

"I need two more packets of sugar, please."

She looks surprised, but gives me two more packets. Then asks sarcastically, "Anything else for your tea? Would you like lemon in it?"

Adding lemon to hot tea with milk! Is she crazy? It will ferment and spoil right away. I shake my head in disbelief. Obviously, she doesn't have a clue. She is about twenty, most likely a student working part-time.

It's good this isn't the lunch rush hour. During that time this place has a long wait with queues reaching almost to the door. They serve food like machines. The typical sounds of cash registers and placing and receiving orders make it very loud and noisy. It would have taken a lot longer to get my tea then.

I learn an introductory lesson: instead of milk I'm to say cream; and ask for three packets of sugar. Also, I have to make sure no lemon is added.

What a hassle to buy merely a cup of tea!

Preaching Religion on Campus

On my way to the computer center on a spring afternoon, while passing the small bridge next to the Student Center, I notice a middle-aged gentleman. He is holding a few copies of the Bible and trying to preach Christianity. He is saying a few words and distributing books to students. Most are walking past him without showing any interest.

Suddenly, a white male student gets into a big argument with him. It gets louder and louder. The vocabulary the student uses is so derogatory and full of slang. I am stunned! Can you address a gentleman in such an un-courteous manner, especially on campus? If nothing else, he is age-wise senior to the student. That alone gives the gentleman the right to be treated respectfully! What a shame!

Treating elders with respect is a basic teaching in Indian culture. Unable to stand witnessing such an obscene scenario, I leave immediately.

Keeping my Distance

One afternoon, Tom comes to my desk and says, "Your hair is gorgeous! When I was in high school, long hair became a fashion trend. Some girls in our school wore long hair. That's not new to me. But your hair is wavy, dense and long. It's beautiful."

In Bengali culture, when given a compliment, a shy and appreciative smile is the expected response. That's what I do.

He continues, "The other day you let your hair down. I kept watching you from behind. I've never seen anything like that before."

Sunil, an Indian student, overhears this from his desk and comments, "In India, Bengali women are well-known for their gorgeous hair. When I visited Calcutta, I used to stare at them."

As usual, I maintain my distance, and the conversation does not go any further.

Food Fight

On my way to the campus post office, I see something weird. A couple of students are laughing and playfully throwing food at each other.

A few more students, standing at a distance, are enjoying and encouraging while clapping hands: "Food fight! Food fight!"

So, is this called a food fight? There is even a designated term for this!

Someone throws a cake at another's face. Though he steps back in self-defense, still the cake lands on his face. It starts running down on his shirt. Oh My God!

He realizes what has happened and uses his hands to wipe his eyes. As soon as he gathers some cake, he tosses it back at his opponent. The saga continues.

Soon more students join them. Hamburgers, fries, and Coke get airborne as the fight continues.

The walkway turns messy. Who is going to clean up?

What a waste of food! Poor people could have consumed it. Are all these students really rich? Even if they are, does that matter? Although we have rich people back home, I have never seen nor heard of them tossing food at each other. In our family excess food was always given away to the maids. They were happy to take it home and share with their families.

I can't even stand to watch it. How can this be fun? What a weird sense of humor!

Vending Machine

A vending machine is like an invisible grocer. Make a selection, pay the price, and the food will be dispensed.

I am craving something sweet. Standing in front of the machine I decide to get a chocolate bar. Once I put in the coins the chocolate bar starts moving, but then gets stuck mid-way. Oh no! I don't have enough to buy another one. I press the coin return button a few times, but that doesn't help. There goes my money and candy. Frustrated, I stare at the vending machine.

A heavy voice asks, "Is there a problem?"

I turn around to find a uniformed campus security officer standing behind me.

Helplessly, I respond, "Yes, I mean, that chocolate bar got stuck."

He slaps the machine a few times like disciplining a disobedient child, without any result. He fetches the price from his purse and says, "Here is your money back."

"No, no," I resist. "That's your money. I don't want it."

"Don't worry about me. I'll get a refund from them." He reassures me and smiles. After some hesitation I accept the money and leave.

Softball Game

Gary Miller, the captain of our departmental softball team, approaches me. "I need a favor—a big one."

The introvert girl in me is truly surprised. "What is it?"

"We need you to join our softball team. Please."

I am stunned. I'm not sure whether I am hearing him right. "WHAT?"

He repeats, "Please join our softball team."

I heard him right, but I'm still not convinced. I know what football is. Calcutta is crazy about football, a male sport. It's called soccer here.

Very reluctantly I admit, "Um…I mean, I don't know what softball is."

Gary, though very surprised, gradually becomes fully convinced about my ignorance. He thinks for a while and then proposes with enthusiasm, "We won't ask you to play. Just wear our uniform and show up at the game."

I am perplexed. "What good is that? Make a fool out of myself?"

"All other departmental teams have both male and female students. Since you are the only female student in our class, please do us this favor."

I should really honor the request. But how is that possible? I have never been to a football field, not even to watch a game. As an adult I have never played any outdoor sports, never worn anything but full-length clothes. I am to wear a short team uniform in front of thousands of people in a softball game?

That's impossible. I can't even perceive doing it. How can I? I shake my head and reject him slowly, "Sorry, I can't do that."

Gary stares at me for a while. Truly disappointed, he leaves with a long face.

I feel guilty, but I am so helpless.

English as a Second Language

I enter the GSA (Graduate Students Association) lounge in the middle of ongoing laughter. Gary, standing close to the entrance, is almost falling apart laughing.

I ask him, "What's going on?"

Unable to speak, he points toward the bulletin board on the wall. There is a picture of a new car with a note in broken English. "Wayne fine, has baby son. Drives BMW that baby looks like."

Wayne graduated from here last year and accepted a job on the West Coast. His friend, a current student, just returned after visiting him. Obviously, the intent was to mean the baby looks like Wayne.

Every one continues laughing. I join them, too.

Later that day the student who wrote the note stops me in the hallway and complains with a heavy Asian accent, "We hear Indians learn English in elementary school. When did you start?"

"Well, my elementary education began in a well-known Catholic school. I started learning English in pre-K, even before I learned to read and write my mother language Bengali."

In a jealous and irritated hissing voice, he comments, "We start English in college. Because of that Indians do better than us here."

The department has a good number of foreign students from this particular country. Time after time I sense that they don't like me. Now I realize they don't like Indian students in general. All the time I hear them socializing only among students from their country, using their own language. It sounds like a second language in the department.

I would like to make a few points to them. If they restrict themselves from speaking English, if they are not interested in learning from their surroundings, how would they get acquainted to a new culture? How would they improve their English?

Before I get into the conversation, he walks away angrily.

Communication is definitely a key to success. But we, the Indians, are efficient professionals, too. Just knowing English does not do it all.

Just a Question

One afternoon while I am busy working in the Digital Circuit Design lab, a white American classmate approaches me.

He says, "I have a question for you. Since all the cars in India are imported from the U.S., how are they transported—via the Atlantic or the Pacific?"

It takes me a while to understand. "Our cars are mostly made in India."

In total disbelief he asks, "What are the cars made there?"

"The most commonly used car is an Ambassador. It is seen all over. There are many other brands and models."

He turns speechless. It's hard for him to accept it. He keeps shaking his head. "Really? Can India make cars?"

Though he doesn't appear to be fully convinced yet, he steps away.

Married Graduate Students

Many of my classmates are married men, as indicated by their wedding rings. Some of them even have kids. Barely in their early twenties, aren't they too young? I am used to seeing men complete their education, get a job and become established before committing to marriage.

In most of the cases the married graduate students' wives work to support the family and the husband's education. Some of the wives plan on going back to school later in life. They all have one thing in common: a dream of a husband getting a well-paid professional job following graduation, a nice house, nice cars, and a good standard of living. Some of them will have their dreams come true.

Others often end up with shattered dreams. Some marriages do not survive the hardship. By the time their husbands graduate and earn well, their marriage falls apart. Poor couples! What a sad ending!

There is a remarkable difference, though. According to my upbringing, we hardly see any divorce. It is almost considered as the end of life. That's not true here. Couples deal with the divorce and start fresh all over again.

Holi Celebrations

In March, as I open my parents' letter, a bright pink dot draws my attention. Instead of a formal date Mom wrote *Holi Purnima*, which means the full-moon on *Holi*, and placed the dot next to it.

Oh, I recognize! It's a dot of *Aabir*, the colored powder predominantly used in *Holi*, a religious and festive occasion.

Many temples as well as households perform special pujas for Radha-Krishna on this day.

Holi, the Hindu festival of colors, is celebrated across the country on the full-moon day in the Bengali month of Falgun in spring. Since the time marks the advent of spring, it is also called *Basanto-Utsab*, the spring festival.

In Calcutta, all schools, markets and businesses are closed on *Holi*. Except for emergency vehicles, transportation is not available until evening, after the wild celebration of playing with colors tapers off.

Neighborhood boys and some men occupy the empty streets, prepared with buckets full of colored water and *pitchkari*, the traditional sprayer, targeting their friends and passers-by. This is the common scene in many streets, back streets and alleys. People react by trying to block colored water being sprayed on their faces and heads but that does not stop it. After a while everyone looks alike: multi-colored from head to toe with pink, red, magenta, green and blue smeared on them. It's customary to wear old clothes that are discarded afterwards.

Doors and windows are kept locked in households to prevent incoming color. Inside the houses, *Holi* is celebrated in courtyards by adults, especially girls and women. It's more common to play with *Aabir*, rather than liquids.

In some temples devotees gather to watch decorations and celebrations in the evening with dancers and singers presenting traditional performances for this event.

Nababarsho Celebrations in Bengal

A letter from my parents conveying their *Nababarsho* blessings reminds me it was on April 16th this year. *Nababarsho*, the Bengali New Year, is celebrated on the first day of *Baisakh*, the first month of the Bengali calendar. My mind drifts away to Calcutta…

People of Bengal also celebrate *Chaitra Sankranti*, the eve of *Nababarsho*, to bid farewell to the past year. Some observe religious rituals such as taking a dip in the river Ganges, going to temples and offering pujas.

An open-air carnival takes place in the local all-dirt playground nearby. If it rains on the day or the day before, sliding down on mud is a common sight. Various rides and magic shows lure the neighborhood children. Though riding *nagar-dola*, the merry-go-round, is fine with me, I am not brave enough to take the up-down vertical rides. We are ecstatic to watch the magic-show performed in a makeshift tent, which has no guarantee of stability in case of a storm or a heavy downpour.

As small kids we cherish the mouth-watering snacks: sliced eggplants or onions deep-fried in a batter, *papads, jalebi,* etc. These are fried in huge iron woks. As we eat, oil drips down running from our palms all the way to our elbows and finally drops to the ground. The accompanying adult in charge, most commonly our J. uncle, Dad's younger brother, is indulgent enough to buy us some of these delicious items. Afterwards, he pulls out a handkerchief from his pocket and wipes our hands.

Inexpensive hand-made toys of clay, paper, wood or plastic are sold directly by the makers. Though these toys do not reflect high class or luxury, we still buy some as part of the festivity. There is a rural and ordinary touch to this fair, but the fun is extra-ordinary and worth waiting for the children.

Nababarsho celebrations are performed with joy, enthusiasm and hope. The rituals start in the morning. Families offer special pujas praying for well-being of the family for the year ahead. Showing respect to elders by offering *pranams* touching their feet, and best-wishes to siblings and cousins are customary. Afterwards, sweets are distributed by the elders. Our sweet-tooth Bengali society is not weight-conscious. Wearing new clothes, generous consumption of sweets, festive meals and seeing favorite relatives are the important attractions to us, the children.

"Shuvo Nababarsho," meaning Auspicious New Year, is the standard greeting exchanged among families, friends and the

entire society. It takes a few weeks to extend greetings to family and friends in person. Writing letters to the ones living out of town also continues over the following weeks. Vice-versa, we receive stacks of letters.

Cultural programs—with the neighborhood kids performing music, dance, songs, drama and recitations welcoming the New Year—are quite common in the evenings.

Haalkhata, the start of a new accounting book, is celebrated by businessmen and traders. They welcome their customers and offer them sweets and calendars. It's usually attended by the man of the house, whose name is listed in the accounting book.

Summer officially starts in *Baisakh.* Temperatures reach the high eighties and nineties, accompanied by high humidity. Homes and schools are equipped with ceiling fans for air circulation.

The heat index keeps rising, making life miserable. The hot and humid weather causes people to sweat heavily. Some get sick due to dehydration. In addition to drinking plenty of plain cool water from earthen vessels, other popular drinks include green coconut water, mango sherbet, lime and lemon water.

The people of greater Calcutta wait eagerly, as thirsty as swallows for rain, to get some relief from the scorching summer heat.

The storm *Kalbaishakhi,* named after *Baisakh,* is expected to make its usual appearance in this month. One afternoon, heavy dark clouds cover the sky, making it appear like nightfall in the middle of the day. The long-awaited *Kalbaisakhi* finally arrives—dust rises, sweeps away everything. Tall trees sway like pendulums, old buildings shake. Thunder, lightning, and a heavy downpour follow. *Kalbaishakhi* dances *Rudra Tandava,* the vigorous Indian dance of destruction—uprooting some old huge landmark trees, a handful of them remnants of British-ruled India.

The fallen trees as well as torn out electric and telephone lines cause major traffic interruptions. Since mass transportation is the way of life in the metropolis, thousands of people are stranded. The backlog ripples all the way to the suburbs.

What a relief from the scorching summer heat! Despite the major inconveniences, people are still happy to welcome the rain…

Gone are those days. I sigh as I look at my parents' *Shuvo Nababarsho* letter on my study table. It's early spring here. I squeeze some time and write a few letters to my extended family. It's time consuming to write the first one. Then it goes faster as I copy the content to others. Going through the address book and writing addresses on the blue air-mail letters also takes time.

Paid Chore

The final week of the spring quarter is approaching fast. It's hectic for most of us. Study, study and study some more. Even then it's not done.

James says, "I really need to do the groceries. I have run out of almost everything. Every day I think about going to the store, but I don't find time."

Gary follows, "It's more urgent for me to do the laundry. Dirty clothes have piled up high. A few grocery items will do for me."

James says, "I need to do laundry, too. But it's not urgent." He pauses, "Let's make a deal. When you do your laundry, do mine, too. I will go to the grocery store and pick up your food also."

Larry interjects, "I am not that busy. I will do the chores for both of you. How much will you pay?"

In the meantime I pick up a book from my desk to return it to the library. As I walk past them Larry asks me, "How much will you charge for doing their laundry?"

Annoyed, I reply, "I will not do it."

Gary jokes, "Not even for five-hundred dollars?"

"No way. Not for any amount of money," I respond, irritated.

Larry looks astonished as he comments, "For one hundred dollars, I will hand wash them one by one."

"I will not. I refuse to do it." I speak in a firm voice and walk out, really upset.

How dare they say this to me? Do they realize how insulted and offended I am? Who does someone else's laundry? The maids. In Calcutta, the maids did our laundry on a daily basis.

An educated person will do someone's laundry for money? What a shame!

If a close friend of mine desperately needs help, I will do it for free. Accepting money like a household attendant? No way!

Undergraduate Course Completion

The official letter from the department stating that my undergraduate requirements have been fulfilled brings me great relief.

Three microelectronics courses and three network analysis courses, a total of twenty-four undergraduate credit hours, have driven me to tears. I am so glad to be able to close that chapter and leave it behind me. In Calcutta, after completing something really challenging, a person is sometimes suggested jokingly to take a dip in the sacred river Ganges to wash off any residue and to rejuvenate. That's applicable to me at this point.

Undergraduate classes have a totally different environment. Students are a bit younger. They are talkative and kind of restless. Even during exams they chew gum and raise a storm with the sound of fast-pressed calculator keys to solve circuit equations. Sometimes they even make joking comments. An average class size is about thirty.

Undergraduate classrooms and laboratories are located on the eighth floor along with their faculty offices. The faculty consists of middle-aged and senior professors. They must have started teaching years ago.

Comparably, the graduate level faculty members are quite young. An average class size includes about fifteen students who act much more maturely. Graduate level courses suit me a lot better.

The university has thirty-six thousand undergraduate students and three thousand graduate students. Consequently, undergraduate classes are larger.

Summer Jobs

About two weeks later I enter the GSA (Graduate Students Association) lounge to check my mailbox. Students are talking about their experiences in summer jobs.

Gary says, "My dad works for the railroad. He helped me get a summer job there when I was in high school. It was really hard work. All day long, strenuous physical labor in scorching summer heat." He shakes his head. "That was a killer job. I wouldn't want to do it again."

Tom adds, "I worked for a construction company a few summers. Carrying heavy loads, demolishing walls, hauling the debris—it was back-breaking hard labor! Once in a while I was asked to paint. That was relatively easier. They paid well, though. I did it for the money."

"I worked in a movie theater concession stand selling tickets, popcorn and drinks," Ben mentions.

Gary comments quickly, "That must have been easy. You stayed indoors in air-conditioning. It was a luxury, I guess."

"Not much money, though," Ben continues, "But I read a lot in my spare time."

While holding a letter, I stand there surprised and listen to them. According to our Indian mentality, physical labor jobs are for the laborer class—the poor and the uneducated.

These engineering students, my classmates, worked as laborers? Why? It's beyond my comprehension!

Suddenly Gary turns toward me and asks, "What kind of work did you do? What's your experience?"

I never thought it would come to this. I try to clarify, "Are you asking me?"

"Yes."

After some hesitation, I respond, "Um…I mean, I never earned any money. I mean, I used to get a scholarship as a student, you may consider that—"

Gary says, "No, not that. What kind of work did you do to earn some pocket money?"

"My parents provided me with everything. I never earned any money."

The scenario reverses, the three of them look at me totally surprised, as if it's beyond their comprehension.

Tom shakes his head in disbelief.

Gary blurts out, "Your parents totally spoiled you."

Their reaction makes me feel so uncomfortable that I can't even make an attempt to provide any further explanation.

Why does it make a day and night difference to them if someone didn't earn money in student life? Why is it so unbelievable? Why is it so hard to accept?"

Perplexed at their reaction, I feel bad and stand silent, like an idiot.

Instantaneously, it becomes crystal-clear to me why they are so comfortable with paid chores.

It occurs to me afterward that I should have clarified the issue.

In our culture, in educated and well-to-do families, students are not expected to earn money. Getting a good job after completing education—is the first time they earn. I am not an exception. There are many others like me.

Co-op Program for Undergraduates

One day Gary mentions to me, "I did my undergraduate studies as a co-op."

I ask, "What's a co-op?"

He replies, "I was in school half the year and worked during the other half. I attended school during the fall and winter quarters, and worked in spring and summer."

"Is that possible, at all?"

"Why not? Some students do that."

In Calcutta we used to get a month-long summer vacation and another month off during religious celebrations around October. We were students year-round. That's the way the curriculum was set. How can someone be a student for just six months a year? That's absurd!

Confused, I ask, "Why would the university allow you? Why would an employer agree?"

Gary looks surprised by my question. He tries to explain, "It's called a co-op program. Both of them agree to make it work."

Without comprehending, I stare at him. "Why would a student want to do this? If you are a student only half of the year, it will take you so much longer to complete the degree. What good is that?"

He explains with a smile, "The student reaps the maximum benefit. Have some money, have some fun. It takes longer to graduate, but the money earned is a big help. Also, the work experience is valuable."

The concept is not yet clear to me. Anyway, I ask, "Where did you work?"

"The local power company has a co-op program. That's where. If I wanted to get a job after my bachelor's degree, they might have hired me. They know me and I am experienced in their line of work. Even if they could not hire me they would have recommended me for other jobs."

"You started graduate school, instead. How did the co-op program help you?"

Gary almost brags, "It really did. I applied to three graduate schools. In all applications I stated my work experience and used them as references. That carried a lot of weight."

"So," I say, "the co-op program is very realistic."

For a while I have been sensing the close connection between the university and industry. Professors mention it while teaching: "This major electronics company just came out with these new microcircuits. They are fast becoming popular for these particular characteristics. In circuit designs you may use them as…"

Professors tend to steer the students toward the ways industries are going. The students graduate well-aware of industry trends. They are highly marketable.

"Are there co-op programs for graduate students?"

"Not really," Gary continues, "The graduate school is an entirely different story. The classes are scheduled in such a sequence that students must stay in school during the fall, winter and spring quarters."

Summer

Unless it storms or rains it's a pleasure to walk to and from the university. There are people everywhere. Sometimes it's too hot. The sun is so strong even past five in the evening when I walk home. On long summer days, it's dusk till eight thirty. Then darkness comes and suddenly it's ten at night. A striking difference from Calcutta! The clock does not change in India. It's the same clock year-round. In Calcutta dusk arrives about 5:30 PM in winter. In summer it may stretch to 6:30 PM.

Swimming Pool

On Memorial Day weekend, the last weekend in May, the swimming pool owned by the apartment building opens. The tenants can barely wait. The pool area gets crowded fast with tenants wearing swimming costumes. At poolside they put on suntan lotion. After swimming for a while, they get up, soak in sun, and then get back in the water again. The same sequence is repeated time after time, hour after hour, irrespective of gender. People who arrive early get to occupy the lounge chairs. Some tenants bring their own light plastic chairs. The rest put towels on the concrete or the adjacent grassy area and lie down. Some read, some listen to music and sway to the tunes, some chat, some just lay quiet. Many sip iced drinks. All of them have the same objective—to get as much suntan as possible. As soon as a group leaves, within a blink of an eye another arrives. They must be watching for availability from their apartments. On weekends, this keeps going all day long from dawn to dusk.

This puts me in a tough situation.

I am taking three courses this summer. As it is, the summer quarter is the shortest, but the same texts and courses like the regular quarters are covered. Classes proceed with lightning speed. I can't even afford to look away from the books. One of the courses, an individual project-oriented lab, is driving the students crazy. Spending hour after hour in the lab, analyzing results and writing the report—pretty much takes all the day.

An irritated student vents in the lab bitterly, "They should have told us this was going to be a full-time load. Why work this hard just for three credit hours?"

I nod in agreement, but make no comment. This is a mandatory lab. I have to get a good grade. The other two courses are not easy either, but less time-consuming than this. I remind myself of a Hindi saying, "*Shir diya to rona kya?*" It means if you are sticking your head out to be chopped, why cry about it?

Under the circumstances studying intensively at home is my only way to succeed. The pool area, located right behind my bedroom, was locked during the winter and spring quarters, giving me the opportunity to study in peace and quiet. Since the pool has opened it's crowded and noisy all the time. No break until it closes after dusk at 9:00 PM. The weekends are festive for pool-goers, but pathetic for me.

Previously I could tilt the shutter in my bedroom and study in daylight on the weekends. Once in a while I could crack the window open for some fresh air. I would love to pull the shutters all the way up and flood the room with fresh air and daylight. But then the interior of the room can be seen from the second and third floor balconies. So I never do that.

It's so pleasant to study in natural light and fresh air. We had enough of that back home in Calcutta. Here I found a chance to do it, but that has to stop. It's fluorescent lighting and air-conditioning all the time in the university as well.

Now it's so noisy in my bedroom I can't even concentrate. Under the circumstances, I bring my books to the dining table in the living room. The table is too small to organize the books the way I like. It's not sturdy, and my writing and drawing often become illegible. What else can I do? As long as summer fun continues I will have to put up with it.

That's not all. There is more to it that makes me uncomfortable. Except in a few foreign movies, I have never seen people this scantily clothed in real life. Out in the public like this! We can't even think of dressing like that, even in the privacy of our own homes. This is the other end of the world, and a totally different culture. I accept that. Instead of being judgmental, I choose to stay away from the pool.

While traveling through some villages in India or watching from a train window, I have seen villagers who use rivers or ponds for daily bath and laundry. They don't have the luxury of running water at home. Even then they, especially the women, take a dip wearing saris. While walking home in a wet sari covered from head to toe, each woman carries a container full of water for household use. Typically, it's a clay container shaped like a round vase. A woman places the full container on her waist and circles a hand around it, as she walks home slowly. There is a sweet and distinct rhythm to this walk, reflected in poems.

Looks

The middle-aged, obese, white American lady, a receptionist at the Student Center, has been absent from work for over a week. She was lying under a tanning lamp for a short-period exposure, but she fell asleep. She is being treated now for burn injuries.

Are people that crazy about getting tanned? That's outrageous!

What a strange choice! In India, we are born tan. If someone is light tan or fair skinned, it's a symbol of beauty. In Calcutta there are women who avoid the bright sunlight like the plague, fearing a tan. Some of them even go to the extent of regular skin conditioning with homemade recipes to protect them from being tanned.

What's the point? Is it because some think being an exception to the general mass earns them the distinct status of being beautiful?

There is also a striking difference in the definition of pretty in India versus the U.S.

A pretty face according to my standards isn't considered pretty here at all. Often in GSA lounge while watching TV or just by talking the students say, "Oh, so and so, is really pretty." "Look at the high cheek bones; she is really beautiful."

The women are far from pretty. Actually they are not even good-looking. How can someone with a big forehead be considered pretty? Similarly, high cheek bones are definitely unattractive; she should eat more to cover them up.

Before final week, I keep thinking about the month's break after the finals, before the fall quarter starts. A whole month? Wow! What will I do during all that time? Just relax, of course. No classes, no homework and projects, no tests, no waking up every morning and rushing. What a pleasure! Just the thought of it makes me happy.

However, I will go to the research lab to work on my thesis. This will keep me occupied. The more I get done, the earlier I will complete it and the better off I will be.

At the end of the final week I come home. In two courses I have done well. But I have some doubts about Dr. Norton's Large Scale Integrated Circuit Design course. He is notorious for twisting questions. Never a single question or a problem is straightforward. It takes longer to decode them than to solve. What a tricky mentality! Hopefully, I did all-right. He is the youngest professor in the department. Actually, he got his Ph.D. here about five years ago and started teaching right away. It hasn't been long enough to forget his student life. Shouldn't he be expected to be more sympathetic to us? But that's far from the reality.

He assigns homework. His Teaching Assistant checks it, but it's not graded. Three tests, each counts as 20%. The remaining

40% from the final exam makes the total grade. I will be happy to score a B, the minimum grade required to pass the course.

Ben Jones' Story

Talk about a brilliant student. I've never seen anyone like Ben. He is significantly overweight, an all-American white student, and the very first one in his family ever to attend a college. His father is a carpenter, and his mother, a store clerk. Neither of them went beyond high school. Though Ben is an exceptionally talented student he has such a down-to-earth personality. He graduated from MIT with highest honors and continued with the Master's program there. Due to family circumstances he moved back with his parents and transferred here. He masters the concepts with lightning speed. Dr. Norton's Digital Design class is a tough one. Each and every test is a killer.

Even Ben comments, "You permanently lose a few brain cells on each of his tests."

Ben finishes the two-hour-long final exam in forty minutes, submits his paper and leaves. The rest of us in the class struggle, pull hair, design circuits, and solve problems the entire two hours and hope merely to pass the course. Needless to mention, Ben scores the highest!

There are quite a few high-achieving students in the department. In general, Indians rank high. But nobody comes close to Ben! Hats off to him!

Derek's Thesis Defense

As I enter the large classroom five minutes before Derek's scheduled thesis defense, I am stunned! Not a single chair is unoccupied. Many of the students are standing by the back wall. Anand gestures at me to stand next to him, and I follow.

What's going on? This classroom is used frequently for theses and dissertation defenses, but I have never seen it crowded like this. Usually, only departmental graduate students and faculties attend. Some students and faculties also come from other departments, depending on their interest in the subject. That is more common for Ph.D. dissertations than M.S. theses.

Most of the people occupying the chairs are unknown to me. They don't look like students, either. It's a combination of those of all ages. Elderly and middle-aged are outnumbering the average students.

Anyway, I pay attention to the presentation, though stay annoyed because of standing. This is absurd!

I whisper to Anand, "Who are these people?"

He whispers back, "Derek's relatives."

That's really weird. I stay surprised, but remain quiet.

Toward the end of the presentation, during the question-answer session, the questions become more and more difficult which is normal.

Derek's family looks so anxious and tense, as if, they would go to any extent to help him answer, if they could. Probably, they are anxious that he may not get his degree if he even misses a single question.

As soon as the defense is over, I ask Anand, "Why are they here? What are they doing?"

"Derek is the very first one in his family to graduate from college. You may imagine, defending a Master's thesis is a dream-world event for them. So his friends and family came. Some of them even drove hundreds of miles to get here."

After a while Derek's advisor tells him that his thesis has been accepted.

Derek has earned a Master's degree in electrical engineering. His relatives hug him and congratulate him. This is a dream come true for them. Derek is their pride and joy!

Deep down I am little bit uncomfortable. Derek is the first one to get a college degree? Without being aware of it I was thinking when did that happen in my family? It's hard to figure out. Grandfather is an attorney, great grandfather was a famous physician. So many uncles and aunts have master's degrees, so many are doctors and engineers. Every one has at least a bachelor's degree. Finally, I conclude that I don't have a clue about when the first college degree was earned. Higher education has been the way of life in our family for generations.

Fall Quarter

It's a great relief to have the required coursework completed for M.S. Now I will focus on research with all my effort.

Two weeks before the fall quarter starts Dr. H. gives me great news. "I have decided to fund you from my research grant. You will no longer be required to perform TA responsibilities. As an RA, I expect you to put 100 percent effort in research."

Excited, I say, "Thank you."

Dr. H. brings in substantial grant money from renowned scientific and industrial research organizations. Consequently, he has the luxury of choosing the best students for his group. Most of them are RAs, research assistants.

The fallen asleep summer campus suddenly wakes up as if touched by a magic wand. New students, mostly undergraduates, are somewhat lost. They glance at the campus map often to get directions.

A skinny girl, a teenager, approaches me in a helpless manner and asks, "Today is my first day here. I am lost. Do you know the campus?"

"Yes."

She shows me her class schedule. "I don't know how to get to my class."

Glancing at her schedule, I see room 212, English building. "That's on the other side of the campus. Follow this road all the way."

Nervously, she says, "I was on that side. Someone told me to come this way. Are you sure?"

"Yes," I nod as I point out the location on the map.

"I arrived on campus about an hour ago. People have been directing me all different ways. They must be joking. Only ten minutes are left before the class begins."

Confusing and misleading a new student does not seem funny to me at all. What a strange sense of humor some of the older students have!

I reassure her, "If you hurry up, you will make it."

"Could you take me there, please?" She appeals.

"OK, I will take you there."

She sounds as if she is on the verge of a breakdown when she says, "I really need to use a restroom."

I direct her to one close by. Then we walk fast, and she barely makes it on time.

She says, "Thank you so much. I really appreciate it." The relief and gratitude on her face speak clearly.

Historic Milestone

The big news circulates through out the university. A couple of people from the People's Republic of China are about to join the university! Since no one has ever seen anyone from China, curiosity and enthusiasm become overwhelming.

"Who are they?" "Which department?" "Undergraduate or graduate program? M.S. or Ph.D.?" Where can we find them?" "How can we meet them?"

Finally, the information is released. The Chinese education system is very different than America's. Two men are coming to join the Chemistry Department as post-doctoral fellows.

On their first day over-enthusiastic students and staff crowd to catch a glimpse of them to be able to claim, "I have seen someone from the People's Republic of China."

Campus security stays alert to keep the situation under control.

Over the next few days students wait in the hallways or stand in front of the elevators in the Chemistry Department, treating the two Chinese fellows as celebrities. After the first week or so, the enthusiasm tapers off gradually.

On my way to the computer center to pick up the printed output of an assignment for my programming class, I run into them. Between 5'8" and 5'10" tall, pale-white complexion, neatly combed black hair and a serious disposition. They almost dress and act like twins.

Keeping their distance from others, they like to stay in their lab most of the time. They are hardly ever seen in common places such as the Student Center or the food court.

We hear they speak heavily accented English. It takes a lot of time and patience to follow them. Though the student circle is overly curious, not much information gets circulated.

Columbus Day

In October Gary asks me, "Do you know it's Columbus Day today?"

"Sure, it's after Christopher Columbus."

With James at his side, Gary continues with a serious face, "You may know already, Christopher Columbus was named after Columbus, Ohio."

I burst into laughter and fall apart laughing. Finally, I pull myself together to tell him, "America became independent in 1776, about two-hundred years ago. Christopher Columbus came here five hundred years ago. That was centuries before Columbus, Ohio was formed." I continue laughing, just can't stop.

James chuckles, "She didn't fall for it."

Gary looks so embarrassed.

Classmates

In Calcutta, I had a few non-Bengali classmates. Gita was from South India, Rajesh from Maharashtra. But they were born and brought up in Calcutta, fluent in Bengali, and they dressed like us. Except for their last names, there was hardly any indication that they were not Bengalis.

I am pleasantly surprised to think I am privileged now to have classmates from so many different nations.

Frederick Petersen: I like Fred. He is polite and reserved. Kathy, his girlfriend, brings him lunch some days and they eat in our graduate students' office.

Fred mentions to me, "All my grandparents are immigrants from Germany. I grew up listening to their stories. Leaving home and going abroad is tough. I somewhat understand your situation."

I listen to him eagerly. A story of immigrants!

He continues, "We are a close-knit family. Three generations stay in close touch. The elderly become the responsibility of the grandchildren. If my grandparents need anything we are the first ones they contact. In our family, lifestyle and core values remain very much like Germany."

Dominique Dermy: A short and skinny French student, Dominique started this fall. Ben comes to my desk and asks me, "Dominique was here, wasn't he?"

"He was discussing an assignment with me a minute ago. Why?"

Laughing, Ben says casually, "The room smells of French after-shave and colognes. If he steps into a room in the morning, you smell it all day."

Really, the room is full of Dominique's fragrance. I start laughing, too.

"You Can't be Too skinny. You Can't be Too Rich."

The graduate students' study area for our research group is spacious. We meet for biweekly group meetings at a table large enough to accommodate 10 to12 students. A white board across from the table enables us to illustrate our issues. Three large, almost ceiling-high bookshelves located next to each other offer some privacy to the four desks on the other side of the bookshelves. One side of the room also has some lab instruments that we use from time to time.

While studying at my desk, I overhear an ongoing conversation from Gary, James and Ben.

Ben says, "The saying is, 'You can't be too skinny. You can't be too rich.'"

Both sayings are new to me; kind of weird.

Others agree right away. "That's right."

I leave my desk and join the conversation.

Ben says, "I would say, you can be too rich."

Gary asks, "Why?"

"Well," Ben says with confidence, "after accumulating a certain amount of wealth, the money controls you. You do not control the money any longer."

"How would you explain that?" James inquires.

"When you have too much money, you have security guards with you. The media follows you around."

Curious, I ask, "Really?"

"You lose a private normal life just because of your money."

Based on my upbringing, I have never put too much emphasis on money. My priorities are different. Since I came to America I have sensed that everybody lusts after money.

Ben's point of view astonishes me. He continues, "I have calculated, if I can save about $250 thousand dollars, I will be able to quit working and enjoy life."

I look at Ben with total disbelief. This is the first time I hear an American say he does not want endless money.

Larry joins our discussion. He reveals his plans. "I will become a millionaire by forty and retire."

I have never heard such a weird thing. Retirement is for elderly people. In India, retirement age ranges from 55 to 60, depending on the profession. I don't know the retirement age here. But he plans to retire at forty! The whole thing is confusing.

I ask, "Is it even possible to become a millionaire by forty, Larry?"

He sounds confident. "Sure. I am twenty-three now. Once I get my M.S. in engineering I will start a job. After a few years I will start my own business and invest in the stock market. The way things are going now, I will reach my goal."

My eyes are popping out. "What will you do after you retire?"

"I love to travel. I love beaches. I will travel and enjoy my life."

I become quiet. What is he planning? Is that even realistic? It's all beyond my imagination.

I guess not all Americans go after money. Some of them want to earn it, and then enjoy other things in life.

"It's very true that 'You can't be too skinny,'" James stresses. Everyone else agrees.

I will oppose that saying all the way. I restrain myself even from uttering a single word. I feel a lump in my throat and return to my desk sadly.

In the streets of Calcutta so many poor people beg for food. Being willfully skinny is a luxury to many of them. It doesn't even come close. Starvation is so vivid. Every time there is a flood or famine, residents flee the affected areas and come to the city in search of food. The number of beggars and street-dwellers multiplies many-fold. Assistance from the government agencies, charitable organizations and the local residents, ends up being nominal compared to the need.

Ribcages barely covered with a layer of skin, kids with pencil-thin arms and legs, people barely clinging to life. Mothers holding skeleton-like babies in their arms, still full of motherly love and optimism…

How would the Americans—who have plenty to eat, and are always worried about gaining weight—imagine that?

Winter Holidays

It's the beginning of December. Occupying my favorite window-side desk at the Engineering library, I am about to study a research article in the Semiconductor Device Electronics Journal.

This needs my undivided attention and effort. I have about an hour-and-a-half that I must utilize.

Two men, most likely undergraduate students, are whispering about their plans to go home for the Christmas holidays.

I have a loving and caring family and friends awaiting me. I want to visit them desperately, but the outrageous plane fares make it impossible. Who knows when it will materialize? I sigh.

I stare outside through the tilted blinds. Large windows allow plenty of daylight. The library can function throughout the day without any electric light. The Engineering building was built in the late nineteenth century. Small red bricks are visible on outside walls.

It's a cold, but sunny and clear afternoon. Calcutta sky is also sunny and clear in winter; it hardly ever rains. My mind travels to Calcutta...

Winter Vacation in Calcutta

Annual exams are completed by early December. The next school year starts in January. The intermediate three to four weeks are precious to us, since this is the only time in a year we enjoy the luxury of total freedom from school work. No school, no homework, is attractive and relaxing enough. Some years we go out of town during the Winter vacation.

A trip to Suri

Though we visit many places in India, one of our favorite trips is to visit our B. uncle, Mom's eldest brother. He lives in Suri, Birbhum, about 120 miles away. Three of us siblings and Mom get there after a couple of hours of train ride. Our maternal cousins as well as the rural atmosphere make the trip attractive to us.

Our city home has a big concrete courtyard, and all the flowers and plants in our verandah and terrace are in clay pots. Growing up in a city amidst concrete and iron structures, walking barefoot on earth is a rare opportunity. Birbhum is known as the land of the red soil. Our long-awaited dream of walking barefoot on red clay comes true. We check the bottoms of our feet quite often to assure they have turned red.

B. uncle's house, a brick ranch, sits on a side of his property, which is enclosed by a brick fence. A huge wood-apple tree on the side is often used as a landmark. Neighbors provide directions as: "Go past the house with the wood-apple tree..."

The kitchen looks strange since it has two built-in clay ovens that use coal or wood as a fuel. An adjacent dining area leads to an all-dirt courtyard. Two brown dogs, devoid of any royal pedigree, take naps in the courtyard and follow us around the neighborhood. Located in the center of the courtyard is a well encircled by a three-foot high concrete siding. I am scared to go near it. Who knows how deep the well is and what will happen if a child accidentally falls in? Water is fetched with an iron bucket attached to a sturdy rope of coconut fiber. A servant fills up the reservoir in the bathroom. Reflection of golden morning sunlight from the trees makes them look pretty. The morning air smells so fresh.

Playing with our cousins and touring the neighborhood visiting their friends is relaxing. Neighbors drop in all the time and chat for hours. No one is ever in a hurry. Many girls get married before completing high school. Most of them start having kids and never graduate. This is strange! Even as children, we know we will be well-educated, and we aren't willing to trade places with them.

The big backyard with various plants and trees has a natural wood look rather than an organized one. Large trees such as jackfruit, guava, mango and palm are there. In summer mango trees get covered with mangoes and the house smells of ripe fruits. The sweet fragrance of jackfruit extends to the neighborhood and attracts humans as well as animals, especially foxes.

The structure of the house, the openness and slow speed lifestyle, are charming to us. Our cousins, who live there, are surprised to hear that.

B. uncle's house has electricity in the building. It lights the courtyard all the way to the well. But beyond that, it's pitch dark at night.

Twilight passes and the evening turns to dusk, as evident by intermittently glowing light bugs. Then it becomes really dark. With monotonously chirping crickets in the background, big trees stand in the dark, branches and leaves swaying in a breeze. On some nights the wooded area is partially visible under a little moonlight. The entire surrounding makes it a heart-throbbing, thrilling place. All the ghost stories take place in these kinds of surroundings, I am sure. I am too scared to look at the backyard, let alone go there.

One day my cousins mention that foxes howling far away can be heard sometimes at nights. After all lights have been switched off and everyone has fallen asleep, an unknown noise wakes me up in the middle of the night. It's coming from a distance, stops for a little while and then starts back again, almost periodic. This must be foxes howling. Trembling in fear, I cover my head with the blanket and block my ears with my hands. With my eyes shut tight, determined not to witness anything scary, I wish to go back home instantly. Eventually I fall asleep. Since some of my cousins are younger than me, I have to retain my seniority. Too embarrassed to mention this the following morning I pretend to act normal. Though deep down, I am ready to return home before nightfall. As the day goes by, I get busy playing, talking, and stay distracted. But somehow, I remember it again as soon as I go to bed at night.

Village Temple Visit

B. uncle's wife, who we call Mamima, mentions to Mom one day, "There is a beautiful deity of Gopal in a temple, I have heard. I would like to visit the temple some day."

Mom says, "Sure, we will join you."

"It's not that easy. The temple is in a remote village," Mamima says. "You city folks may not like the transportation."

Curiously, Mom asks, "How to get there?"

Mamima replies, "A bullock cart is the only way to get to a place that remote."

Mom looks doubtful. Before she gets a chance to say anything, we get excited, "A bullock cart. What fun! We want to ride one for the first time. Please, please, Ma."

Due to our repeated requests and endless whining, Mom agrees most reluctantly.

We keep bubbling with enthusiasm, asking impatiently "When? Why not today?"

Finally, the day arrives. After lunch in the afternoon, a wooden cart with two large wooden wheels, pulled by a pair of bullocks, arrives. One of them is white, and the other one has black patches on white, and each has a bell tied to the neck. Both of them have diagonal horns with pointed ends. I don't want to stand in front of them, let alone get them upset. The driver, a man in his thirties, is wearing a *dhoti*, a traditional men's garment wrapped around the waist and the legs and knotted at the waist. Using his *gamchha*, a thin cotton towel, on his shoulder he wipes his hands and face. He holds a stick to guide the bullocks.

My maternal grandmother, a longtime widow, is short, skinny and really pretty. As a widow, she is a vegetarian, always clad in white saris, and never wears any jewelry. She reflects a pure and sacred look. Very quiet and busy either with her religious rituals or household chores—it's hard to detect her presence.

To avoid the ride, she doesn't accompany us. Bubbling with enthusiasm we, three siblings and two cousins, all under ten years of age, join Mom and Mamima. Sitting within an open front and back enclosure, we stare out at the countryside as we ride.

When the paved roads end, and the cart takes a dirt road, localities become less populated. Farmlands with busy farmers, farm houses, woods, small grocery stores with hay roofs and barren lands are visible. Once in a while passers by, a few bikers, stray dogs, and bullock carts go by. There is not much to see or do; it's boring. After a while we start picking on one another.

After about three hours that seems like days, the cart stops in front of a small, isolated structure adjacent to a wood. We jump down to the dirt road, glad to be able to stand up and move around. The driver helps Mom and Mamima get down safely.

He points to the brick structure and says, "This is the temple."

How disappointing! In Calcutta, temples are well-maintained. Hundreds of devotees visit daily. This is an almost dilapidated structure. It may have been white at one time, now there are scattered grayish-black patches everywhere. Watermarks left by years of rain are prominent. Trees are growing through the cracks in the walls.

A couple of neighborhood kids come running to us. Though they speak Bengali, their dialect is quite difficult to follow. Only Mamima can communicate to them. She asks them about the temple. The oldest boy, about twelve, runs to a nearby mud hut and returns with a skinny, middle-aged man.

As Mamima talks to him, though we don't follow every word, we get the gist of it. He is the priest of the temple. This used to be a well-to-do village. The temple was founded by the affluent Datta family. He remembers festive religious celebrations two generations ago, when his grandfather was the priest. About thirty years ago, during his dad's priesthood the owners moved to the city of Bardhaman. In the beginning they visited frequently and the temple was well maintained. Now-a-days, they mail him a monthly amount that barely covers the daily worship.

Electricity has not reached this far. In the early evening light, he leads us to the temple with a *pradeep*, an oil-lit clay lamp. As he unlocks the door to the half-lit main room we see the clay deity of Gopal, the childhood Lord Krishna.

Mom is the first to comment, "He is beautiful indeed, so expressive. Look at the eyes and the smile; steals my heart."

Mamima agrees. "That's true, he looks so lively."

His friendly attractive smile appeals to me. Mom leaves a one-rupee coin in the temple as an offering. The priest looks happy. He gives each of us a yellow *batasa*, a cheap sweet made from molasses, as a blessing.

We get back to the cart. Mom says sadly, "What a beautiful deity—left uncared for." She sighs. We, the children, feel bad too.

"Don't be too sad. There are many village temples like this," Mamima mentions.

Before dusk sets in, birds return to their nests drawing dark lines across the sky. We hear birds in the nearby woods chirping in their nests. The farmers have gone home for the day leaving their empty farmlands behind.

Evening turns into twilight and eventually deepens and blends into darkness. The soft light from a lantern, swaying below the cart, lights up only a little part of the red dirt road. Once in a while a few dark mud huts become visible.

I move away from the open front of the cart and squeeze next to Mom. My younger brother and one of my cousins have fallen asleep already. Listening to the monotonously chirping crickets, the rhythmic cow-bells, and the periodic squeaking noise of the wooden cart, I doze off.

My cousin pushes me, "Wake up, we are home."

Bakreshwar Temple Visit

One morning we accompany our Mom, Mamima and grandmother on a bus trip to the famous Lord Shiva temple at Bakreshwar.

After they perform the puja and we eat breakfast at a local dessert shop, we walk around the ten hot springs near the temple. I am stunned to see hot springs for the first time in my life! Steam coming out of water without any visible fire! The water temperature is hot in some of them, but one of them is very hot. Looking at the steam I am almost convinced someone is boiling the water underneath the earth. Many believe there are medicinal values in the minerals mixed in the water.

Viswa Bharati University

"We want to see the Nobel Prize." At our repeated request, a trip is planned to the Viswa Bharati University at Shantiniketan.

In 1862 Maharshi Debendranath Tagore, father of famous poet and Nobel laureate Rabindranath Tagore, established Santiniketan, which means The Abode of Peace. He was the first non-European to win the Nobel Prize in literature, in 1913 for *Gitanjali*, a small collection of poems and songs he wrote in Bengali and translated to English.

Jana Gana Mana, the national anthem of India, was also written by him.

We take a train from Suri and get off at the Bolpur station. Our eldest cousin, in her early twenties, is in charge of us, the two sisters.

We can't wait to see the Nobel Prize. We have heard and read so much about it that we are bubbling with excitement. On campus a passer by looks at his watch and tells us, "The building will close in a few minutes. Please hurry."

I get annoyed at our cousin. We could have taken an earlier train. At Bolpur station she wasted at least ten minutes bargaining about the fare with the *rickshaw-walla*, the driver of the *rickshaw*, a two-wheeled passenger vehicle drawn manually.

As we reach the appropriate building, a gentleman steps out and says, "I am about to close the museum now, as scheduled. Please come back another day."

Regretfully, our cousin says, "We don't know when we will be able to come again from Calcutta. What a miss!" She stares at him helplessly.

He hesitates. Then surprising us he says, "Ok, I'll wait a few minutes. Please hurry up."

We run to the spot. Overwhelmed with joy and pride we look at the gold medal and the diploma! So, this is the Nobel Prize!

But we barely get a chance to take a good look at it because our cousin tells us, "Hurry up. We must go now."

Disappointed, we walk around campus. Going past a shaded area my sister asks, "Is this an open-air classroom?"

We have heard about them before. Shaded by a large tree, there is a big circular all-dirt space within a marked boundary. "This can't be a classroom," I reply.

A man walking past us stops and interjects, "Yes, it is."

I am not yet convinced. "How can it be?"

"Students take off their shoes and sit cross-legged on the ground. They hold their books on their laps." He points at a concrete seat about two-feet high: "That's where the teacher sits."

Branches and leaves sway in gentle breeze. Sunlight peaks through the leaves creating moving shadow patterns on the ground. I become jealous and say. "This would be fun."

He nods and leaves smiling. We notice quite a few classrooms similar to this one. The open-air classroom stays vivid in my mind for a long time.

Calcutta in Winter

The winter in Calcutta is mild, and wearing a light sweater or wrapping a shawl is customary. During the winter break, after lunch we relax and read magazines on the balcony or terrace. Warm touch of the afternoon sun, while dwelling in the world of the story and savoring sweet and juicy oranges—is an activity we cherish. Oranges are available in winter only. After almost a year-long wait they arrive from the mountain areas of Darjeeling and its surroundings in North Bengal, where they are grown.

Calcutta Zoo

Visiting the Calcutta Zoo at Alipore in December is our annual attraction. The zoo displays a diversified species of animals: one-horned rhinoceroses, hippopotamuses, lions, Royal Bengal tigers, cheetahs, jaguars, elephants, zebras, camels, giraffes and monkeys. One of our visits was rewarded by seeing the white tiger, which was making headlines in the newspapers at that time.

If there are cubs, we stay glued to their cage.

Sometimes we go on an elephant ride. The mahout, the elephant trainer, rides with us. He talks to the elephant in a code language and guides him effortlessly. Though a short ride on a planned route within the zoo, it makes us feel triumphant looking around from an elevated height. Most of the riders are families with children. Some kids are unwilling to get down when the tour is complete.

Playful monkeys and chimpanzees have always been kids' favorites. Offering them bananas, as they come close on the other side of the fence, and making faces at them are common for children.

It's hard to leave a spot and get to another one.

Among all these we break for a delicious home-made lunch: deep-fried bread, vegetable curry and egg curry followed by a dessert.

The zoo also offers a large collection of birds: various species of parrots and pheasants; ducks and peacocks; all the way to large flightless birds such as emus and ostriches.

Chirping birds in their habitats, owls sleeping during daytime, colorful peacocks walking—all are must-sees. Every year we hope to witness dancing peacocks with spread-out tails displaying the intricate detail of their feathers. Usually, peacocks are known to dance with the sound of thunder before an upcoming rain, but this hardly ever happens in winter.

Migratory birds of various species are also a primary attraction. After flying hundreds of miles they arrive at the zoo's wetland to spend the winter.

Next to the zoo is the National Library. Even as small children we know it's the place for scholars and students of higher studies. On our way out, we stare at it.

The trip never ends with coming home in the evening. We dwell on it week-long…

The loud sixteen bells from the university clock tower indicating the arrival of the next hour startle me. Then they pause for a few seconds, change tune and ring the exact count of the hour. I better concentrate on my studies. Time is running out.

While turning pages of the journal I remember a conversation and smile. Once, to explain the location of my hometown to an American classmate, I asked him, "Have you ever heard of the Bengal tiger?"

"Oh yes," was his prompt response.

"We are from the same state: Bengal."

3. Newcomer, 1982

The beginning of 1982 marks two years living in this apartment. I receive a letter from the electric company stating, "Congratulations on setting a record of paying your bills regularly." I am so surprised. Don't others pay their utility bills on time? Is not to pay on time allowed?

Alice's Story

Alice, a female student from Cyprus, joined our department as a graduate student last fall. Alice spends not only her days, but almost all of her time at the department, sometimes studying, sometimes grading undergraduate tests and homework assignments as her assigned responsibility as a Teaching Assistant.

Valantis, her husband, is a graduate student in Political Science. I feel sorry for him. Day in and day out he carries the sole responsibility for Eda, their two-year-old daughter. Alice dominates their marriage. She gets paid more for her assistantship than him.

Valantis picks up Eda from the baby sitter, goes home to an efficiency apartment on campus and takes care of her. Bathing, feeding, playing with her, and telling bed-time stories—child care is a part of his daily life. He has exams, projects, and homework assignments, too. But he does most of his work at home while minding Eda. Under the circumstances he doesn't have a choice. Otherwise, Eda would spend many more hours with the babysitter and consequently, the babysitting bill would be higher.

He assumed this responsibility when they arrived here from Cyprus to attend graduate school, hoping for a brighter future. No wonder Eda has turned out to be a daddy's girl. I often feel sorry for her. The curly haired, little girl with the doll face never gets a chance to spend time with her mommy. What a tragic childhood!

Alice tells me her father is a tailor in Cyprus. He owns his own tailoring shop and earns an upper middle class living. It wasn't like that always. She remembers how her family struggled when she was a child. As more and more tourists started buying his needle-work as souvenirs, his business bloomed and he hired two more tailors as assistants.

Alice's parents are traditionalists. They stick to the values they were brought up with. They were opposed to Alice going abroad. They have four daughters, no son. Alice is the youngest.

According to their customs, they saved every penny for their daughters' weddings. For the eldest daughter they bought a small house as a dowry. For the other three daughters, money being limited, they built a three-story house with an apartment on each floor. The objective was that each daughter would get her own apartment as a dowry in marriage.

In the meantime the neighborhood of their eldest daughter's home was extensively developed and her house became an expensive property. Now the parents regret not being able to give the other three girls as much. To them, it's depriving their children. They feel so guilty!

My God! This is a part of Cypriot culture! It outweighs the Indian dowry system. How little we know about other cultures.

Alice says, "Every month my parents send us money. Just the other day they sent us two hundred dollars. Their accompanying letter stated to buy Eda clothes or toys on behalf of them."

"That's great! What did you buy her?"

"Are you crazy? We spent the money on groceries. It's the same story all the time." She sighs and then says, "My parents still live in a small home where they always did. I have insisted they move to the apartment they gave me. It's vacant.

"'What?' They asked. 'You think we are going to use something we gave you? It's yours. You may do whatever you want,' was their response."

"Do your parents-in-law send you money, too?"

"Never. Why would they? After all, they are the boy's parents." She runs her fingers through her long curly hair and chuckles. "They expect a financial contribution from us as soon as Valantis gets a job."

Annoyed by her smoking habit, I can't help but say, "Alice, you smoke too many cigarettes. Women shouldn't be smoking at all."

Like a whiplash she answers, "Says who? My mother and mother-in-law smoke; so do my sisters and sister-in-law. My grandmother smoked all her life and nothing happened."

Who am I trying to convince? How defensive and protective she is! She is determined to continue smoking.

Eda is dropped off at the babysitter's dormitory apartment in the morning, and picked up at the end of the workday. Usually, Alice goes home for dinner and then she returns straight back to the lab. Most babysitters charge a dollar per hour, some even less. Many of them are wives of foreign graduate students. They are not allowed to work legally. They babysit cheap and behind the scene.

All payments are required in cash, thus avoiding a paper trail. It's a big risk, though. Any day they may get into legal trouble, which will affect their husbands, too. Most of the babysitters barely speak broken English.

Some of them have two or three kids of their own. On top of that, they babysit as many kids as they can get. The quality of care provided is as much as a mother can offer handling that many pre-school children. The television runs non-stop, irrespective of the quality of the programs. The kids keep watching, whether they understand or not.

The environment is below standard. Hygiene is not kept up well. Coughs and colds, ear and stomach infections spread fast. But because of the cheap rate the student parents put up with these problems without complaint.

Riverside

At lunch I run into Uma at the university food court.

She asks, "I am thinking about going to the Farmers' Market. Would you like to go?"

"What's a Farmers' Market?"

She explains, "A couple of my classmates went shopping there. A variety of farm fresh fruits and vegetables are available; lot cheaper than the grocery stores."

I ask, "Where is it?"

"It's at the end of the town, next to the river," she replies.

"How can we get there?"

"Bus service is available. The commute will be time consuming, though."

I grew up by a river. It has been a long time since I have been to a river, and I really miss it. This is my golden opportunity. "Could we to go to the river, also?"

She assures me, "Sure, we can walk to the river."

Uma sits on a bench looking at the Riverside children's park. It's late-afternoon on a Saturday. Blooming flowers and trimmed bushes make for a picturesque setting. Most of them are unfamiliar to me. The children are noisy and playful.

How long has it been since I have been to a river? Only two years? It feels like ages. I walk forward to get close to the water.

The touch of humidity in the air and the smell of water carry me to my childhood in my home town across the world…

"We want to take a walk to the river." "We want to go to the carnival and ride the merry-go-round." "We want to attend the monsoon-fair and buy clay toys and delicious fresh-fried papads." All these special requests and whining from my brother and sister and myself are lovingly indulged by our J. uncle, father's younger brother. As a bachelor and working full-time, he enjoys spending time with us on holidays and weekends. Every weekend it's a ritual to take evening walks with him.

J. uncle asks us, "Where would you like to go today?"

"To the riverside," I reply fast in hopes to get my way.

We walk past our neighborhood and reach Howrah Maidan, the local park. Various snacks are being sold there by vendors. He buys us warm peanuts in shells, freshly dry-roasted in hot sand. Each of us gets a packet. We enjoy cracking the shells and munching on crunchy peanuts. The vendor offers some hot and spicy jalapeno-salt to go with them. J. Uncle refuses because we won't be able to stand it.

Pretty soon we pass the Howrah Main Post Office and the General Hospital. A left turn leads us to the road next to the huge premises of the Martin Burn Company, the well-known engine makers. Their large compound is surrounded by high walls. Big and strong sentries, with noticeably prominent mustaches, stand guard in brown uniforms at the factory entrance gates. For security they carry *lathis*, heavy sticks made of seasoned wood.

On the roadside there are others, mostly *Biharis*, those from the State of Bihar. They sit around and talk aloud in Hindi, while processing tobacco leaves to make their favorite product *khaini*, chewing tobacco. The leaf is placed on the left palm and crushed by rubbing it with the right thumb. Once it turns into a powder, it is emptied into the mouth. With long time use, their left palm and right thumb become coarse and dark brown. Their teeth and lips turn spotted brown.

The tall buildings of the Calcutta business district are visible across the river. Howrah Bridge is at a distance on the left side. Far to the right, the launches of the regular ferry services are seen helping passengers cross the river. They provide major transportation between Howrah and Calcutta on special events such as football and cricket matches as well as political gatherings.

During the monsoon the Ganges water is muddy and at high level. At other times it's relatively clear. The special touch of the humid breeze, trembling leaves on the big, old bannion tree with a huge trunk, and the river flowing within touching distance make this walk worthwhile.

Concrete steps at the river bank lead all the way to the water. At any time of the day people are taking dips. Many stop by at the nearby small temple to offer their respect.

It's a pleasant evening and a charming sunset by the river. A flock of birds, forming a dark line in the evening sky, are flying back to their nests. Leaving some residual light behind at dusk, the sun is about to set. Soft, golden rays from the setting sun color the western sky. Nature is getting ready to welcome the night…

"We have to leave now. We have to go to the Farmers' Market before catching the return bus." Uma's voice brings me back to the present. She glances at her wristwatch and continues, "I told you we wouldn't be able to stay long."

"OK."

I sigh, and follow her reluctantly. The Farmers' Market does not interest me at all. Spending the evening watching the sunset by the river would have been fulfilling and rewarding to me. Uma would not understand.

Summer

Research

Research becomes an addiction for me. Despite extensive effort and multiple approaches in research lab, sometimes there is no significant outcome. At times I feel frustrated, irritated and hopeless. It takes a toll on me physically and emotionally. I would be better off without this—the thought does cross my mind.

Instead, I convince myself to follow a ray of hope and try again. Maybe one more attempt will lead me to a positive outcome.

With each attempt I write down the detailed procedure and observations in the lab notebook. I review each and every result and make a decision.

As the head of the department, Dr. H. stays very busy with management. Usually, he teaches two courses a year. The rest of his time is for research and management. It's difficult to make an appointment to discuss research with him. Unable to reach him, the junior research students in his group often approach the senior ones for suggestions. I am no exception to that.

Perseverance and optimism, along with months of hard work day after day, forgetting the world, leads me to success every now and then. My world stays strictly confined to the lab.

Almost an entire academic year goes by and the summer of 1982 arrives.

Flute

Hungry and exhausted at the end of the day after working hard in the research lab, I head to the graduate students' office to get my purse and go home.

It's a summer evening about 8:00 PM and the department seems empty. As I open the hallway door leading to our graduate study hall I am spellbound.

Malkaus, my most favorite *Raga*, is playing on a flute. It must be an audio-cassette, but my ears and heart convince me the other way around. This is live!

The music touches my soul—it keeps flowing from my head to my toes, leaving me unable to speak or move. I lose track of time.

How long have I been in this mesmerized state? The wall-clock shows 8:30. I must leave now to reach home before dark.

I tiptoe to my desk. Sunil Malhotra, a doctoral student from Uttar Pradesh, India, is absorbed in playing a flute at his desk. He is a person of multiple talents!

Cautious enough not to make any noise, I proceed to unlock my cabinet to get my purse. But alas! The cabinet makes an annoying metallic sound, and the music stops right away.

Music this excellent came to a halt because of me! I feel so guilty. Through the corner of my eye I glance at Sunil as I tiptoe out. He is resting his head on his desk leaving the flute beside him. He is so shy!

Definitely, I will not reveal to anyone his inner connection to the world of music.

Preparation for Thesis Defense

Finally, Dr. H. allows me to start writing my thesis.

He tells me, "Your research is funded by a famous American research organization. A copy of your thesis will be kept in their library in microfiche. Please use American spelling."

My thesis will belong to the library of such a world renowned research organization! I make an effort to use American spelling, no matter how uncomfortable it is for me. Ionization and synchronization use "z" instead of "s." Color and odor drop their "u." The few spellings that I miss get caught by the scrutinizing eyes of my advisor.

Other students comment about him, "Everything has to be perfect to get his approval."

James, a TA (teaching assistant) in Dr. Norton's group, comments, "You know, they demand extra research work from RAs (research assistant). Had you been a TA, you could have defended your thesis by now."

"Well, I have to work extra hard on research," I answer. "But it goes into my papers and thesis. TAs are assigned to teach undergraduate courses, grade homework and tests and help with the labs. RAs are not."

He argues, "I have done many assignments as a TA. It's not really bad grading tests, homework and lab reports."

I shake my head, expressing disagreement. "Sometimes conflicts take place because a student may not be happy with a grade. Fortunately, I don't have to deal with them. I would much rather be an RA."

There is another very important aspect to this, but I am not comfortable discussing financial issues. During the summer the labs are relatively vacant. It's a golden opportunity to get a lot of research done. For students with good track records in research, professors are willing to continue their research assistantships for the summer.

This is not so with teaching assistantships.

An RA offers me such peace of mind that I don't need to worry about the summer.

In case of unavailability of assistantships in summer American students have the luxury of spending those months with their parents. Alternately, they are more likely to find summer jobs elsewhere. Foreign students are in a helpless situation.

James asks, "So, when are you planning to submit your thesis?"

'Well, I have been fortunate enough to get back the first two chapters corrected by my advisor. I want to work hard and keep submitting to him. Hopefully, he will not get sidetracked and procrastinate. If that happens, I may not be able to submit at the end of the summer."

"Are you planning for end of summer?"

"Yes. Dr. Hewett is very choosy about research results. Unless there is substantial data and strong inferences, he is very reluctant to accept them."

James comments, "That's understandable. The research grants allow him a substantial annual income, along with honor and pride."

I am concerned. "Dr. H. agreed to let me start writing the thesis based on the condition that if he required more results I would have to get back to the lab and continue working again. Hopefully, that will not be the case. "

James tries to encourage me. "Let's hope not. You have worked very hard, I know."

I feel better and smile. "The school will start back full-fledged in the fall. A new academic year will get him more involved again."

James nods, "It will be wiser to defend before that."

In the graduate students' study area, I go to Ben's desk and ask him, "Who should I approach to get my thesis typed?"

Ben says, "Many do that for about a dollar a page."

"On the Student Center bulletin board I have seen advertisements by people who want to do it."

Ben smiles, "Most of them are students or their wives. They do it as a side income. But be careful when it comes to thesis typing."

"What do you mean?"

He suggests, "Choose someone who is reasonable and responsible."

Before I say anything Gary adds, "Ben is right. Last quarter I had a long project report due. It was a bad experience."

"What happened?" I ask.

"Do you know Ed, Dr. Biggs' student?"

Ben and I both nod.

Gary continues, "Ed's wife wanted to type my project. They needed the money." While shaking his head he says regretfully, "The typing was awful—full of misspelled words, and it took too long. Finally, I had to retype the entire report. I submitted it barely on time." He sighs, and then says, "What a waste of money!"

I sympathize. "That's very bad!"

I approach Phyllis, a secretary in our department. "I hear you type theses and dissertations. Would you do mine, please?"

Due to sickness or something she speaks in a high-pitched nasal tone. To avoid any miscommunication, I concentrate hard when she talks.

"Most certainly," she replies. "I charge a dollar a page."

"Would you be able to do it on time, Phyllis?"

"Sure. I would do most of it on weekends; if needed, in the evenings, too. If you are in a hurry, please let me know."

After she types the first two chapters, I read carefully. This is good typing without any spelling mistake. Only two errors in a full page of mathematical expressions! As I point them out, she uses white liquid ink and fixes them.

Phyllis compliments me, "Your handwriting is beautiful. It's so easy to read it, speeds up typing." According to Indian culture I smile shyly to recognize a compliment without saying anything.

She shows me a group photograph. Phyllis is the only one I recognize.

Happily, she describes, "My mom and grandma are on one side of me, and my daughter and granddaughter are on the other."

Impressed, I say, "Five generations of women standing next to one another! I have never seen anything like this before." Actually, I have never known of five generations simultaneously alive. The picture stays in my mind for a long time.

In reality, it doesn't proceed according to my plan to complete by summer's end. One reason follows another. I cannot write as fast as I expected. Dr. H. does not finish correcting as fast, either. Additionally, he accompanies his wife and children on a two-week vacation to California. Subsequently, the fall quarter starts before my thesis is ready.

Thesis Defense

Following each defense there is a get-together for the graduate students. This is a ritual.

Two days before my thesis defense James asks me, "Who will arrange for the party after your thesis defense?"

I hesitate. "I am not sure who to ask."

"I will be happy to do it."

"Really? It will be a big help. Any idea about what to buy?"

"Snacks and drinks; the usual items served for a Master's degree."

"How much will it cost, James?"

He thinks for a while. "Umm, about thirty-five to forty dollars. You can pay me later."

Appreciatively, I say, "Thanks, James."

"Are you nervous about your upcoming thesis defense?"

"Somewhat," I mumble.

James reassures, "Please, don't be nervous. You are the most knowledgeable person in your area of work at this point and time. Keep that in mind."

I defend my thesis in the middle of the fall quarter. In the presence of the departmental faculties, especially members of my graduate committee and my fellow-students, I present my work using the overhead projector.

Last year, before a national conference, I took a bus to the downtown shopping mall. A sales lady helped me choose the appropriate clothes. Though they were outrageously expensive and beyond my means, I wanted to represent the university properly. The research paper, along with my professional presentation, had helped keep Dr. Hewett's grant rolling.

Most of the presentations were by Asian students. The top official of the research organization mentioned in his speech, "We hope the Far East will continue to send us students."

I was impressed by his appreciation.

Today, inside the university, I am dressed in the same formal attire: a gray pant-suit, white dress-blouse and a bow tie. I am somewhat uncomfortable to begin with. But as I start talking about the project—the procedure, observations and conclusions—I become quite comfortable. I enter the world of research that I have been so focused on over the past year. Everything flows easily, at a comfortable pace. I am full of confidence. The hard part waits at the end of the presentation.

First, the faculty members get to ask questions. Nothing seems too difficult or twisted, and I answer well.

The toughest part follows. Students, who work in the research labs, ask in-depth, articulated questions. It's as if they are shooting arrows at me.

"Why did you do this? Why not that? Had you done this instead of that, what would have happened? What would you suggest if…" Their intent is to get some suggestions about how to resolve their problems.

Confidently, I address each issue and respond well. Finally, except for the faculties on my committee, all of us are requested to leave the room.

Within twenty minutes Dr. Hewett, the committee chairman, comes out.

"Congratulations," he says happily, with a firm hand shake. "Your thesis has been accepted."

"Thank you!" I respond, excited.

The quality of research I did in semiconductor device engineering, the effort I put in it, the results I produced—I did not have any doubt that it might have gone the other way. Still, it's a relief to hear the final words. The other members of the committee also congratulate me then leave.

Beaming with happiness, I hurry to the Graduate Students' lounge. James, waiting by the door, asks eagerly, "Everything OK?"

"Yes!"

"Congratulations!" He shakes hands with me and says, "A great presentation, an excellent question and answer session! One of the best defenses I have seen. Clearly, you knew what you were talking about."

The party begins. Not only did he buy the snacks, he also bought small paper plates and cups. Additionally, he organized everything nicely on the big round table in the center of the lounge: roasted-salted nuts, cheese and crackers, chocolate chip cookies, chips, Coke and Sprite.

Students join the party, and chat while enjoying the snacks. The usual questions follow: "Future plans? Which company are you joining? How much is the offer? How many offers do you have?"

This is the golden era for electrical engineers. Offers line up before they graduate. Acceptance is often based not only on the salary and benefits, but the geographic location and weather as well.

I reply, "I am going for a Ph.D."

"So, you are not leaving?"

I shake my head, "No."

This is often beyond the comprehension of American students. Unless a teaching or research career is intended, what good is a Ph.D.?

Universities and research labs are the only places that look for the Ph.D. Regular companies and engineering corporations do not care. An M.S. is more than enough for them. A Ph.D. is such a waste of time and money—another three years in school on a graduate student assistantship.

Realistically, an M.S. is a more employable degree in electrical engineering than a Ph.D. To avoid the higher salary, engineering corporations that do not focus in research and development do not hire Ph.D.s. Also, a Ph.D. has expertise in a particular field, whereas corporations prefer generalists.

I admit, "Yes, I would like to go for university teaching and research. I will be comfortable doing that."

In India, higher education is considered an honor and is of immense pride to the family. It's not necessarily the earning potential associated with the degree, but the degree itself. This thought process does not align well with Americans.

"In a few years you will sponsor a pizza party."

"Hopefully." I smile back.

It's customary, in this department, to have a snack party after an M.S. defense and a pizza party after a Ph.D.

The choice of a career or a job is very much decided by individual situations. A student whose wife is a school teacher turns down a good offer because that city's school system is not hiring. Some graduates like cities with good public schools for the sake of their children. Only a few students do not want to move to West Coast because they want to stay within a couple of hours drive from their parents and extended families.

In India, the general concept is that Americans are not well-bonded with their parents and extended families. Though my experience is limited to my classmates and professors, time after time I find this to be wrong. Many of the Americans I know have close family ties. They may not live at home while going to school, but they stay in touch and go home for holidays.

Eric, with a cup of Coke in his hand, steps forward and congratulates me. At 23, he has two kids: a three-year-old boy and an infant girl.

I ask, "How are your wife and kids, Eric?"

"They are better now. The summer was brutal for them."

"What happened?"

"During scorching-hot summer afternoons I stayed here enjoying the air-conditioning. Our apartment does not have it." Eric shakes his head and says, "I assured my family it was the last time. It will never happen again. I hope to graduate next spring. Then we will have a better life."

At the end of the party James and I clean up the lounge.

He hands me a receipt from Kroger for thirty-nine dollars and some change.

I give him two twenty dollar bills. "Thanks James, I really appreciate it."

"You are welcome. What are you doing the rest of the quarter?"

"I am taking the Optoelectronics I class, but I haven't spent much time on it so far. Now that the thesis defense is over, I will focus on it and make an A. Though it's a new subject and a high-level research-oriented course, I like it a lot. I would like to work in a laser lab in the future. I plan to complete the sequence Optoelectronics II and III in the winter and spring quarters. That will help me with the Ph.D. qualifying exam."

James says, "That's good. I have a suggestion."

"What?"

"You came from India to a new country, a new education system, and a new subject. You adjusted well and you have done great. You should write a book."

I am totally confused. "A book? What kind of book?"

"A book about your experience."

"My experience?" My writing has been limited to scientific and technical articles. This is beyond my comprehension. "This is a joke, isn't it?"

James assures me, "Not at all. I'm serious."

The thought had never crossed my mind.

After the thesis defense, Bonnie, the main secretary in our department, tells me, "You are to pay for the binding charge for four copies of your thesis in bond paper."

I am startled. "Four copies! That many?"

Bonnie explains, "It's the rule. A copy is to be kept in the archive in the university Central Library, a copy in the Engineering Library, a copy for your advisor, and one for yourself."

"OK."

"Bond paper costs more than ordinary paper. If you don't want to spend that much the two copies for your advisor and you may be done using ordinary paper. But the two copies for the library have to be on bond paper." She offers me the choice and waits for my response.

Dr. Hewett is renowned in the university and in the engineering research world. His well-decorated, scholarly office as the departmental head contains a wall-to-wall bookshelf. All the theses and dissertations done under him occupy the top few shelves. They are all bound in black, with the titles in gold.

These easily draw the attention of visitors. My thesis will be there, too. Many times, during research discussions with him, he stands up and pulls a thesis from the shelf as a reference.

In a split second, without any hesitation I reply, "All four in bond paper, please."

A month later, as I enter the graduate students' lounge, I hear the guys giggling. James spots me and warns the others, "Now, be quiet. We have a lady here."

They must have been talking about something inappropriate. Instantaneously, they change the topic. Realizing I have earned this respect, I feel good about it.

Gary says, "I have offers from two companies: one in Denver, Colorado, another in San Diego, California. I can't decide which to accept."

Often, students like to move to the West Coast. San Jose is often mentioned as the pilgrimage for EEs, due to the dense concentration of semiconductor industries in the Silicon Valley. It offers many opportunities to learn, train, and become an expert in the business. Due to tough competition among businesses, they pay well to attract and retain good employees. The saying is that, "In order to move up, you must move around." It's easy to do that in the Silicon Valley.

Surprising me, James remarks, "It's an easy decision, Gary. Who would you like to date and marry? A mountain girl, or a California beach girl who looks like a model?

Gary is too quick to respond, "Of course, a beach girl."

My comment is full of wisdom. "I'm not so sure. A mountain girl may make a better wife than a model-like beach girl."

Gary returns to his original confusion.

Within the past two years a couple of Indian students who graduated from here married American women. Referring to that James says, "Indians are taking away our girls. Have you all noticed?"

I say lightly, "Did you also notice that an Indian woman hardly ever marries an American man?"

Surprised, he asks, "Why not?"

"Maybe we are more traditional." I smile. "We like to marry Indian men."

James sounds irritated. "That's not fair. Your guys will take our girls, but your girls will not marry us. That makes us double-losers."

Instead of sympathizing, I laugh out loud.

Yearbook picture

A photographer is scheduled to take pictures of the students for the yearbook. I meet him in a room in the Student Center as scheduled. He is a white American man in his mid-thirties. He is carrying a camera with a big flash.

He asks me, "Where are you from? How long have you been here?"

"About three years ago I came from India."

He continues, "Really? How do you like it here?"

Usually, I am not comfortable talking to a stranger. "It's OK," I reply.

"What's the place that you liked the best?"

His question confuses me. Noticing that, he explains further, "What did you like the best out of all the places you have visited?"

My honest answer follows. "I walk from my apartment to the university. I have been to the downtown a few times."

He rephrases his question, "I mean travelling and sight-seeing."

"I haven't gone anywhere."

It appears to be beyond his comprehension. Apparently, he is having a hard time believing me. He shakes his head and asks, "You never left town in thr-e-e y-ea-r-s! Are you kidding?"

Is he questioning my honesty or my sanity? To change the subject I say, "I may go to India in summer."

"Going home? That's good."

He takes three pictures of me, and I leave at the first opportunity.

How would he know about foreign students' lifestyles: how they suffer from missing their family as well as the lack of their time and money?

Financially, I am much better off than many foreign students. There are families where a husband, wife and a child or two survive on a single assistantship. On the other hand, engineering is a very challenging subject. I know female foreign students studying English, political science, etc. They have more free time. Consequently, they are more relaxed than me. Some foreign students have family and friends in the U.S. They are not as lonely.

The International Folk Festival

At the end of November every year, The International Folk Festival is celebrated throughout a weekend in downtown. The objective is to honor diversity among people and cultures. It also reflects the commonality among different cultures and traditions. The festival connects people from all around the world through cultural performances, food and merchandise.

Our student circle talks about the festival. The university newspaper mentions it. Since it is so close to final week, the heavy load of studies has kept me from attending. But this year I have only one final, and I am prepared for it. So I plan to go to the festival with Uma.

On Saturday afternoon we ride a bus to downtown and show up at the convention center. Tickets are affordable due to the students' discount. We get day tickets because we need to spend tomorrow studying for the finals.

A glance at the brochure reveals the merchandise booths and food court are on the first floor. The cultural program, hosted on the second floor, will start shortly. Sitar and flute recitals and other instrumental programs are scheduled for tomorrow afternoon.

We are absorbed, almost mesmerized, watching the multicultural dances. Though I do not follow the songs in different foreign languages, I get the gist of it by watching the dancers. Facial expressions and body language provide quite powerful communication. Depending on the country and the culture, some dances are performed by males and some by females. Most of the dances include both men and women. The dance groups range from five-year-olds to adults.

A very attractive feature is the diverse costumes. Some wear formal attires: pressed shirts, bow ties, suits and jackets. Many European female dancers wear skirts and blouses. But each country has a distinct style and blend to its costume.

Bharatnatyam, the South-Indian classical dance, performed by a group of teenage Indian girls, turns out to be an instant winner. The bright colored, long silk costumes are so attractive. The audience claps for a while to show their appreciation.

A Jewish dance, performed by a couple, ends with a lot of appreciative laughter from the audience because of the funny story involved.

It has been a long time since I have been to a cultural program. I am enjoying every minute of it.

Uma interrupts my attention and says, "I am hungry. Let's go to the food court."

Annoyed, I reply, "I am willing to skip a meal to watch this."

She sounds serious. "I am not. My stomach is growling. It's almost eight o'clock."

That startles me. "Really? Has it been that long?"

We enter the food court. What a diverse choice: Indian, Mexican, Italian, Chinese and American cuisines and snack bars! The smell of food really makes me hungry. The large dining hall has rows of tables and chairs, many of which are occupied.

We buy some Indian snacks: hot fried *samosas* and *pakoras*. It turns out cheaper to share two slices of cheese pizza from the Italian cuisine. Due to the multi-cultural environment, people dressed in their authentic clothes and speaking different languages, dinner becomes such a pleasure.

While eating Uma mentions, "My tooth on the lower left side has been hurting off and on."

Concerned, I ask, "Did you go to a dentist?"

"No. I will go to New Delhi on winter break. I will get it checked then."

I say, "Growing up, we went to the dentist only if needed. Visiting the dentist regularly was not the way of life."

Uma nods and asks, "Did you ever visit a dentist here?"

"Only once. Looking at my dental X-rays the dentist asked me, 'What kind of diet do you have?'

"I was concerned. 'Diet, why?'

"He replied, 'You don't get teeth this strong and healthy from our diet.'

"Surprised, I said, 'A typical Bengali diet consists of fish and rice, lentils, veggies, milk and milk products. We used to chew fresh fruits all the way to sugar-cane, stems of cooked veggies, cooked fish bones, chicken and goat bones. Actually, there was a competition among the youngsters about who could chew the best. '

"The dentist said, 'It's not a surprise that you have strong teeth.'"

Uma nods. "Food seems too soft here. Not much chewing at all."

"Fish and meat are either boneless, or it's not customary to chew the bone. I miss chewing," I comment.

Then I smile and continue, "Did you notice something else? In India, a smile is expected to show only a little bit of teeth, if any. It's supposed to look sweet and attractive, mild in nature, but not all the way exposed. I guess that goes well with our culture."

She agrees. "Americans smile showing off all of their teeth."

Uma glances at her watch. "Our bus will arrive in less than half-an-hour. No point in returning to the cultural program upstairs."

"I really want to go back," I insist.

She says casually, "We don't have the luxury of a car. We have to follow the bus schedule."

Disappointed, I follow her as we stroll through merchandise booths from different countries. All of them have a common theme: handicrafts from the specific country, and photographs displaying traditions and famous tourist locations. In the Indian booth a photograph of the famous Taj Mahal is exhibited. Pictures of traditional Indian weddings are also displayed. The jewelry and the unique silk costumes look colorful and vibrant.

The handicrafts available for sale consist of beautiful dolls from different states, and decorated elephants made of white stone. The peacock is the national bird of India. Metal peacocks with multi-color feathers are also for sale.

The bus travels through the almost empty downtown. Though the shops are closed, the displays in the windows are brightly illuminated.

"Uma, look at the showcase in that clothing store."

"Nice dress suits; must be very expensive. Look at the shoe store next door."

"Fashionable high-heel shoes. A pair costs seventy-five dollars!"

Uma shakes her head. "Unbelievable! Leather is outrageously expensive here."

I want to attend the festival tomorrow. Uma has three finals. She may not want to come.

Hesitating, I say, "I wish we could come back again tomorrow."

She looks annoyed as well as surprised. "Tomorrow?"

"Just for the afternoon concerts; won't take very long," I say, trying to sound optimistic.

"Downtown bus service is not available on Sundays."

That settles the issue.

Diploma

In December, at the end of this fall quarter, the university sends me a letter. They want to know whether I would like to receive my diploma by mail now, or wait for the regular commencement in June?

Next summer I will not be here. I plan on going to India to visit my family and friends after a long three-and-a-half years. My advisor has approved of this already.

I reply, "I would like to get it now."

On a sunny and bright Saturday afternoon a few weeks later, the highly awaited big brown envelope from the "Office of the Registrar" of the university arrives in the mail. In big, dark letters it is stated outside: "DO NOT BEND – DIPLOMA ENCLOSED." My M.S. diploma is secured inside it. Using a knife, I open the envelope slowly and carefully, not to damage the contents.

Looking at my name and the degree displayed on the diploma, I get emotional right away. This is the official proof—formal recognition of my hard work. I read it over and over again. I left my family and dear ones behind, and came to the other end of the world to achieve this. I stare at the university seal for a while. It looks so different from the Calcutta University's seal on my previous diplomas.

The mixed emotions of happiness, achievement, gratitude and relief overwhelm me and bring tears to my eyes. I miss my parents, my brother and my sister, and my grandparents. I wish they were present to share this moment. They would have been very happy and proud. I can't wait to show it to them.

I am indebted to my family and grateful to all my teachers who helped me achieve this—from preschool to today.

4. Newcomer, 1983

After my M.S. in electrical engineering, I am admitted to the Ph.D. program in January, 1983. It's the same department and professors, but a more advanced curriculum. Since Dr. H. is very pleased with my research performance, he continues to fund me as an RA.

Transition

Following the final week of the winter quarter I go to Dr. Hewett to ask him a question about a research issue.

He asks me, "Have you received your grade sheet yet?"

"No, I will get it in the mail in a few days." Though I think I did all right in the finals, I become anxious. What happened?

He continues, "Do you know your grade for the CMOS circuit design class?"

"No." Scared, I shake my head and mumble, "But I did well throughout the quarter."

"Congratulations! You scored the highest marks in the class."

Is that true? I have a hard time believing it. I was expecting an "A" though.

Dr. Hewett explains, "This is kind of rare for a non-traditional student. We focus on the grades in the CMOS circuit design course and the integrated circuit design lab course to measure how well a non-traditional student has transitioned to engineering. You made an "A" in that lab last quarter. You have transitioned very well. No one is happier than me."

Everybody knows Dr. Hewett is very hard to please. A compliment like this from him is above and beyond my expectation. It's like a dream come true—too hard to believe!

Watching me standing still, he assures me, "Not every student who attempts to make the transition succeeds. You did."

It takes me a few minutes to accept it. After I leave his office I go back to my desk upstairs, hopping a few steps at a time and singing in joy and excitement.

International Women's Program

The university has decided to do a special program this year to promote better understanding of international women's issues. Showing international movies is an integral part of this program. The Bengali movie "Devi" has been selected.

An Indian professor from the physics department contacts me. He says, "We are trying to form a group of experts who will be responsible for answering questions in a panel discussion following the movie. The International Students Office referred me to you as a Bengali woman. Would you like to be an expert?"

Oh no! I have neither read the book nor watched the movie. Serving as an expert? I can't do this. I better get out of it right away. But a part of me reminds me of my Bengali heritage and my love for the language and the literature. To show respect to my heritage, I have to do it.

I admit, "I have not read it. Could you get me the book?"

He is quick to respond, "No, I don't have it."

"Before serving as an expert, I have to read the book. I cannot do a good job just by walking into it."

The professor stresses, "I have discussed this with other Indian women. Your response is the best and the most reasonable one I've heard. You can do it. I will arrange for you to view the movie beforehand."

"When?"

"After we receive the movie; maybe a few days before the showing."

On a Wednesday afternoon I show up in the specified classroom to watch the movie. Dr Saxena, a non-Bengali Indian woman in her mid-forties, joins me. A psychologist, she will also serve as an expert. The noisy projector runs, the reel rotates and the black-and-white movie is shown on a white-board screen.

The author is Pravat Mukhopadhyay. The story is based on a Bengali teenage housewife's issues in a landlord family in a Bengal village. The Bengali language, the Bengali actors and actresses, the countryside of Bengal—all absorb me and float me away to a different world.

Such a tragic story! It consumes me over the next few days.

More than a hundred people show up at the Student Center auditorium on the following Saturday afternoon to watch the movie. Most of them are Americans.

I am the only Bengali woman serving as an expert. Dressed in a beautiful, blue, Murshidabad silk sari, I represent a traditional Bengali woman.

Sitting at a table with three other experts I am scared to death.

Most of the people leave at the end of the movie. Still, about thirty stay behind for the panel discussion.

"Why did she do it?" "Why not that?" "What role did her husband play?" "Why didn't he…" "Could you explain the father-in-law's action?" Questions are directed to me like arrows.

My throat is dry. I am so nervous that I can't even come up with appropriate English words to communicate. Still, I keep trying to explain to get my point across.

Then Dr. Saxena starts. She uses psychology to explain the father-in-law's behavior in such a derogatory way! I can't even think of portraying a respectable senior landlord with such a distorted mentality. What a pity! Is that what psychology is all about?

A Bengali gentleman present in the audience, a professor in the University Medical Center, enters the conversation. He supports my point of view and provides elaborate explanations. I feel so grateful to him.

A few days later I receive a letter from the president of the International program committee praising and thanking me for my participation and expertise, and inviting me to attend their future programs.

Ben and Anand

Ben finishes his thesis work in the winter quarter. He will graduate in the spring. As an American citizen, it's easy for him to get job offers. He has three offers lined up, but all are out-of-state. But because he doesn't want to leave his hometown, he is hesitating. He has applied to two local companies. Hopefully, one of them will offer him a position.

Ben has never mentioned having a girlfriend. Out of curiosity, I ask him, "Don't you want to get married, Ben?"

"I am not opposed to getting married." He pauses then adds, "So far, the women I've liked were either married or not interested in me. The women who were interested in me, I did not like them."

I am disappointed. "Oh, really?"

Truly, I feel sorry for Ben. He is definitely obese. This society looks down upon obese people. Would-be girlfriends avoid them like the plague. Many of our classmates got married as graduate students. All of them found girlfriends, why not Ben? He is a fine man, so intelligent and considerate.

Within a month Ben says, "I am about to buy a new car."

This topic is outside my jurisdiction. I am totally ignorant about buying a car.

Other students—all men—become instantly interested in the make, model, price-range, etc. They express opinions about good buys and bad buys.

In a few weeks Ben buys a Ford Escort with two-percent financing. Our classmates congratulate and assure him, "It's a great deal."

"I will start buying furniture once I start working," Ben tells me. "I am looking at catalogs now to choose some."

"Why buy furniture now?" I ask. "After you get married, do it together."

"Why?"

"Suppose you buy furniture now and your wife doesn't like it after you get married. That will be a hassle."

Very calmly, he comments, "She may not like me after the wedding. Then what?"

Is that even a possibility? "Once married, married forever"—is what I grew up watching and believing. I stare at him speechless, like an idiot.

I realize, after being in the U.S. three years, my core values still remain strong and unchanged. I am determined to complete higher studies and go back to India to settle down.

Before Ben leaves I invite him and Anand to lunch at India Palace, the only Indian restaurant in town. The three of us started the graduate program the very same day. Though we are from three different countries and cultures, despite our differences we have been friends all along.

We get a ride in Ben's brand new car. The smell of paint, shiny exterior, and spotless interior, impress me. Totally unlike the old and used cars that are commonly seen in the university parking lot.

Buffet lunch. Ben is not familiar with Indian dishes. Anand has a good idea, though. Thai food and Indian food have much in common. I explain each and every item on the menu as Ben serves himself. Pulao, daal, mixed vegetables, Tandoori-chicken, lamb curry, and chutney—all the way to the dessert: gulab-jamun and rice-pudding.

According to Indian hospitality, I keep requesting them to eat well.

Anand relishes each and every item, Ben picks and chooses. Overall, all of us eat well. After such a long time I really enjoy every bit of a good Indian meal.

I say, "Ben, I wish you a bright future and a successful life." But deep-down, I am also sad about his departure. I will miss him.

Anand has been looking sad and serious over the past few days. He has forgotten to smile, never talks to me, and avoids eye contact. I can sense that he is acting very differently.

What's wrong? Bad grades? Poor performance in research? Any bad news from his family in Thailand?

I keep thinking give him a few days and he will turn around. A week passes by. He doesn't change. I want to ask him, but hesitate. Maybe it's best to leave him alone. I don't want to put unnecessary pressure on him.

Unexpectedly, during my lunch at the fast food place at the Student Center, Anand shows up and asks me in a tired voice, "Mind if I join you?"

Though I have almost finished eating, I welcome him. "Please, do sit down."

He sets his lunch on the table: a hamburger, a small serving of French fries and an extra-large cup of Coke. He picks up the Coke and takes a long drink.

While smearing ketchup on the hamburger and avoiding looking at me, he asks in a sad tone, "How are you?"

"I'm fine. How are you these days, Anand?" I look him straight in the eye.

He stares at me as if trying to understand something. A long sigh follows before he responds, "Not well." He pauses. "Remember Souda, who was my girlfriend?"

Was? I become alert. Is she dead? My heart starts pounding.

She was his high school sweetheart. When Anand came here for higher studies, she stayed behind in Thailand as a medical student.

I swallow and manage to say, "Sure, you introduced her to me when she visited you last summer. Is she well?"

"Probably," he says in a low, deep voice. "But I am not well—not at all."

The food court is too crowded and noisy at lunch time. I can barely hear him. But I don't want to request him to speak louder.

I am concerned. "What do you mean?"

He picks a French fry, takes another big swallow of Coke and keeps staring at me.

I am getting restless and impatient. What's going on?

"She broke up with me." Anand pauses. Then he clears his throat and continues sadly, "She wrote that it had become hard for her to keep going year after year without me."

"That's all?" In India, I have heard women waiting for years when their future husbands went abroad for higher studies.

"Additionally, after she graduates from medical school, if she comes to the U.S., it will take her a couple of years to fulfill the requirements of a foreign medical graduate, you know."

"Yes, I know."

Anand shakes his head and says, "Souda, I mean, um…She doesn't want to go through that any longer."

Every word sounds like it is covered in tears. It must be ripping his heart apart to reveal this.

"Really?" I feel so bad, but can't find words to express it. I sit helpless.

"You realize my situation," he comments in frustration. "Who knows how many more years before I complete the M.S. and Ph.D. and settle down?"

"Certainly," I nod. "It's not easy for the foreign students. An employer has to deal with legal paperwork and process them. Sometimes it takes years."

"How can I blame her?" He asks, and becomes quiet again.

Anand does have a big heart. He didn't even utter a single negative word about her.

"Souda mentioned being good friends with a male classmate," Anand mumbles, "I think they have become closer." A deep sigh follows. That expresses his loss beyond words.

Eventually he finishes the drink then stands up. "Let's go back."

"Aren't you going to eat? You didn't even take a bite."

"I haven't been able to eat lately."

"Anand, what if you get really weak and sick? As foreign students, we don't have family support. Please, try to eat something. Please."

At my earnest request, he wraps the food and picks it up. "Maybe later."

We walk side-by-side past the clock tower, the ATM and the bookstore.

He stares at the sky and like a monologue, he whispers, "Had I known this was going to happen, I wouldn't have come. NEVER. It was not worth it. What a loss!"

I want to offer him consolation. But I can't come up with the appropriate words to express my sympathy and compassion. I let the silence convey my feelings. In our Eastern culture, that's acceptable.

Afterward, I notice the golden-framed photograph of a smiling Souda that has occupied the center of his desk over the years has been removed.

Within a month Anand buys a Volkswagen Rabbit, a used car in good condition. He confides in me, "When Souda left last summer, she said she would visit me again in two years. I was waiting to buy the car together. The wait has ended." He sighs.

Anand babies his car, repeatedly dusting, washing, drying and vacuuming, though it's needless most of the time. He joins an auto club to take better care of his car.

Poor man! Trying to keep himself distracted in order to deal with the loss of his teenage sweetheart. He came abroad for higher studies, to achieve a better and brighter future for both of them. A shattered dream!

Will he recover from the deep wound some day? He may stay scarred the rest of his life.

Hassan, a doctoral student in the physics department, went through a similar situation. He came from the Middle East. He finished his Ph.D. last year, and accepted a teaching position at a university in Florida.

At his farewell party I asked him, "Is someone waiting for you back home?"

He stared at me quietly. I thought he was too shy to admit it.

"When are you going home to marry her?"

Regretfully, he said, "That was six years ago when I came here. She gave me three years to finish."

"Well, it took you longer. She would understand."

He almost cried. "She had younger sisters waiting for her to get married first. She wanted to, but she could not wait for me."

"Uh?"

His face became clouded with sorrow. "She is the mother of two kids now."

I felt so guilty about bringing it up.

Sunil and Usha

Sunil is a few years senior to me, about to complete his Ph.D. A graduate of one of the prestigious I.I.T.s (Indian Institute of Technology), the one at Kanpur, he is a brilliant research scholar. A number of his papers have been published in IEEE (Institute of Electrical and Electronics Engineers) already, though he is still a student. Sunil is very good at discussing research problems. Besides that, he hardly ever speaks to me. I guess he is shy.

Our professor often mentions, "We have had great luck with the I.I.T.s. Whenever we get applicants from there we try to accept them."

Usha, Sunil's white American girlfriend, is an undergraduate student in the English Department. She was born in India during her father's sabbatical and given the Indian name Usha, meaning dawn. Her straight blonde hair is elbow-length. She is slightly overweight, but not obese. In India, slim is not considered beautiful, slender is.

Usha often brings lunch and she and Sunil eat at our group-discussion lab table. While passing by, I have noticed they eat fruits and vegetables mostly. Sunil keeps munching on crunchy carrots. When I visited New Delhi I saw locals enjoying raw carrots with coriander leaf chutney as a favorite snack. He reminds me of that.

I have overheard him saying, "I was a non-vegetarian in India. I became a vegetarian here."

That is contrary to the normal trend. Many who are strict vegetarians in India become non-vegetarian after they come to America.

In the absence of Sunil, a discussion takes place in our study hall.

Gary asks, "Will Sunil and Usha ever get married?"

James replies, "I am not sure."

I comment, "Why not? Many Indian men marry American women."

James stresses, "It's somewhat different, though."

I have seen many differences wash away when it comes to love and marriage. I ask, "How?"

"Usha belongs to a staunch Catholic family. Religion means so much to her."

"There are many people like that. Sunil will compromise," I assure.

James remarks, "Though Sunil is not a staunch Hindu, he has made it clear that he would maintain Hinduism in his family."

Without even a second thought I comment, "Apparently, they really like each other a lot. I'm sure they will come to a compromise."

James shakes his head. "Sunil is a good friend of mine. I doubt that he would make a compromise about religion."

In summer, Usha takes a two-month-long trip to Pakistan to visit her parents. Her dad is working there.

Our professor jokes about it, "Sunil, being an Indian, has let his girlfriend go to Pakistan? How strange!"

A few months later, Sunil graduates and leaves for San Jose, California. He starts a highly paid job in a research group owned by a well-known corporation.

About a year down the road, Sunil drops by accompanied by his newlywed wife, a skinny, dark-tan Indian woman! He introduces her to us.

Trying to get over the initial shock, I swallow. Finally, I manage to say hello.

I am heart-broken. Sadness overwhelms me. Over and over again I visualize Usha and Sunil chatting, having lunch, and walking on campus holding hands.

It all ended like this?

Going Home in Summer

My two-and-a-half-month trip home to Calcutta is this summer! Unlimited freedom! All the constraints that restrict me to loneliness and immobility will be gone.

The most cherishing thought is that I will always be surrounded by my immediate family. No more coming home to an empty apartment and living an isolated life. My parents, grandparents and siblings mean a lot to me. We are all looking forward to the long-awaited family reunion. It will be ecstatic.

My sister and brother-in-law's son was barely a toddler with a limited vocabulary when I left. Afterwards, he used to go to my room, point at my study table and enquire about me. Poor baby! He has written to me a few lines now and then in his preschooler handwriting. As a kindergartener now, I doubt he will recognize me.

During this trip I will not do any cooking, cleaning, laundry or grocery shopping. It seems like a dream—almost unbelievable! Bed tea will be served to me in the morning. I will read Bengali literature or listen to my favorite music sitting or lying half-way on the sofa. The thought makes me cheerful.

I will visit friends and family as I please. The question will not arise about how to get around. What a mobility! It's something I really miss here. Accompanied by my mother or my sister I will watch good movies and attend concerts in famous theatres such as the Academy of Fine Arts. Also, there may be a few out-of-town trips with my parents.

I have made a wish-list of dishes that I would like to enjoy. I have badly missed various vegetable curries, and fishes like *hilsa, mourala, parshe, topshe, pomphret, bata and koi*. I can't wait to enjoy a variety of desserts: *jalebi, sandesh, sweet pink-yogurt* and especially *gulab-jamun*. Just the thought is causing my mouth to water.

The loneliness and boredom of eating alone will not happen. Family meals! In our culture food is always served an item at a time accompanied by requests to eat more. It establishes such a heart-to-heart connection. An everyday meal is multi-course. The mother always starts eating after serving everyone else.

It's a pleasure to chat while enjoying a cup of tea. Conversations during meals! A luxury I almost forgot. Cordial requests from my family will accompany, "Have some more. Come on, this is your favorite fish *pomphret* cooked the way you like; one more helping at least." "Freshly made *gulab-jamuns* in syrup are your favorite dessert. They are still warm. Have some now." "Here's some pink-yogurt from Mollarchak, the famous confectioner." "You are not eating well. Any problem? Feeling all right?"

I am really looking forward to being pampered. I am thrilled thinking about it!

If a wedding of a close relative or friend takes place while I am there, that will be great. After such a long time I will get a chance to dress up in a *Benarasi* sari, wear a lot of gold jewelry and make an impressive appearance. That will be a-dream-come true.

Shopping

The Indian grocery store near the university recommends an out-of-state Indian travel agent to me. The agent tells me over the telephone, "Traveling on weekends is more expensive due to the weekend surcharge on airfare."

To avoid this I get a ticket to leave on a Wednesday at the beginning of June, the day after my spring quarter finals will end.

I start shopping in the middle of the spring quarter because there will be no time after finals. I have written my parents, brother and sister about the gifts they would like me to bring. Their flat response, "Just bring yourself."

I am sure my brother, a college student, has something in mind. He has hesitated to express it—that's all.

Two Japanese printed synthetic saris, an orange one for my sister and a beige one for my mother from the Indian grocery store. Besides that, my shopping stays limited to the strip mall next to the university. A Parker pen for my dad. Shirts for my dad, brother and brother-in-law. Legos for my nephew.

Mom always likes perfumes; a Cachet perfume for her. Small bottles of deodorants, a couple of pens, and a few small items as gifts for extended family and friends.

I wish I could buy a lot more. But after paying almost twelve-hundred-dollars airfare, I am in a tight situation and can't afford very much.

On my Trip

I have prepared a list of things to do while I'm in India. First and foremost is learning to cook a few Indian dishes. I made sure ingredients are available here; especially fish and gravy and chicken. We grew up eating goat meat. It's unavailable here. The horizon of my eating choices has to be expanded. I am sick and tired of sticking to the same foods all the time, because that's all I can fix in a hurry without burning them.

A small frozen fish called smelt is available in grocery stores. I have heard it can be used to fix a delicious fish curry with eggplant. My mom has always been a good cook, especially for fish dishes and desserts. What I need is hands-on training.

An excellent *Paneer*-curry can be made from the Ricotta cheese available in local grocery stores. A Bengali housewife brought it to a potluck dinner.

Besides this, *gulab-jamun* is my favorite. I would like to make it if it's not too much of a hassle. Many Indian desserts are labor-intensive and time-consuming.

Bengalis always wanted me to bring a freshly chopped salad to the potluck lunches and dinners I have attended. Right before a party I used my regular knife and spent about an hour chopping cucumber, lettuce, tomato, carrot and green pepper for the entire gathering of forty or so. At times I arrived with hurting fingers and a clear conscience that, though I did not cook, I did fix something. After I learn to make a few of Mom's recipes I may volunteer to cook.

Calcutta is well-known for stainless utensils, from pressure cookers to pots and pans, skillets, and dinner sets all the way to lunch boxes, spatulas and spoons. I will bring back everyday usable stuff. Most of these are available here at the Indian grocery store, but at an outrageous price.

Among the books I will bring are *Sanchayita* and *Gitanjali* by the Nobel laureate Tagore. They will help me stay connected to Bengali poems and songs. In other words, they will help me stay connected to my inner-self—my soul.

I will bring back some audio-cassette recordings of Tagore songs, primarily by my favorite singers Suchitra Mitra and Kanika Bannerjee, and some *Nazrulgeeti* by Feroza Begum. Maybe a few Sitar recitals by Ravi Shankar, and some other instrumental music. All of them must be classical, my favorite. When I return, I will buy a cassette player from the bookstore. They have it available for thirty dollars.

My list also contains a couple of sweaters and a leather handbag big enough to hold my lunch and everyday stuff. Two pairs of leather sandals and two pairs of leather shoes from Bata Company, the famous leather shoemaker.

Uma points out to me, "While you're in India make sure to get your dental and eye-checkups done. Also buy your eyeglasses."

"Definitely. Eyeglasses are very expensive here. I will bring back two pairs of regular glasses and a pair of sun-glasses. Everything together will cost less than one pair here."

Pre-departure

Letters from my parents state how excited they are. Just like me, they are impatiently counting down the days. Every day seems too long of a wait to them, too.

For the last few weeks the wait seems never-ending. I have waited for this since I arrived here three-and-a-half years ago. I have been counting weeks since the beginning of the spring quarter. Now I'm counting days, and the count-down is about to roll-over to hours.

James says, "I will be happy to give you a ride to the airport. I don't mind at all."

"It's final week. Don't worry, James. I will get a cab."

"My finals will end Tuesday, too."

"Just relax, then."

James says, "Renew all your acquaintances while you are there."

I smile. "My acquaintances? Most of my female classmates and friends are married by now. They live with their husbands. I don't know their addresses. Most of my male classmates moved wherever they found employment. There are a few working on their Ph.D. degrees in research labs, and I may be able to get in touch with them."

"They will connect you to others," James reassures.

"Hopefully."

"Have a great trip. We will wait for your safe return."

"Thanks, James. Bye."

"Bye." James shakes my hand.

Anand also offers, "Let me take you to the airport."

"Don't worry about it, I will manage."

After being exhausted from studying hard and sleep deprivation for weeks, students dream about relaxing after finals. Sleeping till noon and not being under any constraint are integral parts of that. I feel bad to steal any of that treasured time away from them.

The rental office at the apartment complex has been notified about the availability of my apartment. I will lock my books, research materials and important stuff in the steel cabinet next to my desk. My clothes and household items will be stacked in a corner in Uma's apartment.

After I return, it will be more realistic to move closer to the university. The Ph.D. comprehensive examination and doctoral research will keep me more involved in the department.

Departure

The taxi arrives to take me to the airport. I open my purse and make sure that I have the passport, ticket and cab fare readily available. Unlike India, cab-drivers are to be tipped ten-percent.

A glance at my HMT (Hindusthan Motor Tools) wrist-watch that my parents gave me as a birthday gift years ago, assures there is enough time before my domestic flight to New York. Then I will take the shuttle to JFK airport to board an Air-India flight home.

The elderly cab driver places my big suitcase in the luggage compartment and asks, "Are you ready, madam?"

For the last time, I look at my apartment—my home of past three-and-a-half years—as tears fill my eyes.

Julie, the caretaker at the apartment house, has just finished inspecting the apartment. She assures me, "It's in good condition. You will get most of the damage-deposit refunded."

She steps forward and says, "You have been a great tenant. You always paid your rent on time, and hardly ever complained about anything. Please call us if you need a place when you return."

I nod and board the taxi.

Julie wishes loudly, "Have a safe trip. Bye."

I want to say bye, but I feel lumps in my throat and nod instead.

The taxi goes past the swimming pool and the premises of our apartment house, and gets to the main road—the uphill road I walked every day, the Italian grocery, the old peoples' home.

A strong smell of tar fills the air. Construction crews are busy with maintenance work.

The university and the Engineering building are on the right-hand-side and Bishop Woods is on the left. I turn around and stare at the Engineering building until it goes out of sight. That's the place my life revolved around. Tears roll down my cheeks.

The driver, stopped at a traffic light, looks back and asks, "Madam, are you OK? Is everything all right?"

Embarrassed, I reply in a broken voice, "Yes."

All these years I have counted the days to go home. After a long and hard wait, this is my dream come true. But why am I crying? When did I get so attached? How did I get tied by an invisible emotional string?

Whenever any foreign student went home, I offered myself consolation that my turn would come. So why am I sad? I should be ecstatic.

We pass the major crossing near the university hospital, and continue on McMillan Avenue leading to downtown.

Skyscrapers and the business district, the conference center and government buildings, courts and hospitals and finally, the Springdale mall—all pass one after another. All of them look hazy due to my blurry vision, even on this nice and clear sunny afternoon.

A brown sign indicating a recreation area appears. I can't read the sign. This may be the well-known park where the students come for picnics.

A winery sign-board stands tall. The air is saturated with a sweet aroma.

The cab drives past the farmers' market and the train tracks. Then it enters the highway and picks up speed. We get on the bridge to cross the river that divides the two states.

While sobbing I turn around to look back through the windshield. Looking at the fast-disappearing town I whisper, "Bye."

Epilogue

After enjoying summer vacation with my family and friends in my hometown of Calcutta in 1983, I returned to the university and continued working as a doctoral student.

Following graduation an excellent job offer from a well-known high-tech corporation landed me in California. My intention was to get a few years of work experience to make myself more marketable and then return to India.

The work environment with new computer systems, new technologies, new designs and products presented me with a wide range of opportunities for learning and development. It made my familiar university laboratories look old.

My professional life and Indian social life kept me busy. At an Indian wedding ceremony I met a gentleman, an assistant professor of chemistry in the university. Not only did we share the same mother language and hometown, but also both of us were determined to return to Calcutta.

We got married the following year. Three years later, after our son was born, we missed our families in India so badly that we started searching for jobs in Calcutta.

In the following few years I mourned the loss of my grandparents while my husband mourned his parents. Every time we visited India, as I boarded the return flight from Calcutta, I hoped that was going to be the last time. Next time we would come to Calcutta with jobs and would never leave.

Our son started kindergarten and he became comfortable in his own little world of school, classmates and friends. Without even realizing it, we got more and more involved every step of the way.

Due to the loss of my parents and sale of the family home, the only home where I lived before coming to the U.S., my longing to return diminished.

We came to realize this is our home, our country.

Today, more than 30 years since my arrival as a newcomer, the world has changed a lot. My hometown has changed very much due to construction of high rise buildings, schools, hospitals, new subway systems and bridges, etc., to accommodate more residents and businesses. It's hard for me to relate to my childhood and I feel like a newcomer there though I still love India.

About the author

 Mahasweta Ghosh was born and raised in greater Calcutta, India. She is a writer and an engineer, a Senior Member of IEEE (Institute of Electrical and Electronics Engineers.) A long time member of the Atlanta Writers Club, her book of short stories, *E Parabase (In this Foreign Country)*, was published in Calcutta in 2009. She lives in suburban Atlanta.

Additional information about Mahasweta and her writing can be found at her web page: www.mahaswetaghosh.com